ALSO BY
Sherrhonda Denice

PATHWAYS

When your life is falling apart ...

Glue

A Novel

SHERRHONDA DENICE

LILY BIRD PRESS • UTICA, MICHIGAN

Glue: A Novel

© 2012 by Sherrhonda Denice
www.sherrhondadenice.com

Published by
Lily Bird Press, LLC
P.O. Box 180971
Utica, MI 48318

Cover & Interior Design: Selah Branding and Design LLC
www.iselah.com

Pre-Press Layout: Donna Kitchen of deetoo Design

Edited by: Amanda Johnson

Library of Congress Control Number: 2009912763

ISBN 978-0-9801028-1-9

Printed in the United States of America

This book is dedicated to every woman who has ever endured the pain and shame of divorce. God loves you.

For I know the thoughts that I think toward you, says the LORD, thoughts of peace and not of evil, to give you a future and a hope.

Jeremiah 29:11

In Loving Memory of
Willie "Nilly" Neloms,
who served Jesus Christ, his country, his family and friends, and his loving wife faithfully.
See you in heaven . . .

1
White Picket Fence

Debra Prince-Myles sat on the edge of her bed holding the small item she'd found in her husband's suitcase. Her soft brown eyes narrowed with defeat and spilled over with tears. The glow of her light brown skin vanished. Paralyzed by what she'd found, she cried silently, knowing that this small item was going to change her life in a profound way. No, she hadn't been snooping like she'd done many times in the past—with good reason. This time it was an honest discovery. Debra had simply unpacked the suitcase he'd taken on his business trip so she could clean their walk-in closet. He'd left the suitcase open in the middle of the floor with half his clothes spilling out onto the carpet. Debra had planned to wash whatever needed to be washed and hang up the rest of the items—housework. Now, she wished she had done some other menial chore. Because now, Debra couldn't pretend anymore. It was real. Why had she married him in the first place?

Debra met Bryce at church. He had honey-brown skin and an average build. He stood six feet tall with dark brown eyes. His dark curly hair was cut close to his scalp creating gentle waves. His skin was baby smooth, a characteristic that made him look younger. He was a handsome man with a bright smile. And he had a sense of humor—not stuffy like some of the other men Debra had met. Most of all, he was kind and more sensitive than any man Debra had known.

He had been candid with Debra, admitting that he'd once been in a long-term relationship with his high school sweetheart. They'd gotten engaged when he was twenty-seven and still immature. He said that he had practically destroyed that relationship single-handedly with infidelity, but that he was a different man now. And it seemed that way, too. He attended church regularly and seemed to be committed to growing in Christ. They were both thirty years old and were gym rats. They both loved to travel. Their rhythm was synced. Debra and Bryce dated just eight months before he'd asked her to be his wife. He said that he was ready. That his past was behind him. Pre-marital counseling had gone well. And the forty-thousand dollar wedding and honeymoon were beautiful.

Surprisingly, their first two years together had been unbelievably peaceful—not at all like the older sisters at church had warned her about. Debra had dreadfully anticipated the arguments that the older sisters vowed would happen over minute matters— like Bryce leaving the toilet seat up, or her forgetting to put the top back on the toothpaste. They said that married life would be an "adjustment." That living with a man would be the biggest challenge she'd ever face—in love or not, but for those first two years, Bryce proved those church ladies wrong. The two of them lived in tranquility. Debra couldn't think of a disagreement that could be classified as an "official" argument. The lovemaking was still passionate.

Communication had been good. Bryce sent roses to Debra's job at least once a month, making her co-workers envious. He helped out around the house by picking up after himself, and he cooked a couple times a week to relieve Debra. Within the last three years, however, that had all dissolved.

It was a struggle living with Bryce now. Uncertainty and mistrust. Lies and insecurity. All the things that slowly destroyed a beautiful love story, like a cancer, but Debra loved him. Still loved him. Still wanted to make it work despite their issues that could not be rationalized away. The truth was the truth.

Debra couldn't call her mother. She'd shared too much with Sheila in the past and believed that it hadn't been held in confidence. Her father, Daniel, had a different attitude toward Bryce now. No harsh words had been spoken, but an invisible wall had been erected. Indifference replaced that fatherly, man-to-man relationship that they'd had in the beginning. Daniel's conversations were short and stayed in the safe zone of small talk, discussing things like weather and sports—not his little girl, who Daniel would still kill for. He'd said that with stares.

Debra had to deal with this alone. She wasn't even sure if she could share this with Sandy, a neighbor she'd become fast friends with over the last five years. Sandy was a saved woman who walked the walk, and she gave good, sound, godly advice supported by Scripture and didn't just shoot from the hip like some Christians had a tendency to do. Debra had to be a big girl and confront this head-on—see where her marriage was going. She believed in those vows she spoke. Debra promised God. She intended to keep her promise. Maybe counseling—again.

She stood up and wiped her face with the back of her hand

before walking over to her chest and placing the little "destroyer" in her third drawer where she kept her lingerie. It was an ironic hiding place for it. She didn't know what moved her to place it there. It just seemed like it should go there. Debra wouldn't deal with it today. No. Today was a beautiful spring day. The air was filled with all the fragrances of May flowers. The sun was shining and the delicate blue sky was so serene with plush white clouds. She'd just gotten her hair done yesterday. She looked and felt good. Debra and Bryce were supposed to go ballroom dancing tonight. She'd bought a new dress and shoes to surprise him—get his attention.

She had stopped by Target and picked up several sandalwood scented candles for their return home. Debra wasn't going to throw all that out the window because of what she'd found. She would deal with that later—some other time when she wasn't so fragile, when she could handle the barrage of questions the "destroyer" required, and the answers she didn't necessarily want to hear. *White picket fence . . .*

Before her disillusionment got the best of her, Debra prayed. "Lord, I need you." It was a short cry for help. She stood up and walked over to the window where she watched Bryce mow the lawn. His muscles flexed tenaciously in the white tank he wore as moisture drizzled down his brow. His honey-brown skin bronzed in the sun. Debra pushed her forehead gently against the glass and stole glimpses of the masked man cutting her lawn. Bryce looked up instinctively, as if he could feel her presence and tossed his hand up in a wave. Debra smiled an innocuous smile to hide the thoughts that were bombarding her head. *White picket fence . . .*

* * *

Debra lay in the afterglow. Indulging in dinner and dancing

had been an easy way for her to delude herself into thinking that maybe life was normal—maybe there was a reasonable explanation for what she'd found. Maybe it was some joke one of his co-workers had played on him. Maybe. She listened to Bryce's light snore, relishing the mental snapshot of his peacefully sleeping face, wondering how he could be so deceitful...wondering how he repeatedly took a sledge hammer to their union with his indiscretions and lies. Lies. That's what he told mostly. The lies were necessary to cover up the parts of life that he didn't want to admit existed.

Sleep evaded her. Debra rose from the bed and went down to the kitchen to meditate until she couldn't hold her eyes open another minute. She'd fallen asleep with her head buried in the Bible when Bryce awakened her.

"Debbie . . . get up," he said shaking her. "Debbie! Come on babe, go back to bed."

Debra rubbed her lids to focus on Bryce as her vision sharpened. She watched a blur transform into the man she loved. "Umm . . . " she stretched. "What time is it?"

"It's 5:00 a.m. What are you doing down here?"

"I couldn't sleep."

"After all that good lovin'?" he joked.

She couldn't force a smile. Thoughts of the dream she had devoured it. She tilted her head and stared at him.

"What's the matter, babe, you okay?"

Debra should have lied. She wasn't ready for this right before church. "No, not really, Bryce. No. I'm not." She couldn't hold it in. The thought was eating away at her conscience.

"We've still got a few more hours before church. You can get another couple hours of sleep. I'll wake you up in time for early service."

"No, I'm tired of *you*, Bryce," she said. Debra stood and walked toward the staircase. She climbed the stairs slowly, waiting for the *truth*.

Bryce followed her. "Babe, what are you talking about? I thought we had a good time."

Debra stopped on the ledge. "Who are you seeing?" Her voice was calm. She had breathed slowly and spoke perfunctorily, as if she had asked him the time.

"WHAT?! Debbie, come on, babe . . . what are you talking about?!"

Again, her voice was calm. "Who is she?"

"Who is *who*, Deb?"

"The woman you're seeing. The one who was on the trip with you."

"Debbie, where is all this coming from? I was on a business trip. You *know* that, Debbie. I don't know what *she* you're talking about."

"If you're not going to be honest Bryce, I don't want you here anymore. I can't keep living with you lying." Her voice hadn't raised an octave.

It was unnerving to Bryce. *But how could she have known?* Her calmness was scaring him. "Debbie, I don't know what you're talking about."

"You don't?"

Stick to the story. "No, babe, I don't. I wasn't with anyone but my co-workers."

"I want you gone. *Today*," she said walking into the second floor laundry room.

"Deb—"

"Today, Bryce," she said resolutely. No tears. No crying. She plugged the iron into the wall and walked past him, careful to avoid touching him. She went into their master suite and into the closet to retrieve the dress she was going to wear to church. It was a flowing yellow sundress that didn't quite fit Debra's gray mood. She left Bryce standing in that spot at the doorway of the laundry room. Reentering with her dress in hand, she passed him again, and laid her dress on the ironing board. She poured water into the spout on the iron and tried to focus on the gurgling sound it made—anything but what was happening right now. She separated the panels on the window to let the morning light in, and pressed the iron against her dress.

Bryce stood in the door way, carefully calculating his words. "Deb—"

"Nothing but the truth, Bryce," she interrupted, sitting the iron up. She held it firmly—almost threateningly.

"Okay, Debbie . . . I'm confused, babe. I'm sorry. I'm . . . I'm . . ." he stuttered. "I'm just really confused right now," he admitted ruefully.

"Who is she?"

"I've been soul searching, Debbie."

"Bryce, I'm going to ask you one more time. *Who* is she?" Her eyes were angry.

Bryce laid his forearm against the doorpost and rested his head on it. He let out a sigh of disgust. His words were muffled. "Suzette . . . I was with Suzette. I think I'm still in love with her."

Had she heard him correctly? Certainly he hadn't said what she thought she had heard. She snatched the iron cord from the wall to silence the room from any distractions that would keep her from hearing Bryce. "*Excuse* me?! You were with *whom*?"

Bryce moved his arm from the doorpost and looked Debra in her eyes, stabbing her with the words she thought she'd heard in the first place. "I was with Suzette. I think I still love her. I'm just confused right now, Deb. I never meant to hurt you."

Debra sucked in a breath and let it out slowly. She wanted to attack him with the iron that her fingers were inching near, but she pulled them back. She crossed her arms over her chest and rubbed the sweat from her palms. Her response was graceful. She bit back every vile word she wanted to spew. "I want you and everything that belongs to you out of this house by the time I get home from church. You can leave your key on the counter in the kitchen." Her quiet voice was final. Gingerly she lifted her dress from the ironing board, hung it on a hanger, and toted it gracefully past Bryce.

His eyes revealed the shame he felt. "Debbie, I'm so sorry . . ."

Debra turned around fiercely. "For what, Bryce? Wasting five years of my life?"

"It's never been like that, Deb. You know that."

"All I know, Bryce, is that after all we've been through—after all I've dealt with—you tell me you love someone *else*?"

"Debbie, I didn't plan any of this."

"How long have you been seeing her, Bryce?"

"Debbie, don't do this."

Her tone rose. "How long have you been seeing her, Bryce?"

"Babe . . . I'm sorry."

"How long?!"

Bryce spoke the words quietly, sneaking them out. "A few months," he said swallowing hard.

Debra let go of the tear that fought its way out of her eyes, and it cascaded down her soft cheek. She shook her head and smiled an ironic smile. "You took her on a *vacation*? You lied about the business trip?"

He couldn't respond to that loaded question.

Debra closed her eyes and wished it all away. She spoke without opening them. "So all the late hours at work—everything for the last few months has been one big lie?" She ached inside. She'd given herself to him just hours ago. Why had she done that after what she'd found? He'd held Suzette in the same arms he'd caressed Debra with last night. Kissed her with those same lying lips. Shared the kind of passion with Suzette that should have been exclusively reserved for his wife.

"Right now, Bryce. I want you to go. Right now." Debra went into their bedroom and took a pair of shoes from the closet. She opened her dresser and took her undergarments and slip out before going into the guest bedroom. She closed the door softly behind her.

Bryce's eyes poured out his pain and embarrassment. His confusion. His loss. He packed the same suitcase that he'd used to betray his wife. Then he loaded his stereo equipment and computers into the car. He took a few things from his office, and as many of his clothes and belongings that could fit into his black Yukon Denali XL.

Debra lay lifeless across the bed in the guest bedroom. She wasn't coming out until she heard Bryce load the last of his belongings and was gone out of her life for good. It had taken her an hour to stop crying and get herself together after Bryce had finally left. It was 8:00 a.m. She was going to be late for service. She tried to make her body move faster through the house, down the stairs, and out the door, but Bryce had shocked it into slow motion. She walked past the black granite counter where Bryce's house key lay. She picked it up and tossed it into the waste paper basket. She would call a locksmith as soon as she returned home from church. Bryce wasn't coming back. Debra wouldn't allow it. What was this, his second affair in five years? Two too many.

She knew why she had stayed after the first one, but now, she was going to be a statistic after all, joining ranks with the fifty percent of the population that was divorced.

*   *   *

Debra sat in the balcony of Morning Star Baptist Church crying weary tears, while Pastor Joseph Kelley preached a sermon that seemed to have everyone else shouting and laughing. The stadium seating sanctuary was packed with what seemed like all two thousand members present and accounted for. Debra couldn't make out Pastor Kelley's words over the loud noise in her head. All the conversations she'd had with Bryce. All the times he'd made her laugh. All the times they'd shared each other's love in the last few months. She wondered how many times he had been intimate with Suzette in that time. How many times had Bryce *claimed* that he was working on a project for his job, but was really with Suzette? How many times had he left his marriage bed to be with Suzette? When did he and Suzette start seeing each other again? *How* did they start seeing each other again?

Debra couldn't make out Pastor Kelley anymore. Her eyes were blurred with tears. The roar of praise sounded more like noise. She grabbed her purse and scooted her way down and out of the aisle. Sandy and B J McKenzie sat in the row across the aisle from her with their two toddlers, and their newborn twins resting peacefully in their carriers. Sandy was so overly protective, that she kept the children with her throughout the service unless they were fussy. Then she'd take them to the infant and toddler room. She noticed Debra and followed her out of the sanctuary. Debra had run into the restroom and pressed herself into a corner.

"Debbie, you okay—?"

Debra responded with more crying. Somehow Sandy knew *that* cry. She'd been there before. It pierced her on the inside. She pulled Debra from the wall and wrapped her arms around her. "It's going to be alright, Debbie. I'm right here for you."

"Oh, I hurt . . . so badly right now . . . Lord, Jesus please . . . " Debra cried on Sandy's pink and white flower printed dress.

"It's okay. God knows, Debbie. He can fix whatever it is."

"I don't even want it fixed!" Her cry grew louder.

"Debbie, what's wrong?"

It took a few minutes before Debra could calm herself enough for her words to be understood. "It's Bryce . . . he has been cheating on me . . . again. I just don't know why God let this happen to me, Sandy. I've been trying so . . . so hard to make this thing work."

Every word Sandy wanted to say evaporated in her mind. She couldn't think of anything that would console Debra. It was as if her thoughts were being stolen as they formed, so she just hugged Debra and prayed for her.

2
Relic

ebra's mother, Sheila, had called four times in the last
few hours. Debra and Bryce had skipped Sunday dinner
at her home, which was unusual as a total eclipse. It was
Debra's practice to call when they couldn't make it. Sheila knew
something was wrong. The marriage had been rocky in the past,
and Debra always seemed to withdraw when it got that way so she
wouldn't be compelled to tell her mother anything else that could
add fuel to her father's building fire.

Debra still had on the dress she'd worn to church. She lay in
the guest bedroom flipping through the cable channels on the high
definition plasma screen that Bryce had bought for company—
especially his older brother, Calvin, who along with his wife,
visited him and Debra at least once a year. It seemed that Bryce
was always trying to keep up with Calvin who ran a successful
medical practice in San Diego and had made some shrewd real-

estate investments that afforded him a lavish lifestyle.

The guest bedroom looked almost as nice as the master suite. After visiting his brother's impressive six million dollar home in La Jolla, Bryce had come home and ordered new furniture for the guest room and hired an interior decorator to duplicate a swanky Venice, Italy hotel suite. It had olive-colored silk wallpaper with delicate cream antique furnishings. The only thing truly modern in the room was the plasma screen. It seemed that Calvin and his wife Jessica had them all over their house. Even in the bathrooms, of all places. Bryce was adamant about not having Calvin show him up, which was hard to do, considering the fact that as a plastic surgeon, Calvin made triple Bryce's salary. Although his computer programming and design firm earned a little over two million the previous year, Bryce was a long way from his big brother, financially speaking.

Debra couldn't stand to be in the master suite. She looked around the guest room glad that Bryce had outfitted it so nicely, although she thought it was ridiculous at the time. She looked at the silk wallpaper on the walls and the antique furniture and remembered her and Bryce's honeymoon in Venice. Their marriage was full of passion and promise that night. A sad five years later it was dissolving.

Debra felt foolish. How could she have thought that Bryce was going to change his ways? She had believed him after the first affair, two years into their marriage. She had tried to empathize with him then and watched him come undone as he watched his mother lose her fight with ovarian cancer. Debra was a helpless witness as her new husband withdrew from everyone and everything—even her. She rationalized that the trauma of losing a parent made him act outside of himself. She witnessed the emotional rawness and anger Bryce had toward God. He'd never had a relationship with his father, and Diana was all the family Bryce had ever known before his marriage to Debra. So she tried to make herself understand that his affair was a result of his emotional instability at the time. Debra erased his extra-marital indiscretion from her mind as if it had never happened. This time she couldn't pretend.

She went down to the family room and looked in the trunk where she and Bryce kept their photo albums. He hadn't thought to take any of them with him. Debra searched through the numerous albums until she found the worn green and black one that represented Bryce's life with Suzette "Zee" Peters.

Debra had to look at Suzette's face and see what Bryce saw in the chocolate complexioned woman with the long, jet-black hair and eyes. Suzette was a tall, shapely, exotic looking woman with the kind of curves men loved. She reminded Debra of the singer, Sade, with darker skin. Debra knew Suzette's whole life story.

Suzette was born in Germany, a military brat who had lived all over the world. Her father was a high-ranking military officer. Her mother was a homemaker, who sewed beautifully. She met Bryce in middle school, and then her family moved away. They re-connected in high school, but Suzette always had to move when their relationship was deepening. The two maintained contact in college. Suzette had studied abroad in Paris and Italy. Bryce and Suzette's timing never seemed to be right. Her parents were still together. Like Debra, she was a daddy's girl, having an ongoing rivalry with her mother, and she was *beautiful*.

Debra took the album up the stairs with her and lay back across the bed in the guest room. There they were, Suzette and Bryce years ago, smiling, kissing, and hugging on various photographs. Debra felt a kick in the pit of her stomach. Did Bryce think Suzette was more beautiful than she was? Was it her exotic look that kept him desiring her after all these years? Was it her curvaceous body, or did the two of them have some sort of deep soul connection that still drew Bryce? Was it a connection that he couldn't shake after all these years—even after being married?

Debra remembered once when Bryce had had some of his buddies over for Monday Night Football. Chris Porter, one of Bryce's long time friends asked him about Suzette. Debra was on her way back down to the basement with more buffalo wings when she overheard the conversation:

"So Bryce, man, whatever happened to Suzette—Zee? You ever talk to her?"

Bryce hadn't responded, which caused a sly laughter from the rest of his Monday night crew.

"That silence must mean yes," Chris had said. He lowered his voice. "I ain't mad at you if you have, and I definitely ain't mad at you for not telling!"

Again, the men laughed. Debra had stood still near the top of the stairs to hear what Bryce had to say. She couldn't control her curiosity. She could just imagine the wicked grin on her husband's face at the mention of an old flame like Suzette. She had heard the stories of how beautiful she was.

"Man, that's one of the finest women I have ever seen in my life. Sexy, chocolate thing. I mean, if you weren't my boy, I would have tried to creep behind your back on that one. Every time you walked in a room with her dudes' mouths would just drop open," Chris said.

"Yeah. Bryce always gets the fine ones. Deb is fine too." Leon had interjected.

"Man, but Suzette, this chick was *f-i-n-e* . . . looked like she stepped off a magazine cover or somethin'. I used to envy you back then, man." Chris continued.

Back then. It was apparent that Bryce wasn't going to comment. He had enough sense to keep his mouth shut while Debra was there. If she hadn't been, he might have given in to his male ego and shared a bit—just enough to make the rest of the men jealous, but he wouldn't take that chance while Debra was there. Besides, his silence gave him more status with them and created a certain amount of intrigue. They figured his silence meant that he still had *that* bird in the hand. They envied him anyway.

Bryce liked to be envied. He'd once told Debra that he got a kick out of being with Suzette because she was so beautiful. Men gawked at her when she was with him. He was always the topic of conversation because of it. It was a natural man-thing to be puffed up about his woman—especially when he had one that everyone else wished they had. It was like dating a movie star.

Debra wondered. Was that what his relationship with Suzette was about? She looked through the pictures and cried. Was Bryce's need to be envied or applauded by his peers more important than their marriage? It had to be deeper than that. When the time came, she would surely find out.

Debra was fast asleep when the phone in the guest bedroom awakened her. She didn't answer it. It was probably her mother anyway. She shifted, and a picture that she had lifted from the protective film of the photo album slid to the floor. Sleepily Debra rolled over and reached down to pick it up. It was a picture of Suzette on a beach wearing a white bikini. She could tell by the enticing look in Suzette's eyes that Bryce had taken the photo. It was as if Suzette was inviting him closer with the tilt of her head. The sun eased down behind her giving her skin a sensuous glaze. Debra studied the thief of her husband's heart "What kind of hold do you have on my husband?" she said aloud, returning the photo to its proper place in the photo album.

She picked up the phone and dialed the voice mail. It was Bryce. *"Debbie, I know you may not want to talk to me right now, but I want to get some household things straightened out with you."* Bills. He was anal like that. *" . . . Listen . . . I don't want to stress you or anything. Just wanted to sit down and let you know how I think we can handle things. I just want to keep you in the loop. The house is a big responsibility. I'm not going to stick you with a bunch of bills. I wanted to work it all out with you. Call me on my cell when you get a chance, please. Bye."*

Did he think she cared about managing the house right now? Is that all he could think about? Debra would deplete every dime she had in her 403b before she ruined her credit or slacked on the household bills. *Fine. That's all he can think of?! He has nothing to say about messing up my life? Lying? Cheating? He wants to discuss check writing? Fine.* "Whatever," she said aloud. She hung up the phone, bypassing all of her mother's messages.

3
Manic Monday

M *anic Monday.* Debra hurried up the stairs to the second floor of Peace Valley High School. The four-story hi-tech glass structure was a stand-in for a fortune 500 company office complex, with immaculately landscaped lawns, dramatically designed outdoor fountains, stone paved walk-ways and winding garden trails. At Peace Valley, the cars parked on the student lot mimicked those driven by six-figure-earning CEOs and company presidents. It was just one of the privileges of indulged youth living a suburban upper-class lifestyle. Located in an area where hefty property taxes afforded such extravagant luxuries, the campus was complete with two Olympic size pools, a full size professional football field and basketball court, and a tennis court that rivaled that of Centre court at Wimbledon. The library and computer lab were unrivaled university equivalents. Needless to say, the students at Peace Valley came from upper-crust families who felt entitled and deserving of the spoils.

Debra navigated through the crowded hallway that was alive with the familiar sound of excited, high-pitched screeches and weekend chatter, filled with the tales that only a Monday could conjure up. Cliques congregated at lockers and near the stairwell recanting the happenings of their lives during the two-day furlough. The P.V. athletes and movie stars-in-the-making crowded around Jason Lockmore's locker. He was Peace Valley's young Michael Jordan. The geeks hovered near the stairwell, while the *different* kids sort of walked together down the hall. The "in-betweens" congregated at lockers where they could easily observe the jocks and the wanna-be stars.

Debra was late. Her normal arrival time was thirty-minutes *before* school started. She liked to spend quiet meditation time in her office with a cup of coffee and her 'Daily Bread' devotional before being bombarded with the problems of this affluent high school world. Her denim bag swung fiercely back and forth across her right hip as she bumped her way through the swirl of students and into the health wing of the school where her office was located.

"Hey, Mrs. Myles! Can I come see you this afternoon? I need to talk about that *little situation* we discussed last week," Jeremy Manning yelled to her.

"After lunch. Get a pass."

"Cool." Jeremy returned, nodding.

How was she supposed to be any help to Jeremy who was trying to cope with his parents' pending divorce, when she might be getting a divorce herself? What encouragement could she offer today, after what had happened between her and Bryce over the week-end? Debra slid the electronic key in the door and unlocked the wing. The door slammed shut, locking automatically. She went into her office and sat her bag down in a chair and hung up her coat. She placed her bag underneath her desk then started coffee. All of the offices in the clinic wing had been painted in a mundane beige color and appointed with brown furniture. Bryce had re-painted her walls a light pink. Debra bought pink and brown striped curtains, and pink throw pillows for the brown sofa. Debra thought the pink would be perfect for the girls and the brown worked for the guys. She had artwork and student collages on her walls and desk. It was a friendly, relaxed environment; a retreat that offered respite and reassurance for teen-sized problems and crises.

While she waited, she booted up the computer and looked at the To-Do list she'd left for herself on Friday. She didn't feel like doing any one of the seven items on the list. She especially didn't feel like seeing any students today. Mondays were always packed. Debra looked on her e-calendar. All the tough students were on Monday. She couldn't remember why she'd scheduled them that way. It just seemed that she needed to touch base with them after the weekend. They were the ones who had serious problems like addictions, depression, and bipolar disorder. She sighed. Affluence sometimes gave the illusion of perfection. Even though most of her kids were from well-to-do homes, they had just as many, if not more problems than teens Debra had worked with in the inner city. Every now and then she questioned her decision to become a school social worker. It had to be one of the most stressful jobs there was, second only to the work of an air traffic controller. However, it definitely was rewarding at times.

The tardy bell rang. Debra got up and poured herself a cup of coffee. She put extra sugar in it. She needed the extra energy, although she realized it was going to send her crashing before lunch. Sugar always had that effect on her. It hyped her up then let her down hard. She pulled her snack drawer open and prayed that there was one of those energy bars the school nurse told her she should stop eating. She moved her hand around underneath all the other junk food in the drawer and found one. She handled it as if it were 14K gold, placing it on top of her desk photo collage cube.

Debra sat down at her desk and stared out the window, sipping her coffee. Her gaze was broken by her audio e-mail alert: *"Hey, baby, you've got mail,"* a deep Barry White sounding voice said from the computer. She twisted her rolling chair around to face the screen and clicked the mail button. It was an email from Bryce. She clicked the mouse and read.

You haven't answered any of my calls. I'm not trying to stress you, but there are some things we need to talk about, baby. I need you to call me.

Debra sat back in the chair and re-lived Sunday morning all over again. She put her head down on her desk and sobbed. Her life wasn't normal. Why was she at work trying to act as if it was? Her telephone rang. She inhaled, sucked up her pain and cleared her throat. She picked up on the fourth ring.

"Hello, Peace Valley High School Health Clinic, Mrs. Myles speaking." She immediately wished she hadn't answered when she heard his voice.

"Deb, we need to talk."

"I'm listening, Bryce."

"I electronically transferred some money into our joint account this morning so that you can take care of the bills. I'm going to be doing that for the next few months, Deb. Like I said, I'm not trying to stress you."

"Humph. I'd think stress would come natural to someone who'd been cheated on."

"Deb, I don't want to get into it with you this morning, babe. I'm trying to do the right thing by you—believe that."

"Was that what you were thinking, every time you laid up with Suzette, Bryce? You were doing the right thing by me?" The pain she felt just moments ago had caramelized into a sweet, menacing anger.

He was silent a moment before saying, "I'm just trying to figure things out Deb—get my head clear."

"You plan to stay gone Bryce? You said a few months. How long does it take to decide if you are going to be with your wife or lay up with some tramp?"

"She's not a tramp, Deb. It's not like that."

The nerve of him defending Suzette. That one act of treason sent Debra springing up out of her chair. "What is she to you then, Bryce? Because I thought I was your wife!"

The bile that shot out of her mouth afterward shocked her. Though fiercely repugnant, she couldn't stop it. It was like a busted fountain that sprayed water out mercilessly. She slammed the phone down hard and screamed as if she was attempting to scare some huge, horrific monster away from her. Debra stood frozen in her spot behind her desk squeezing back a weekend's worth of tears, five years in the making. Her eyes stung like they'd been assaulted with pepper spray.

Virginia Carlton, the school nurse, had entered the wing and was walking toward her office when she heard Debra screaming. Debra's screams had both frightened and shocked Virginia. When she gathered that it was safe, Virginia took it upon herself to walk in and gently say, "Debra, sit down for a moment and calm down." Like Debra, Virginia was accustomed to handling all kinds of student problems, including mental health issues. She knew how to de-escalate a situation.

Debra plopped down like an obedient mental patient climbing out of a moment of rage. She rocked back and forth in her chair as if her life depended on it, rattling the items on her desk.

Virginia went to Debra's door, closed it shut and pulled the shade in case anyone else entered the wing. It was obvious that this wasn't a work-related matter. Virginia claimed the seat across from Debra.

"I want to help you. Tell me how I can do that," Virginia said gently. "Whatever it is, we can work it out together—if you like." Her non-threatening, southern drawl was soothing to Debra, even at a time like this.

It was easy to see how, despite the obvious age gap, the students still took to Nurse Carlton. At sixty, she was old enough to be their grandmother. However, that didn't stop them from bonding with her. In fact, her genuinely caring attitude made her sort of a mother-figure among them. She was a slender woman of medium height. Her silver hair was cut into a sharp, angular bob. She dressed fashionably underneath her lab coat, and Virginia Carlton kept up with the latest happenings in the students' world; it helped to keep her young at heart.

Debra squeezed her eyes closed, wringing the last of the tears out. She focused on Nurse Carlton. "My husband is cheating on me . . . and my marriage is a mess," Debra managed stoically.

"My, Lord. I'm so sorry to hear that, Debbie. I want you to know that I will be here for you. God is here for you."

"Thank you, Virginia. I just don't feel like *me* today. I don't know why I came in."

"Sometimes we feel like we can handle things, when we really need a minute to regroup. I think today might be one of those days that you need to regroup. You can't counsel a soul in this building unless *self* is together."

"I know. I just have to get through this."

"In time. Now listen, God is a God who can handle all manner of problems, you hear me? What appears to be un-fixable to us, isn't to God. Lasting marriages go through all sorts of trials. Believe me. I was the trial queen," Virginia chuckled a bit.

Debra blew into a tissue, and wiped escaping tears. "Right now, I feel worthless. Gosh, this was not how my life was supposed to go, Virginia. I was supposed to be *happy*," Debra cried.

"*Happy?* That word, you know, can be a weapon against a sane mind."

Debra looked puzzled. "That's what everybody lives for."

"I don't want to get all soupy on you, Debbie, because God knows I hate when people get soupy on me. I know that you realize *joy*—not happiness comes from God, so I'm not going to tell you that. What I will tell you is to pursue *peace*, not happiness. The word 'happiness' can be a villain. It changes over the years— what makes you happy. I think when you have God's peace—in any situation, you'll be okay. Now, does that mean that life won't hurt? Lord, no. It means that you have rested in the assurance that God is in control—He's with you."

"You don't understand, Virginia. This is not the *first* time Bryce has been with another woman. I'm beginning to think that he just doesn't want me—doesn't love me. He's not the man I thought he was."

"You know, sometimes in our foolishness, we make terrible mistakes Debbie—mistakes that cost us more than we planned to pay, and we have to deal with the consequences. Bryce has to work some things out in his mind. Lord knows you are a wonderful woman. He has to be convinced of that."

"I thought being his wife and loving him was convincing enough."

"No, no, no. It's not about *you* convincing him. It's about him convincing himself."

"I don't know if I can ever forgive him for this. I don't want to forgive him for this. He keeps hurting me like I don't matter to him."

"In time, you'll be able to forgive him and work through it. Mike stayed with me," Virginia confessed holding Debra's gaze.

"Virginia, you cheated?"

"I'm not proud of it, but yes. I thought 'happy' was in the arms of an old flame who never gave a hoot about me. Nearly tore my marriage apart, Debbie—emotionally killing the man who has always loved me. I was too young and too dumb to realize the gravity of what I'd done back then. You see, my daughter, Margaret, is not Mike's *biological* daughter."

"I was a typical naïve southern girl—high school cheerleader. Good girl. I fell for Thomas Ray, our quarterback. I was seventeen years old and green as ever. Well, I let Thomas Ray get me in a whirlwind of trouble right in the back of his father's old Ford pick-up truck. Next thing you know, I was pregnant. I'd just graduated and was planning to go to college to become a nurse."

"I thought Thomas and I would be a family, but honey, Thomas stopped speaking to me way before I ever told him I was pregnant. He'd walk past me like I was invisible. I put up with the shame of being pregnant and being dumped. My daddy had too much pride and too much love for me to make me have a shotgun wedding. He told me before he died that I deserved *good love*. I didn't understand what he meant until years later," Virginia said.

She told Debra how she'd met her husband Mike while she was seven months pregnant. While all the other people in her small town shunned her, Mike engaged her in conversation whenever he'd see her. She vaguely remembered him from her biology class in tenth grade. He'd admitted to having a crush on her since then. He said he'd always been in love with her. She couldn't help but feel secure with Mike. He married her in two months, right before Margaret was born.

They were married two years when Thomas Ray crept back into her thoughts. She'd seen him around town and the attention he'd given her seemed to make up for the broken heart she'd suffered at his hands before. Virginia loved Mike, but Thomas was something that she'd never been able to have. The excitement of his attention caused her to stray away from the man God had sent her.

"Virginia, I can't imagine *you* doing something like that," Debra said, shocked.

"Well now, I'm human like everyone else, Miss Debra. I thought that maybe Thomas and I were meant to be—after all Margaret was his daughter. I loved Mike, but being with Thomas made me feel *happy*—worthy. It was all foolishness of course. I'll never forget the look on Mike's face when he came to Thomas Ray's house looking for me, toting Margaret. He looked as if life itself had been sucked out of him. His skin was pale white. He knew what I'd been doing with Thomas. He just looked at me and said, 'I love you. We need you. Come on home, Virginia.' His face was soaked with tears, but I saw true love in those eyes, love I didn't deserve. I looked back at Thomas. He had a mischievous, boyish grin on his face, like he'd been caught with his hand in a cookie jar. His eyes were empty—uncaring—nothing like the man that was standing there holding our daughter. I never looked back, Debbie. That was nearly forty years ago. That's why when people ask me how is it that I left Florida to come to cold Michigan, I tell them my husband wanted to be close to his grandson—Margaret's firstborn, and that was it. I would follow Mike Carlton to the ends of the earth."

Debra soaked it in. Looking at Virginia she never would have guessed she'd done something like that. Still, where did that leave her and Bryce? He seemed to have made up his mind that he was going to be gone for a few months, as if he didn't even want to be married. All he wanted to talk about was bills.

Debra stayed at work, but the only student she saw was Jeremy Manning. The poor kid had been so depressed, she had to talk to him. He was feeling guilty about his parents divorcing, but he was glad too. He'd seen his father beat his mother more times than he cared to remember. The last incident had turned into a family spectacle when Jeremy tried to help his mother. He'd knocked his father unconscious with a lamp. Consequently, Jeremy was assigned a juvenile probation officer. There was so much documentation of domestic violence complaints against his father, however, that the judge gave Jeremy a break. Initially, during the altercation, Jeremy had thought he'd killed his father. He admitted to being relieved for those few moments. He was still struggling with that guilt. Jeremy and his mother were moving back to Arizona with relatives.

"Mrs. Myles, talking to you has helped me a lot," Jeremy said. He held back his tears cleverly in front of Debra.

"I'm glad Jeremy. And remember what I said. Don't be afraid of your feelings. It's okay that you *wished* your father was dead. That was a normal reaction to what you've seen him do to your mother over the years. We just can't always *act* on our feelings, understand?"

"Yeah. I'm really gonna miss you, Mrs. Myles. I've never been able to talk to anyone like I can talk to you."

"I'm glad you feel that way."

"I'm kinda excited about going someplace new, though— living closer to my cousins and all, and Arizona is warm . . . "

"You can always email me, Jeremy. I promise to write back."

"Thanks, Mrs. Myles. I'm gonna write you—I promise."

"I'll be looking forward to your emails. Well, it's almost time for the bell to ring. Good luck with everything."

"Okay, bye."

Debra had made it through an entire school day. It was a quarter 'til three. She had the rest of the day to regroup. She thought about just walking around at the mall. That always seemed to calm her down. If she went home right now, she'd just spend the rest of the day crying. There were too many reminders of Bryce at home. She packed her things and prepared to leave, when her principal, Mrs. Daughtry, came in.

"Hi, Mrs. Myles, I'm sorry to bother you at the end of the day, and I'm not going keep you long. We have a new student who just enrolled today. This student is dealing with some very serious grief issues. She lost both her parents in a robbery and is living with her aunt. I promised her aunt that we would be able help her here. This young lady won't talk to anyone. Her aunt has tried to get her to see a therapist that a family friend recommended, but she has totally shut down since the tragedy of what happened to her parents." Mrs. Daughtry flipped through her note pad that she toted around with her everywhere she went. "Let me see . . . her name is . . . Wynona Garrett. She's fifteen."

Debra's face looked contorted. How could she add yet another student to her caseload? She already had forty-five students. Debra feared that adding more would make her less effective. What did the people in administration think? You could just lump a bunch of kids with serious mental health issues up on one worker, provide *effective* treatment and expect all the bureaucratic paper work to be done too?

"Gosh, Mrs. Daughtry, I am full. I mean, I actually don't know where I could squeeze Wynona in without needing some counseling myself."

"Mrs. Myles, I truly do understand your predicament. I know you are overworked, but as principal, you are the only option I can offer this young lady. She's not going to be academically successful if we don't help her deal with all that she's got going on. Being a new student and all . . . I just don't want to see her fail before she gets a chance to get started. If there is anything I can offer you—like some compensation time or something . . . you know I am more than willing."

"I'll see her tomorrow," Debra conceded. She knew that Karen Daughtry was the real deal. She definitely cared about the students. Although the school's standardized test scores were higher than the state average before Mrs. Daughtry had come on board, she was committed to being involved in the students' lives as much as she could be. Debra didn't want to think about it too long; it would just stress her out more. She had more pressing issues going on right now.

"Again, I really appreciate you, Mrs. Myles."

"Okay, see you tomorrow," Debra said zipping her bag. She needed to get out of the building before anyone else needed *something*. She didn't know what she could accomplish significantly with Wynona. There were only three weeks of school left, and the last week was always *crazy*.

4
The Truth of the Matter

It was ten thirty when Debra finally arrived home. She'd gone
to the mall and shopped until it closed, then she'd gone to Target where she stayed until it closed at ten o'clock. She carried
all of her bags upstairs and tossed them onto the guest bed. She
went into the master suite, plopped down on the bed and clicked
on the plasma screen television. She looked at the blinking light of
the digital recorder and scrolled through the caller ID before placing the phone back on the base. Sheila had been calling her like
a maniac. Debra wasn't in the mood for questions or accusations.
She turned on the television—a supposed-to-be love story. After
seeing the main character get excitedly nervous over some guy
that wasn't her husband, she turned it off. The story of someone
feeling trapped in an unfulfilling relationship, and subsequently
having an affair while their spouse was away, wasn't romantic. It
was downright adulterous. It didn't matter what the reason was.
All Debra could think about was Bryce being with Suzette—shar-

ing a love that wasn't theirs to share—probably at this very moment. The thought of it made Debra's stomach sick. She crawled into bed and cried weakly on her pillow.

When the phone rang, a part of her hoped it was Bryce. At least then she'd know that he wasn't making love to Suzette at that moment. She looked at the caller ID and was disappointed by the number. It wasn't Bryce. It was Tyler, Bryce's best friend, but for reasons unknown to Debra, their friendship hadn't been the same in recent years. Bryce talked about Tyler less, and Tyler didn't call or visit as frequently as he used to. Debra didn't know what that was about, and Bryce was short on answers when Debra inquired about his friendship with Tyler. Debra answered the phone.

"What's up brown sugar? Where's that ol' man of yours?" Tyler asked. His words were heavily sprinkled with a Brooklyn accent. Living in Michigan over the last twenty years hadn't tamed it that much.

Debra didn't want to go through this right now. "He's not here, Ty," she said casually, trying to sound normal.

"What do you mean, he's not there? It's almost eleven o'clock."

Debra took a deep breath. If she got this over with now, she wouldn't have to do it later. "Ty, Bryce doesn't live here anymore."

Tyler laughed. "Girl, stop trippin' on me. Where is your man?"

"Ty, I'm serious. Bryce moved out yesterday, and to tell you the truth, I don't know where he is—probably somewhere with Suzette. If you know how to find her, you could probably find my husband." The tears came and her voice wavered. "I'm very serious."

"What the—*What* is on that *boy's* mind?" Tyler hadn't even questioned Debra's statements—as if he expected this kind of behavior from his best friend.

"I don't know, Ty, but I do know he's been seeing Suzette.

He told me that himself. They just came back from a week-long vacation in Arizona. He told me he was going on a business trip. He lied."

Tyler was speechless. "Man, I . . . I don't even know what to say, Deb. I'm sorry. I didn't know anything about *this*. I don't know what's up with Bryce anymore. He can't just walk out on his wife for some chick he had a thing for way back in the day. That's *crazy*."

"Well, he did. I did ask him to leave, but that was after he told me he was confused—that he still loved her." Debra was crying so hard, it was hard for Tyler to decipher what she was saying.

"Deb, don't cry . . . I'm so sorry. God can work this thing out, for real."

"This is the second time, Ty. I can't keep doing this."

"I know, Deb." Tyler let out a frustrated breath and waited for Debra to compose herself.

Debra wondered if Tyler saying "*I know*" meant that he understood that she couldn't do this anymore, or if he knew that Bryce had cheated on her before. "Maybe you could try him on his cell, Ty. My head is hurting. I gotta get some sleep."

"I called that fool all day yesterday and today. He's avoiding me. He doesn't want to hear what I have to say. I knew something was wrong. But you listen to me, it's gonna be alright. One way or another. You don't have to keep putting up with adultery. Unh-uh." Tyler said the word *keep*. He knew something.

"Ty, you know about Bryce, don't you?

"Deb, I don't want to get in the middle."

"Ty, did he ever tell you about the time before—or Suzette?"

"Deb, listen. Bryce and I have talked about a lot of things. It wouldn't be right for me to discuss anything with you that he and I dealt with on a man-to-man level, but I will tell you this: You can rest assured that if Bryce ever came to me about a situation where he was out of line, I took him straight to the Word. I would never go along with a man cheating on his wife—or leaving her. I wouldn't do that to you, Deb. You're just like a sister to me. You are family."

Honor among men. It was fair. Tyler's skirting of the question told her all that she needed to know. Maybe that's why Bryce and Tyler's relationship had deteriorated. They just weren't the same type of men. "I know. Thanks for listening, Ty. I gotta go. Take care."

"Take care, Debra. I'm praying for you."

5

Grieving

Debra waited for her new student, Wynona Garrett, but pulling *herself* together every day was a chore, now that she had come to the realization that her marriage was in serious trouble. She knew that Bryce would be the key factor in whether or not the marriage made it. Even though she was hurt, deep down in her heart, Debra wanted to stick it out. If he came back home, she'd work on it.

Suzette had her beat hands-down. Debra asking him to move out had given him the freedom to love Suzette—to lay with her. Debra doubted herself. Maybe *she* should have left, and allowed Bryce to stay at the house. There was no way he would have brought Suzette to their home. Asking him to leave just seemed to have pushed Bryce into Suzette's arms—right where he wanted to be anyway. Debra looked out the window, thinking about her life—how screwed up it was. She heard voices in the wing and stepped into the hallway. She saw a thick, caramel-colored young lady with a wavy bush of hair walking toward her. Debra smiled.

"You must be Wynona?"

"Yes," the young lady replied somewhat uncomfortably.

"I'm Mrs. Myles. Come on in," Debra said, allowing her into the suite.

Wynona looked around at the sofa, group table, and Debra, then said, "Mrs. Myles, you have a nice office."

"Thanks, Wynona. I try to make it comfortable for you guys."

Wynona took a seat on the sofa and picked up a magazine from the coffee table. Debra waited for Wynona's comfort level to rise before she began asking questions. Wynona was easy going, but Debra could tell by her presence that she had a very boisterous side. Debra busied herself at her desk while Wynona looked through a magazine. Several minutes passed before either one of them spoke.

"This is therapy, right?" Wynona chuckled. "How come you're not asking me any questions?" Her smile was beautiful. She twirled a strand of her bushy hair.

"I was waiting on you to get comfortable, sweetie. I wasn't ignoring you," Debra smiled. This was a tactic she'd used for years with students she didn't know that well. It went against some of the things she'd learned in grad school, but it worked. This strategy gave the students more control and prevented them from feeling like they were being bombarded as soon as they walked in her door. It wasn't easy sharing your business with a stranger. Debra understood them.

"This is about the third time I've been in somebody's office for therapy. I really don't want to talk about what you want me to talk about, Mrs. Myles," Wynona said honestly.

"Really? Well, my first question is, what is it exactly that you *think* I want you to talk about, Wynona?" Debra was good at what she did. She kept an indifferent look on her face—not too pressed, not too laid back.

Wynona let out an exasperated breath of air. "My *parents*?"

"Oh. Well, actually, I didn't want you to talk about them today—unless you want to talk about them."

Wynona's tone was flat and final. "I don't."

"Okay," Debra said nonchalantly. "I need to ask you some other easy questions then." She observed Wynona's responses as she went through a student questionnaire she'd developed, which enabled her to obtain non-threatening information, like their favorite color, what kinds of foods they liked, their favorite movies and other seemingly insignificant information, which always opened doors to other conversation.

Wynona relaxed immediately. Afterward, when Debra felt that Wynona was comfortable, she shared some information with her on grief, explaining in depth the stages of grief, and the feelings Wynona may experience, as well as certain behaviors associated with those feelings. Wynona paid attention as Debra talked, but offered very little conversation.

There was something about Wynona that Debra liked. She had such a pleasant spirit. Debra could sense that even through the steel guarded doors Wynona had erected to protect herself, she was transparent. Debra could see right through her stand-offish attitude. She was in a lot of pain. There was a small dimmer in the bright, light brown eyes that were warming Debra's heart. Hidden behind those eyes, was a broken heart. Debra tried hard to avoid getting attached to the students, but it was almost impossible working at a school, especially when she saw most of them every day from ninth through twelfth grade.

Their first session lasted an hour. Debra was satisfied with the information she gained, and was confident that a therapeutic alliance was forming. She learned a great deal in the hour she spent with the beautiful young butterfly. It was Wynona's preference to be called by her nickname, "Noni." Noni indicated that on the "All About Me" questionnaire she filled out. She loved to cook, dance, and roller skate. She wrote poems. Four had been published in a teen magazine. Noni was a delightful girl. Debra watched her as she left the health wing. Noni had a better shape than some grown women Debra knew—thick and curvy. She was just fifteen years old, about a size twelve and very voluptuous. She was well proportioned, with a double scoop of everything. Somehow, she caused Debra to think of Suzette. Debra squashed the thought.

The mysteries of the bombshell butterfly unfolded over the next several sessions they had. Debra saw her twice a week. Noni was beginning to open up and work through her grief by acknowledging it, journaling, and talking about it. Her aunt, Elaine Hudson, was her mother's sister. She called Debra at least once a week to see how things were going. She told Debra that she saw a change in Noni. She was starting to awaken—talk to people again and smile. She'd lost her parents just a few weeks before she began seeing Debra. It took a lot of strength for Noni to talk about her parents' brutal murder. She trusted Debra, and even shared that her faith in God had been wavering. She was raised a Christian. Now, she was confused. Debra discovered that Noni's disillusionment with God was the source of much of her guilt.

Lately, Noni had been questioning whether God was real or not. Her parents had taught her that He was, and Noni believed them, until they were murdered. The tragedy had shaken her— made her doubt. Someone broke into their home, shot both of her parents at close range and robbed them. There was no forced entry. It was someone they knew, and had willingly allowed into the house.

They lived in "the hood" for as long as Noni could remember. Her Father, Judge Joseph Garrett, used to tell her, "Never be afraid to be around your own people." And even though they could have moved somewhere else, he chose to stay in the old neighborhood. Joseph Garrett had been a judge at the juvenile court in Detroit for over twenty years. Her mother, Andrea, had been a kindergarten teacher. Joseph had been convinced that living on Collingwood Street showed the kids in the neighborhood that they could be anything they wanted to be. He believed in community. Noni grew up spending holidays at the soup kitchens with her parents, feeding the homeless. She couldn't remember a holiday that the family didn't go to a soup kitchen or homeless shelter first. Joseph said that was what God called them to do. Andrea went right along with him. As Noni grew older, she figured out that the two of them liked spending the extra time together anyway. Even though she found it sort of gross to see them all "lovey-dovey," Noni missed it now that they were gone.

Her aunt Elaine had legal custody of her now. Noni told Debra she loved her aunt almost as much as she had loved her parents, as she sat on the sofa with her legs propped up on Debra's ottoman.

"That's good, Noni. I'm glad that you feel safe with Ms. Hudson."

"Yeah, she's got a bunch of plans for us this summer, but some days, I just don't feel like doing nothin'. I just want to stay in bed and cry," Noni said somberly.

"I know, sweetie, but sometimes you've got to make yourself get up and walk around—get outside. Go to the park. *Cook*," Debra said smiling. "If you give in to depression too much, it can take over. There has to be some balance."

Noni nodded. Her eyes lit up. "Hey, Principal Daughtry told

me we were going to have a cooking class in the fall, but there's going to be a special summer program with this chef that owns a restaurant."

Debra smiled, knowing how much Noni enjoyed cooking. "That's great."

"I've already signed up for the summer workshop."

"Well, let me know how it goes."

"I will." Noni got up and gathered her cotton tote. She looked carefree today. Debra eyed her scoop-neck top and faded Capri pants that fit snuggly on her well-proportioned figure. A huge set of pink pearls dipped to her stomach and were tied in a knot. She had earrings to match. She'd wrapped a pink scarf around her bushy mane that poofed into an afro puff. She had on light pink sequined gym shoes. Debra liked the throw back look of the sixties. Noni was so stylish and confident. Debra had fallen in love with her already.

6
Summer Madness

The last day of school came and went. Debra was glad to say good-bye to her students, but what was she going to do at home? It was the one place she spent more time crying than anywhere else. Her only reprieve was work. So, for the first time in a long while, she allowed someone—who just happened to be Principal Daughtry—talk her into working summer school. Something she'd sworn off years ago so that she could use the time to regroup before the next school year.

The school had started a new enrichment program, which mainly served the students who weren't vacationing in exotic places with their parents. Ms. Daughtry had snagged Debra to run a life-skills class, because although most of the kids were well-off financially, some of them lacked the basic skills necessary for real-life success—like creating a budget, developing character, and being socially responsible. Debra taught a life skills class and

saw a few students for therapy sessions. Wynona Garrett was one
of the students who had summer sessions with her. She'd taken a
liking to the young bombshell, so at least that part of her life had
some joy in it. There were two other young women she saw for
therapy as well: Corey Hunt and Maya McIntyre, both of them
were a handful.

Corey's parents, like most of the parents at Peace Valley, were
upper-crust. Her father, Corey David Hunt, owned Hunt Capital
Management, and her mother, Dr. Vanessa Hunt, was an emergency surgeon. Mrs. Hunt had freaked out when she'd found marijuana in Corey's drawer, and subsequently read her journal and
found out that her little princess wasn't as innocent as she'd believed. She discovered that the beautiful little siren had long since
lost her virginity to a young man her mother knew nothing about.
Mr. Hunt was adamant about not having Corey treated at one of
the clinics in the area for fear of putting a stain on his perfect little
life. Vanessa was more reasonable, but she gave in to her husband.
After discovering that Debra was also a certified addictions counselor, they made the decision for Corey to be seen at school, which
to them seemed less intrusive and more ordinary than letting the
world know that their family didn't quite measure up to the image
they portrayed.

Maya, the most troubled of them all, just seemed to be suf-
fering from an identity crisis, along with the more noticeable
problem of anorexia bulimia. She was a African American girl
who had lived in Colorado for most of her life—gone to mostly
predominately white schools where she never felt fully accepted.
Before her father, Greg, a construction engineer, moved to Michigan, they'd had a brief stay in New York where it seemed to be
more culturally diverse. That proved to be an unsuccessful social
venture for Maya as well, because of her diction and use of proper

English, she never fit it with the black or Latina girls. They often called her offensive names, like "white-girl Maya." She wasn't "street" enough to hang with them. The most devastating truth was that she wasn't quite accepted by the white students either, which had made school a miserable experience for most of her life.

A wild party is what landed her in Debra's office. Maya completely trashed her father's house. Being a single parent and raising a young woman with an eating disorder was a constant challenge for her father, who had simply tried to give his daughter a better life than he'd had as a young African American male. He'd found a church that was predominately African-American, in an attempt to try and provide her with more social outlets, but found that he just wasn't helping his little girl to connect at all. He trusted that Debra was going to be that bridge, but all Debra could seem to focus on was the fact that her husband was gone.

*   *   *

The life skills session was over and Debra was glad. She wanted to steal away to her office where she could just think to herself for a moment. She didn't know how teachers stood up and talked most of the day. She was burned out after two hours straight. She found the second part of the workshop to be easier because it gave the students an opportunity to actually work on projects in groups. Debra eased her way out of the home economics wing and started up the stairs to the clinic. A voice slowed her stride.

"Hi, excuse me, I'm Chef Chase . . . I'm looking for the culinary class that I'm supposed to be teaching. Someone sent me to the cafeteria and I was told down there, that's not where I'm supposed to be . . . ?" He was a medium built brother with a light complexion. He had jet-black eyes and coarse jet-black hair that was cut in a close fade. He looked dumbfounded, but harmless.

"Actually the home economics wing is right around the corner. They're probably expecting you in the last room on the right," Debra said pointing.

"Thanks."

Debra was so consumed with her thoughts that she didn't notice that the man was handsome, or that she hadn't even been polite enough to say a courteous "you're welcome" to the lost soul. Before she knew it, she was back at her desk. She sat for a moment before she packed her things. She only taught for two hours a day Monday thru Wednesday. Debra had therapy sessions with her students right after her classes. She'd left Thursdays and Fridays open for the weekend getaways she was sure to need now that her life was falling apart. Her two-hour-a-day classes, along with therapy sessions, were a nice compromise. It kept her from sitting around crying for at least two hours a day. She needed to figure out what she was going to do with the rest of the day. She couldn't sit around crying again like she'd done yesterday.

She drove home, stopping at the mailbox in front of the house to get the mail. She got out of the car hurriedly and took the mail out of the wrought iron antique-looking mailbox stand that was reminiscent of the roaring twenties. She pulled the car into the garage and started searching through the mail as she entered the house. Bryce's American Express Black Card statement had arrived. Her curiosity made her open it. She slammed her fist on the table and swore. "I hate you, Bryce!" The statement wasn't a lie. Her marriage was a lie. Certainly Bryce was in love with Suzette. Purchases from the Louis Vuitton store at Somerset. Hotel suites. Dinner at places he'd never taken Debra. A twelve hundred dollar purchase at Saks—shoes. And Debra could just scream. She knew what that purchase was for. A pair of Giuseppe Zanotti heels she and Bryce had seen. He was so adamant about her having them. Debra had complained that the heels were too high and that the shoes were too "high fashion" for her taste. She was a modest sophisticate. Bryce had kept on about how sexy and feminine they looked. It was like he was imagining things just holding the shoes. Debra had declined, and she didn't know why Bryce was so dismayed about her not spending over a thousand dollars of his money on some stupid shoes.

Maybe Suzette was everything she wasn't. Maybe they looked sexy on *her.* Maybe Suzette was the epitome of sexiness. After all, he had left his wife for her. Debra imagined Suzette modeling those heels for Bryce, wearing next to nothing. She tortured herself with all kinds of thoughts of what her husband might be doing with another woman. "Lord, are you this cruel!" she screamed, staring at that statement until her eyes burned. "What have I done, Lord, to deserve this—Why!" she cried. There was no answer. How could her loving God be silent at a time like this? She thought she knew Him, but it felt like she didn't really know her God at all.

Every insecure thought Debra had was magnified seven-fold. She criticized her hair. Her face. Her thinness. Maybe if she was more voluptuous—maybe Bryce wouldn't have had the desire to be with another woman—to leave her for another woman. Debra berated herself until her head pounded. All the details that made her the woman she was harassed her into a migraine. It took 800 milligrams of Ibuprofen to chase the pain away so that she could get some sleep. A nap in the middle of an 80 degree day to escape what was real. She was at the epicenter of a crumbling catastrophe.

7
On and Poppin'

Noni strolled into Debra's office with Corey Hunt of all people. Debra never would have guessed that the two had *anything* in common. Corey was a little more "worldly" than Noni—a lot more according to her mother. Corey's big brown eyes made her look innocent. Her smooth creamy complexion was to die for. She was a beautiful girl. Debra could imagine her being an actress or someone who worked in the entertainment industry, and from what Debra heard from the other kids at school, Corey had a voice that was just simply divine. Debra understood why she was so popular with the boys at the school.

"Hey, what can I do for you ladies?"

"Well, Mrs. Myles . . . Corey has something she wants to discuss with you. She just needs some moral support. That's why I'm here," Noni explained.

"You're the moral support?" Debra asked Noni, smiling.

Noni nodded. "Yep."

"Corey, are you sure you don't want to wait until you have your session, so that you can talk in private?"

"No, it's cool. I've already told Noni mostly everything. She's the first female I've met at this school who's *real*. I don't mind if she knows. We have cooking class together. She's good people."

"That she is," Debra said wondering what was going on. "Okay . . . so what's up you two?"

"Mrs. Myles, I hate to admit this—and I feel really bad for saying this, but I wasn't completely honest when I talked to you with my mother. I mean, I didn't clarify some things I should have. I wanted to, but my mother just kept on at me—not listening like always. The guy I'm with isn't some older guy. The journal is just fantasy stuff. I've never even had sex before. I wrote that stuff like last year sometime. I was just imagining how it would be to be with someone. Since then, I have given my life to Christ. I didn't know my mother was gonna go readin' my stuff. When I tried to explain she just said I was lying. Right now, I'm seeing someone who goes to this school, but we've been keeping it quiet because of our parents. The joint—marijuana was mine. I tried it *once* with Scotlyn—months ago—before I started trying to live for God. I haven't touched it since then. I don't even want Todd to know I did that. He might be really disappointed and upset."

Debra focused in on the one thing that intrigued her most. "Todd? Would this be Todd Clark?"

Noni and Corey smiled at each other. "Uh-huh," Corey said. "Yep. He's *white*. And I know my dad would trip to no-end. Todd's mother is cool. She's a Christian—but his dad, he ain't goin' for it. So we just see each other on the low, you know? But I'm not some drug addict. I swear I only tried it once. It was stupid, I know. My *real problem* is that I have to hide a relationship that I shouldn't have to hide."

Corey's words took Debra aback. She could sense that Corey was telling the truth. Most young people her age did fantasize about what sex is like. With all the music, television, and movies being so sexually focused, Debra understood how the thought of sex could constantly be on their minds. "Okay, well it seems that we've got ourselves a little situation here . . . and I don't have a quick answer right now, but I do know you are going to have to give some thought to being honest with your mother and father, Corey—even about Todd."

"Yeah. That's what Noni said."

"Oh, so you're trying to do my job?" Debra joked with Noni.

"Just tryin' to help out."

"Mrs. Myles, I'm not some loose cannon. You can ask any guy here at school. Todd is only the second person I've ever *kissed*. He loves the Lord, and he is a sweetheart. He's the kind of guy that's a keeper."

Debra smiled. "I understand, but give some thought to what I said about honesty."

The three of them were interrupted by a knock on Debra's door.

"Yes?" Debra asked politely.

"It's Maya, Mrs. Myles."

"Give me a couple of minutes," Debra said through the door. She looked down at her desk calendar realizing it was time for Maya's appointment. She eyed Noni and Corey. "Ladies, I have to think over what you've shared with me today, so that I can process it properly—and help Corey make the best decision possible, okay? Like I said, no quick-fix answers today."

"Okay," the two of them said in unison.

"Alright, I'll see you two tomorrow. Let Maya in for me,

please."

Maya sauntered in Debra's office unassumingly, looking demure in a baby-blue sundress, flat white sandals, and a white straw flop-hat. She was toting a white Dooney and Burke bag. She looked like a young southern bell. She had her own unique way of dressing that reminded Debra of a well put-together woman, rather than a sixteen year-old girl. She was always faithfully clad in the latest high-fashion clothing, and carried expensive handbags with names Debra had only spotted from the pages of the high-fashion magazines she browsed through when she was at doctors' offices, spas, and other places where those kinds of magazines were plentiful. It was hard to believe that Maya had thrown a party that had completely trashed her dad's home.

"I know I don't know you that well, but you should have said something back to Millicent," Noni said to Maya without warning.

"It wasn't a big deal," Maya said shrugging her shoulders nonchalantly.

"Oh, yes it was! She always does that because people let her get away with it. It was really mean. Somebody needs to tell that girl something!"

"What are you two talking about?" Debra's curiosity was piqued.

"Nothing," Maya said quickly. "It's not a big deal."

"Well, Noni seems to be pretty riled up about it."

"I just don't like to see people try to walk all over other people, that's all. I'm like my daddy when it comes to stuff like that."

"Millicent is just stupid anyway. It doesn't matter. I should have never told Scotlyn. Then, Millicent wouldn't have even known."

"I don't care *who* you told. It wasn't her place to say anything about it."

"About what?" Debra asked impatiently.

Noni looked as if she'd said too much. She eyed Maya silently, as if to say *"You tell her."*

"Yes . . . ?" Debra said.

Maya exhaled. "Millicent made a comment about me throwing up my food. I told Scotlyn about my problem before I knew she had the biggest mouth in the school—my bad."

"I'd give Scotlyn a piece of my mind too," Noni interjected.

Debra studied Maya. The hurt look on her face revealed her true feelings, even though she claimed it had been no big deal. "Maya, why *didn't* you tell Millicent to back off?"

"Because I figured it was my fault for telling Scotlyn, anyway."

"Miss Scotlyn seems to be making a real name for herself lately," Debra said.

"Scotlyn and Millicent are just alike, Mrs. Myles. They gossip about everyone and keep up a bunch of mess—and both of them have nasty attitudes. I can't stand either one of them. I swear, if she does one more thing, It's gon' be on and poppin' I'm gon' put my foot—"

"Noni, remember who you belong to," Debra cautioned. Yes, her young bombshell had plenty of fire—that needed to be contained.

"Noni is right," Corey defended. "Scotlyn pretends to be friends with people so that she can find out information about them. And then she just talks about them behind their backs. I'm so glad I didn't tell her about my *situation*," she said careful not to say too much in front of Maya.

"I see . . . " Debra said. "You two let me talk to Maya alone. I'll see you tomorrow. And watch that temper, Miss Noni."

"Alright."

Corey and Noni exited, leaving Debra alone with the fragile creature who was fighting her way through the world—and losing the battle. Out of the three of them, Debra felt most sorry for Maya. She was like a lost soul. So many times Debra wanted to share her faith with Maya, despite what the district's rules were, but Debra knew that she could only do so much for her students. Maya McIntyre was definitely "a job for Jesus."

Debra spent the next hour with Maya working on her self-esteem. She'd learned that one of Maya's biggest issues was the fact that she didn't know her mother. Her mother had chosen to be single—leaving Maya's father Greg to raise Maya by himself. Her parents had divorced when she was just three years old. She'd seen her mother twice since then. She'd gone from school to school trying to fit in and find the acceptance she wanted from her mother. Now she was a shell.

Maya had been sexually active since age thirteen. Debra thought she was going to have to pick Greg McIntyre off the floor when that had come out during their weekly family session. He'd done all the right things, and yet he felt that he'd somehow failed his little girl. And if he could get his hands on any of the punks she'd slept with, well . . . he'd make them wish they'd never even heard of Maya Marie McIntyre. And Debra had the most daunting task—help Maya somehow piece herself together, stay healthy, and communicate better with her father, not to mention the fact that she was trying to keep herself together in the process. It was going to be a steep hike up a high mountain judging from where they stood at the moment.

8
The Interview

Summer break faded like an old-school tune. School was back in session, and Debra had been given the task of scoping out the chef who had headed the school's culinary class during the summer enrichment program. He owned a successful restaurant in downtown Detroit called Chase on the River. It was just off the waterfront. Noni had done so well in class that the chef had offered to hire and mentor her. Her sixteenth birthday had just passed and she was excited about being independent and having her own money—most of all, doing something she absolutely loved.

Debra sat nervously in her car. She didn't know why she was nervous. It was stupid. She was just going to check things out for Wynona's aunt—make sure Chef Chase Martin wasn't some creep who preyed on teen girls. In recent years, those kinds of situations seemed to be more prevalent. Wynona was a rather curvaceous thing. Her body was voluptuous. It was enough to give a creep some incentive.

Debra checked her make-up and slid out of the car and up to the front door of Chase on The River, one of Detroit's premiere riverfront establishments. Debra pushed the door open lightly. The grey brick restaurant was chic, decorated in black and white. The walls were painted a charcoal-grey color that was accented with black drapes with white sheers. The furnishings were black lacquer chairs with black suede seats and oval lacquer tables covered with white linens. Chase was waiting at the door for Debra. He was dressed in a pair of Levis and a white polo shirt. Debra smiled nervously as she extended her hand.

"Hi . . . I'm Mrs. Myles. I'm here to see Chef Chase."

"Hello Mrs. Myles, that would be me," he said smiling, giving Debra a firm hand shake. He loved Noni. He had already been grilled by Noni's aunt, but it wasn't often that he met young ladies whose career aspirations were to become a chef. "Well, why don't we go back to my office. You said you had a few questions to ask me. And Noni's aunt, Ms. Hudson, was adamant about her *not* working here until things were clear with you too."

Debra smiled knowingly. "She trusts my opinion."

"That's great. This way please," Chase said leading Debra down a long corridor where there was a set of white French doors at the end. The black and white restaurant decorum continued in Chef Chase's luxurious office suite. He had a huge smoked-glass, L-shaped desk and several built-in book shelves along the walls. There was a white kidney-shape ultra suede sofa and two white oversized arm chairs with high asymmetrically designed backs. Chef Chase seated Debra in one of the chairs facing his desk. He walked behind the desk sat down. He looked relaxed and confident. "Okay Mrs. Myles, shoot."

Debra felt herself staring hard, but where else was she supposed to look? She squirmed a bit in her seat. "Well, first, I would like to know why you've chosen Noni out of all the other students in the class to work at your restaurant."

Chase didn't have to think about that question long to answer it. "It's simple. Noni is a wonderful cook at her age—she's creative and she has a business mind. Smart girl. I like working with kids. She's got a lot of potential. I want to give her an opportunity to grow. You know in other ethnic groups, mentoring is very important. If a couple has a son who wants to be a doctor, there's a doctor within that family or group who'll take that child under his wing. We don't do that enough in the black community. Noni wants to be a chef. I'm going to give her some experience—mentor her."

Debra nodded. "Okay," she said satisfied with his response. But the real concern had to be spoken directly—straight with no "chaser" as her uncle Chuck would say. Debra paused for a moment then said, "Noni's very fond of you, Chef Chase. I think she might even have a school-girl crush on you. I want to know how you might handle that in the event she steps out of line with you."

"I see where this is going," he smiled, not the least bit offended by Debra's directness. "Mrs. Myles, if Noni ever stepped out of line with me, I would immediately check her on it, without crushing her spirit, and I would let her aunt and you know right away so that you'd know where I was coming from. And depending on what the situation was, I'd have to decide if she could continue to work here. And more than likely, I would be against that. I understand the dynamics of our society. It's screwed up. There are some men who prey on young girls. I'm not one of them. I assure you my intentions with Noni are for the purpose of mentoring only. For *my* safety, Noni will never be alone with me at *anytime* for *any* reason. That has always been my policy with female students—and as of late, males too, with all the down-low business going on. I always try to avoid putting myself in a position where my integrity can be questioned or my actions misconstrued. I have a younger sister who works with me handling the business end. She's almost always here."

"Oh, excuse me, I didn't know you were in a *meeting*," a very attractive woman said after she'd waltzed into his office unannounced.

"Speaking of the *saint*," he said to Debra. "This is my business manager and younger sister, Mona. Mona, this is Mrs. Myles, she is helping to coordinate my mentoring of a young future chef—Noni."

"So nice to meet you," Mona said extending her hand. She shook Debra's hand firmly and gave her brother a sly look. "I'm sorry for interrupting. If you don't mind I'd just like to make sure some very important information is synced on your computer. Won't take but a second."

Chase moved out of the way as Mona scooted behind his desk and bent down in front of his computer. "Please excuse us for a minute, Mrs. Myles," he said.

"No problem," Debra returned, eyeing Mona. She was a short vanilla complexioned woman with a short tapered hair cut. Her natural waves lay perfectly. She wore a gray suit with a skirt that came just above her knee, and four-inch black leather heels.

"Everything's fine," she said. "And once again, I'm so sorry for interrupting. I'll be back in a couple of hours, Chase."

"Really? Where you headed to?"

Mona winked. "Lunch date."

"Uh-huh. We'll talk later." Chase said with his brows raised just a bit. Mona smiled before darting out of the office. "Where were we Mrs. Myles?"

"Oh, you were telling me about your policy on female men-tees—and males too."

"Yes. I understand that you all want to make sure that I'm on the up and up. Mona will be the one actually scheduling Noni's hours, most of the time she will be in Mona's care. She'll only be with me in the kitchen with plenty other people around."

Debra was satisfied after talking with Chase for over half an hour. "Okay, Chef Chase. Everything sounds good. I think this is a really good opportunity for Noni. It has given her something to concentrate on besides her losses."

"Well, great. And please, call me Chase. Only the students call me Chef Chase out of respect since I don't like to use my last name—Martin—it's rather common. Maybe you and your hus-band can visit us sometime." He reached in a drawer and took out a dinner certificate. "This is for one hundred dollars—you guys should be able to eat pretty decently around here with this," he smiled, knowing that some of the menu prices were a little expen-sive.

"Well, it'll be enough for *me*. My husband and I are sepa-rated." It hurt to say those words. She didn't even know why she'd blurted that out. It was sitting somewhere in her gut, and seemed better out than in.

"Sorry to hear that. Maybe you and a friend could come." He regretted bringing up the subject of *husband* to her. He wouldn't have made that assumption if it hadn't been for the fact that Debra was still sporting a wedding ring and using the pre-fix *Mrs.*

"Thank you," Debra said politely.

"It was a pleasure meeting you, Mrs. Myles," Chase returned shaking her hand again firmly. He was amazed by her dedication to Noni. He could tell that her concern extended far beyond her professional title. Too many people in the world were apathetic. It was refreshing to meet someone with a cause bigger than themselves. He wondered if she had a personal relationship with Christ.

"Same here."

9
Dancing Hearts

The second Friday in October was alive with expectation. The junior class's highly anticipated Fall Ball was commencing in the Gold Room of the Green Hills Country Club. The extravagantly decorated banquet hall blared with the sounds of Omarion's "Ice Box." Debra patted her feet to the music, identifying with the words of the song. She knew exactly what it felt like to have an ice box where there was once a heart. "I hear you," she mumbled to herself. Watching the students dance so freely made Debra smile. They were released from inhibitions and worries. Adult problems. They were enjoying themselves immensely, frolicking with one another, temporarily suspended from structure and order, giving the chaperones an opportunity to peek inside their world for a couple of hours.

Chase sat on the other side of the room studying everyone. Mrs. Daughtry had asked him to cater the event. He agreed, but

tonight he was not *working*. He'd placed his right-hand man, Chef
Stevens in charge. Chase periodically consulted with him during
the evening and spoke with the student servers, but he was not in
the world of "chefdom" tonight.

"Chef Chase, you ain't heard a word I said," Noni complained
with feigned anger.

"Huh?"

"Who you lookin' at over there?" she asked looking in the
direction of his gaze.

Chase smiled. "*Ms. Noni*, I'm just enjoying the ball."

"Look like you was . . . checkin' somebody out to me," she
laughed.

Chase smiled. "What can I do for you?"

"I was trying to tell you that I'm nervous about the pies."

"Why? They're delicious. I've told you that. We wouldn't be
serving them if I didn't think they were good. I told you, you've
got to be confident in your abilities. You can't doubt yourself all
the time. They'll love 'em," he said, encouraging her. Noni had
developed a delicious recipe for individual sweet potato pies that
were being served for desert. Chase was proud of her.

"Thanks, Chef Chase. I feel better already." Her attention was
diverted as she noticed Jason Lockmore approaching the table
where she had scooted in next to Chef Chase. It seemed that every
other girl in the room was staring in her direction now as well. Her
eyes widened.

"Excuse me Chef Chase, Noni," Jason said politely. "I just
wanted to know if you'd like to dance with me," he said looking
directly at Noni.

Shocked, Noni hesitated. " . . . Uh . . . yeah." Her eyes widened a few more centimeters.

Jason extended his hand. Noni rose from the chair laying her hand softly in his following him bashfully. Blushing girlishly, she looked back at Chase as Jason led her to the floor where they danced to Rueben Studdard's "Make You Feel Beautiful."

Chase shook his head smiling. He remembered those days of asking a girl to dance—the nervousness and anticipation all wrapped together turning him into walking jelly. He looked across the room at Debra who was now chatting with Mr. King, the chemistry teacher. She looked as if her mind was someplace else.

After dancing to three songs with Jason Lockmore, Noni came and sat next to Debra.

"Oh, my goodness, Mrs. Myles, did you see me?"

"Uh-huh. I saw you lookin' all googley-eyed at Jason Lockmore."

"He asked me to dance."

"So I saw."

"He seems really nice."

"Um-hmm."

Noni lowered her voice. "He is sooo cute. I can't believe he asked me to dance."

"Why not?

"You know, Mrs. Myles. I wasn't expecting him to be interested in me. I mean, I think I'm cute and all, but most of these guys—they like really petite, *skinny* girls—the video babes."

"Well, I think Jason is *different*," Debra said.

"You see all those chicks checkin' me out?"

"Yes, I did."

"Humph. They better watch out."

"I think they know that, Noni," Debra said smiling, glad to see the depression cloud lifting from Noni's life. She had only worked with Noni a short while, but Noni was definitely blossoming, healing.

"Mrs. Myles, I think somebody has been checkin' you out too."

"What are you talking about young lady?"

"Chef Chase was over there lookin' at you like you was a triple layer chocolate cake."

"Girl, get away from this table," Debra said jokingly. She hid her smile.

"For real, Mrs. Myles."

"Here comes Jason. Bye," Debra said, shooing Noni away, eager to get rid of her with her instigating self. Jason walked up and asked Noni to take a walk outside with him. Debra started to ask if there was a chaperone outside, but she looked out of the floor-to-ceiling windows and saw several staff members outside. They had to keep their eyes on the young adults that were pulsating with hormones.

Debra's curiosity caused her to look in Chase's direction. Their eyes met. Debra smiled politely and nodded her head. It was nice to be noticed by someone. She thought of Bryce. When was he coming home? Did she even want him back? He'd been gone all summer doing only God knew what with some other woman. It was devastating. The thought caused her eyes to mist. It was so embarrassing. How many times had she lied to someone at church when they'd asked her where Bryce was?

Debra slid her hand across the table and pulled Mr. King's pie in front of her. He was a diabetic and couldn't eat it. He had brought it to her, knowing that she loved sweet potato pie. It was absolutely delectable. She savored each bite, hoping there would be some left over to take home.

"I see you're enjoying Ms. Noni's sweet delight," Chase said.

Debra had been enjoying her pie so much she hadn't noticed him approaching the table. "Oh, hello Chase. You caught me right in the act. These things are scrumptious," Debra said.

Chase took a seat at the table. "They are. Did I tell you, we've put them on the menu at the restaurant?"

"No. But that is wonderful. I know Noni is happy about that."

"Yes, she's blossomed a great deal."

"I was just thinking that myself."

Chase had been watching all the students come over and talk with Debra, how she interacted with them. How they made her smile, and how comfortable they seemed with her. He could tell she had a genuine love for them. She made working with teens look easy when he knew it was anything but that. He'd come over to her table with innocent intentions. It was getting pretty boring sitting there alone. Now he had run out of words to say. They sat uncomfortably for a few moments before he thought of a conversation starter. "So they do this Fall Ball every year?"

"Yes. It's a tradition. This is how the juniors raise money for their senior events. They sell ads for this Fall Ball to get sponsors and donations.

"I think it's a wonderful idea to introduce them to formal dining. A lot of business deals are made during social events like golfing and charity balls and stuff," Chase said.

"You're right. And tonight is very nice. They all look so good in their tuxes and gowns."

Chase nodded. He had fallen in love with some of the students at Peace Valley High since his cooking program began. Normally, he focused his attention on inner city schools, where he felt his services were needed more. It seemed that children in the inner city always had a lack of programs and resources. But bureaucracy and red tape had interfered with his plan this year as the city school system had hired its third superintendent in five years. The changing of the guard caused a breakdown of communication. In the meanwhile, Principal Daughtry had asked Chase to assist at Peace Valley, and they had the facilities and resources he needed to make the program successful.

Debra almost fainted when Chase asked her to dance to an upbeat Sade tune. The D.J. was doing a pretty good job of mixing old school and new school tunes, so that the chaperones could have a little fun too. Turning Chase down would make it seem as though there was something wrong with dancing with him. Accepting his invitation would make Debra feel like a nervous little schoolgirl, but she accepted anyway and for a few minutes, she enjoyed the freedom of not thinking about the things that had kept her worried almost every day. Chase seemed like a nice man. It was just a harmless dance. Neither one of them was that good at it, so Debra didn't feel as foolish as she would have if Chase had been more coordinated. They managed to stay on beat and find out some trivial information about one another in the process.

Bryce was an exceptional dancer. Debra guessed it was a part of his charm. His smooth movements were effortless. He had ballroom dancing or stepping, as they called it in Chicago, down to a science. He looked suave whenever he danced. He'd tried to teach Debra several times, and although she knew what steps to execute, she never seemed to be as flawless as Bryce.

Debra remembered one night when they'd gone to a wedding reception and Bryce had ballroom danced with one of the older ladies in the room. It looked as if he was wooing the woman the way he moved her and bid her to follow him with soft directions that were patted out in Morse code on her lower back. One touch. *Come forward.* Two pats. *Move backward.* A slight pull on the waist. *Turn.* The woman had caught on easily, and looked like she was enjoying being charmed by a younger man.

It was all done innocently, but it had made Debra jealous

because she wished she could move that smoothly with him. He was *her* husband. Debra was an awkward dancer at best, especially when it came to ballroom dancing and salsa, dances that required a good deal of rhythm and coordination. The woman had come back to the table and told Debra, "Girl, I know that you know you've got one good looking and charming man! He had me thinking I was twenty-one. Ain't too many men that can dance like that. You better hold on to him." It seemed like every woman in the room wanted to dance with Bryce. Debra had danced with him that night, but she knew she didn't look as good with him as some of the other women he had danced with. Bryce was the star Debra couldn't keep up with when it came to dancing. She guessed it was natural for a woman to want to be led by a man. To be enchanted by his confidence, especially when dancing.

Debra imagined Bryce and Suzette out dancing somewhere tonight. Maybe at the Salsa club he had taken Debra to on a few occasions. Maybe at some other smoky club where he and Suzette could ballroom dance in perfect harmony with one another—Bryce leading, Suzette following. Debra imagined Bryce's hands sensuously placed on Suzette's lower back. He wouldn't have to tap codes on it, because Suzette would already know them. She would anticipate his movements, and submissively sway in whatever direction he wanted her to. Debra envisioned Bryce lowering his hands to Suzette's behind until they were barely positioned appropriately enough for public viewing. Suzette would perhaps laugh and tell him to stop being naughty, like Debra had often done. But unlike Debra, Suzette wouldn't make a fuss if he didn't move them. She'd relax in his power, in his will to touch her however he wanted—like she belonged to him.

Debra cringed.

"Are you getting tired?" Chase asked, noticing Debra had

mentally disconnected.

"Yes," Debra lied. "I think it's time for me to get on home."

"Okay. I'll walk you to your car."

"No thanks, I'm fine. The kids will just make a big deal out of it on Monday."

"Yeah, you're probably right," Chase acquiesced. "See you later. Be safe out there."

"I will. Thank you."

Debra had barely gotten her key in the ignition before she burst into tears. Her head was throbbing terribly. She couldn't pull herself together. She didn't even remember the fifteen minute drive home, or taking off her clothes and getting into bed. She could only see Bryce with his body pressed up against Suzette's, dancing close. She cried out to the Lord and soaked her pillow with tears—on her side of the bed.

10

Love is Scary

Debra stayed at school later than she'd anticipated. Part of it was her reluctance to go home—because home wasn't the same anymore without her husband. And she understood God less and less these days. It was getting dark. Debra headed to her car with a brisk walk. She'd worn a thin jacket and it was beginning to get chilly. The wind was stirring up a colder temperature. The multi-colored tree leaves whipped to and fro as if they were in a frantic dance. She stopped before she neared her car noticing something stuck under her left windshield blade. Debra curiously pulled the white envelope from the blade and looked around to see if she had an audience. The students could be real pranksters at times. Satisfied that she was alone, she threw her bag into the back seat, got into the car and started the ignition. She turned on the heat and opened the envelope. It was a note from Bryce.

They hadn't had a *real* conversation all summer long, and now it was the third week of October. It would be Halloween soon—something Debra had never celebrated because of the pagan origins and witchcraft associated with the day. It was an insignificant day as far as she was concerned. Now, it would mark the time her husband had been gone. Nothing was scarier than that—not all the ghouls and goblins in the world. Debra felt like Bryce had been out of her life forever. The memories that she had of the two of them together under one roof were just that—memories. She didn't know if life would ever be the same again. And she didn't want to think about it tonight.

Deb, I just want to say that I love you and I miss you. Please give me a call so that we can talk about saving our marriage. I need to see you. I've made some mistakes, but I don't want to throw us away. I hope you don't either.

Bryce

Debra tossed the note into the passenger seat and pulled out of her parking space. Her heart crumbled into a lifeless, useless glob. As much as she had prayed for God to restore her and Bryce's marriage, she feared seeing him again, loving him again—needing him again. It wasn't fair that Bryce owned her heart this way and had the power to lift or crush it at whim. It wasn't fair that his love was the only love she'd ever known and now she couldn't bring herself to think of not loving him—no matter what he'd done or who he'd done it with.

It frightened her to think that her life was wrapped around

Bryce, intertwined with his. He'd all but destroyed her when he'd left to be with Suzette. Now, here he was talking about *saving* their marriage. Her love and fear were equal monsters, waiting for the opportunity to tear her apart for good, and leave her as a woman who had been murdered by her own heart.

Who was she kidding? She still loved Bryce. And she was sure that would be the death of her. It was funny that the very thing she'd been praying for could be happening—Bryce coming to his senses and realizing that they had too much invested to just walk away from their marriage, but another part of her longed to let go. It wasn't like this was her first time dealing with Bryce's infidelity. Was she going to be dealing with this every few years or so? She couldn't live out the rest of her marriage that way.

11

Maybe We Can Work it Out

Bryce stood when a restaurant host escorted Debra to his table at Big Rock Chophouse in Birmingham. She looked fresh. Her skin glowed. She'd pinned up her shoulder length hair. Bryce couldn't tell if Debra was wearing make-up or not. She looked good either way. She sported an alluring royal blue dress with black air brushed flowers splashed over it. It fit her body superbly, tracing her curves. She had draped a black silk-knit shawl around her shoulders. She wore a pair of three-inch black patent leather sandals with single toe loops that left her pretty toes fully exposed, showing appreciation for Michigan's fickle weather— 76 degrees in the middle of October. The sexy, three-inch heels brought out the definition of her calves. Bryce hadn't seen Debra in five months. It was like being on a first-date with a stranger. He desired her. Anticipated her. He couldn't keep the heat of his thoughts from surfacing.

He smiled. "Hey . . . you look really nice baby,"

"Thank you," Debra said taking a seat at the table. She scooted closer to the table. She was nervous. She felt strange. She was on a date with her estranged husband—a man that she still didn't know after cohabitating with him for five years.

Dinner was awkward. Each of them tried to stay away from topics that would ruin the evening—like, *"What have you been doing lately?"* and all the other paltry conversations that could remind them that their lives were disjointed.

"So, how has work been going?" Bryce asked, picking over his steak.

"Pretty much the same. I've got three new students—some pretty intriguing girls."

"Really? How so?"

"Well, they're all different. They come from totally different backgrounds, yet they're all alike in a lot of ways—I mean the pain they've experienced to be so young, just blows me away."

Bryce nodded. "I never did understand how you could deal with listening to other people's problems all day long. I think that would drain me, but you do a wonderful job. I could tell from the few times that I've been at your school that your 'babies' love you."

Debra smiled. "Thanks. I love them too," she said.

Bryce's eyes were telling. "I still love you too, Deb."

"Bryce, don't . . . "

"Don't do what, Deb—tell you I love you? I thought that's why we agreed to this date, Deb, so we could talk about us—see where we're going."

Tears stung her eyes. "Bryce, to tell you the truth, I'm not sure *why* I agreed to this. Part of me loves you—misses you. Another part of me keeps telling me that the man I love ran off to be with some other woman, and I need to let go." Her voice trembled. She wiped the tears from her face with her napkin.

Bryce leaned in and spoke quietly. "I didn't run off, baby. You told me to leave."

"Yeah, right after you told me that you were in love with someone *else*, Bryce."

"I didn't say that. I said, 'I *think* I'm in still in love with her.' I said I was confused. It's not the same thing, Deb."

"It doesn't matter. All that matters is that you told your *wife* that you were in love with someone else!" The elevation of her voice stirred the patrons in their immediate area. Fiery tears flowed. Debra scooted her seat away from the table and stood up. "I can't do this Bryce. Do whatever you want to do, okay?"

"Deb, sit down . . . please."

"No . . . I'm going home." She walked away from the table.

"Debbie!" Bryce fumbled with his wallet, removing three fifty-dollar bills. He laid them on the table and rushed out of the restaurant after her.

Debra stood out front with a teary face, waiting for the valet to bring her car around.

"Debbie, baby, please, let's just go somewhere we can talk. Let me follow you home and then we can just go for a ride someplace like we used to do."

"I can't do this . . . I want some peace . . . I need some sleep . . . please," she pleaded.

Bryce cupped Debra's face in his hands. His own eyes were swollen with tears. "Debbie, just let me take you for a ride. Let's just talk. Let's not throw it away. I'm wrong, okay? I was wrong. Don't throw us away, Deb."

"You've got her. Why don't you just leave me alone, Bryce?"

"Because you're my *wife*, Deb. I haven't been with *her* in over a month. I told you. I've been trying to sort my life out. Just give us a chance to talk, Deb."

The valet eased Debra's silver Lexus coupe close to the curb, hopped out and swung the door open for her. She turned and walked toward him. Bryce pulled her back.

"Debbie, don't . . . " he said.

She snatched away. "No, Bryce. I'm tired. I just want to go home."

The valet was protective of her. "Is everything okay?" Bryce fought back his own tears. "We're fine. This is my *wife*. I'm just talking to my wife." He gently took Debra's hand. "Please, Deb."

She nodded reluctantly. "Whatever we don't straighten out tonight, will never be straightened out. Do you hear me?"

"Yes." He handed the valet his ticket. Within minutes he was pulling into the driveway behind Debra.

Debra eased her car into the garage. Bryce left his engine running. When she got out and walked toward the door that led to the mudroom, Bryce got out of his car. "Debbie, I thought we were going to go for a ride and talk." He wondered how she had changed her mind so quickly.

"I'm tired, Bryce. We'll talk right here and then you can go back to your life."

Bryce turned the ignition off and followed her into the house. Debra sat at the kitchen table. Bryce sat across from her.

"You want to talk? Talk."

"Debbie, I love you."

"You cheated on me Bryce—for the second time. Obviously, you love her too. Is she worth our marriage?"

"No, baby, I don't love her. I was just confused . . . and no, there is nothing worth our marriage. Since I've been by myself, Deb, I've had a chance to think about it. Every married couple goes through changes, Deb. You see all those people standing up at church who've been married fifty and sixty years. We all give them standing ovations, but nobody thinks about what happened in between those fifty or sixty years. Somebody messed up. Somebody left. Somebody came back home. They worked it out, Deb. I made a mistake. I've made mistakes, but I love my wife. I want my wife."

"What do you think I'm supposed to do just because you walk in here and say you want your marriage?"

"Deb, I don't know. All I know is that I love you and I don't want to lose you. It was stupid, baby. If I knew what was wrong with me, I would change, Deb. I'm not trying to hurt you. I never meant to hurt you." His sincere words shocked both of them.

"Have you always kept in contact with her?"

"No."

"I heard your friends ask you about her before. You didn't say anything. Was it because you were seeing her?"

"No, it wasn't anything like that. I ran into her at lunch one day and we just reconnected. I hadn't seen her or talked to her before then."

"Bryce, don't lie to me."

"I'm not lying, Deb. That's how it happened. I swear. I saw her at lunch. We went out after work that evening and I stepped into dangerous territory. I put myself in a bad situation—a situation that a married man should never put himself in . . . and I fell."

"Does she make you happier than me? Do you like her physically—being with her more than me?" She shouldn't have asked him those questions because she didn't know if she could handle the answers.

"Deb, it's nothing like that. It was just stupid male ego. It was just because I'm a man who is weak and flawed, Deb. Because

I didn't allow God to lead me out of temptation. Because I was selfish, baby." He reached across the table and held her hands in his. There was no warmth in her hands. They were limp in his. He covered them with kisses and cried. "I'm so sorry, baby . . . I'm so sorry . . . I love you. I want you in my life. I'm sorry I hurt you."

Now, she was confused. Stubborn tears crawled slowly down her cheeks. She laid her head on the kitchen table and cried. Bryce got up and held her until there was stillness in the room. Until the only sound he could hear was the faint melody of Debra's breathing next to him.

*   *   *

Morning came quickly. Sunlight infiltrated the darkened space that had hid all of Bryce's fears and shortcomings. Debra slept next to him. The warmth of her body ushered in the return of his soul. He watched her stir. She twisted, and then spiraled back to sleep, sliding down a peaceful funnel where they lived happily. How could he have been such an idiot? Why had he risked her? Looking at her, he couldn't comprehend his own wayward actions. Of the crimes he had committed against her, none had been justifiable. Yet, he was still unsure how to love her. He knew only that he did.

Still sleeping, Debra flung her leg over Bryce's thigh. A passionate heat tingled in him. She hadn't allowed him to make love to her last night. That he regretted. The cruelty of his adultery was made manifest when she'd denied him. Her body wasn't his to pleasure or to be pleasured by—not anymore. His physical right as a husband dissolved in the pain he'd caused her—severed by the soul tie he'd made with another woman.

After his first indiscretion, she'd denied him almost eight months.

He'd suffered it without complaint. He'd only told her about the betrayal because guilt had gotten the better of him and he truly wanted them to move forward. It was the hardest thing he'd ever had to do—sit his wife down and tell her that he hadn't been faithful. There'd been no reason then either, except that the reality of being married had left him feeling choked at first, even though he loved her. The idea of spending the rest of his life with her and only her, made him fear. It was a rebellious attitude that caused him to seek the affection of another woman that time. It was intensified by the anger he felt toward God about his mother's death. Being with someone else seemed to mask his pain . . . and then there was Suzette, a relic of the past that wouldn't remain in its place. How long would it be before they could move beyond this damaging stalemate?

Debra shifted and sat up on her elbow and stared at her husband. The moment felt like any other moment they'd shared in the morning. Except, this morning, Bryce was here stealthily. Debra wondered how Suzette would feel if she knew that Bryce had spent the night at home with her, slept next to her, and was now lying next to her. Was Suzette in love with him? Would the revelation hurt Suzette as much as Debra had hurt when she'd found out that Bryce had been intimate with her? The moment was stolen. Debra likened it to fornication—intimacy without right. Although she hadn't given herself to him, just being with him made Debra feel that *she* was cheating. The legality of Bryce being her husband did not erase that thought.

"You hungry, baby?" Bryce asked, gently moving Debra's hair from her face.

She smiled amidst her confusion. "You know the answer to that."

"Yes, yes, and yes?"

"Correct."

"Do we—you have breakfast food?"

"Uh-huh."

"I'll make breakfast."

Debra watched Bryce rise from the bed. He'd slept in his dress slacks without his shirt. His hard chiseled chest was inviting. She felt guilty about wanting him. She pushed the covers back to get out of bed and exposed her taut thighs that extended from under the T-shirt and shorts she'd worn to bed. Singed by desire, Bryce feasted on Debra's thighs for a moment too long, and then looked into Debra's eyes. He shook it off.

"I've got some sweats in my gym bag in the car. I'm gonna go out and get it. I'll shower in the guest room. Then I'll make us some breakfast."

Debra nodded. What was she supposed to say? What were they doing? What was *she* doing? She walked into the master bath thinking.

Bryce exited the house through the garage. He hit the switch on the wall and the garage door lifted. He saw Mr. Craiggs, their across-the-street neighbor, preparing to mow his lawn. Mr. Craiggs looked surprised to see Bryce. He smiled awkwardly. The two of them had had a five-year history of carrying on conversations before they beautified their landscapes.

Mr. Craiggs and his wife, Leona, had lived on the block seven years before Bryce and Debra had moved in. They were one of the first black families to build in the area. Mr. Craiggs made it his business to help get the young newlyweds acclimated to the neighborhood and share his aged wisdom with them. Bryce enjoyed talking to him, and looked forward to his early morning lessons on most Saturdays. Leona spent time with Debra helping her to get the flower garden prepared each year.

Mr. Craiggs threw his arm up and waved. "Morning."

"Morning."

Mr. Craiggs had a curious look on his face. He wanted to tell Bryce that he hoped that he and Debra worked out their marital problems. He wanted to see the young couple make it. He was fond of both of them, but he didn't want to let on that Debra had told Leona anything personal; he knew how that could strain the trust in a marriage.

Bryce felt Mr. Craiggs' suspicion. In lieu of a full-fledged conversation, he said, "I'm working on it, Mr. Craiggs."

"Good enough," Mr. Craiggs offered back with a thumbs-up sign.

Bryce went into the house and showered in the guest room. Then he and Debra ate breakfast together. They took a walk around their master-planned community, which included a park, basketball, baseball, and tennis court as well as a children's play area. He and Debra rested on the swings in the play area. They used to come in the afternoon when Bryce wasn't working late, and look at all the children playing, both of them dreaming about having a family. Debra stirred her feet in the playground sand causing her swing to twist gently. She bumped into Bryce. He held the chains of her swing and stilled it. He was serious.

"Debbie, I want to work it out. I love you, baby. I told Suzette that it was over between us a month ago. I've been using the time to think."

"It's not that easy, Bryce. I don't know if I can ever trust you again."

"I know it won't be easy, Deb, and there is nothing I can say right now that can make you feel secure. I haven't proven myself trustworthy since we've been married, baby. But, I can say that I am going to put in the effort to gain your trust back. I mean, I think counseling can help us.

"Bryce, I don't know . . . "

"Do you still love me, baby?'

"Yes . . . but that doesn't matter, Bryce. What matters is, can I trust you *now*? And I can't. I don't know if I will ever be able to. I can't pretend that you haven't cheated on me *twice*."

"Are you telling me you want a divorce, Deb? 'Cause I don't want a divorce, baby."

"You can't have me *and* Suzette, Bryce."

"I don't want you and Suzette. I want *you*."

"What made you come to that conclusion all of a sudden? You mean to tell me you never thought about that when you were—" She stopped abruptly in order to stifle a foul word. "Did you ever think about that when you were layin' up with her?"

"Deb, I was confused. Can we try counseling?"

"Again? What good is it going to do if you're going to keep doing the same thing? A therapist can't follow you around and make you keep your pants up, Bryce."

"I'm asking you to *try*. I believe we've got years ahead, Deb—good years."

"I'm sure we do. But maybe it's not meant for us to spend those years *together*."

"I want to spend them together."

Debra toyed with the string of her hoodie. The sun was coming up. It was getting warm. "I'd really have to think about that, Bryce. I'm not sure. I've been thinking about getting a divorce. I saw an attorney."

"Deb, don't. You'd be making a big mistake if you did that. I love you. I want this."

"You've got a strange way of showing it, Bryce."

"Listen, can we just see each other again? Just let me date you for a little while. I don't have to move back in or anything right now. Let me just start over, Deb. Like today—let me take you shopping and to the movies—spend some time."

He was her husband. She did love him. Maybe they could work it out. The pain was too fresh to make a decision. She looked into his eyes and all she could see was a vision of him and Suzette locked in passion, kissing and caressing—making love, sharing a gift that hadn't been given to them. She would have to sort out the defeating thoughts that beat down on her.

It was eleven o'clock. Debra had forgotten that she and her father had made plans to shop for her Mother's birthday gift. Daniel felt safer shopping with Debra. That way, Sheila couldn't blame him alone if she didn't get what she wanted.

Debra and Bryce hurried down the block toward the house. Daniel was in the driveway sitting in his Cadillac DTS next to Bryce's Denali. He smiled when he saw his baby girl in the distance, coming towards him. When Daniel realized Debra was with Bryce, his smile faded. He plastered it back when Debra walked up close enough for her to see the expression on his face. He hopped out of the car.

"Hey, Daddy," Debra kissed him.

He kissed her on the cheek. "Hey, sugar. Did you forget we had a date today?"

"Not really—sort of, but I'm ready, Daddy. I just need to go in and get my purse." She ran up the walk way and into the house.

"Hey, Dad," Bryce said uncomfortably. He could feel Daniel's ire.

"Call me Daniel. That's what I want you to do from now on." That calmness Daniel possessed wasn't present. "That's my baby girl you're messin' over, and I want you to know I don't like it. I think you're full of it, Bryce. I didn't raise some common, trashy woman with whom you can come and go as you please. If you're going to be a man, be a man. If you're not, leave Debbie alone, because you don't want to have to deal with me. Believe that." Daniel went into his pocket and removed a stick of gum. He unwrapped it and leaned against his car.

" . . . Daniel, I love Debbie. I messed up. I'm trying to work it out."

"We'll see. I'm done talking to you, Bryce," Daniel said with finality, folding the gum into his mouth.

Debra came out of the front door toting Bryce's gym bag and his keys. "Here you go, Bryce. I'll talk to you later." She got into the car with Daniel, without giving Bryce a hug or a kiss good-bye.

12
Therapy

Bryce had taken on the responsibility of securing a good therapist for him and Debra. He decided against being counseled by one of the ministers at their church. He wanted someone who he felt could be totally objective. His choice was Dr. Sylvester Buckley, a licensed psychologist and certified Christian counselor who had an office near downtown Birmingham. He had gotten the reference from a co-worker. Meanwhile, Bryce kept his apartment and Debra continued to live at home. They decided to keep things that way until it was comfortable for both of them to reunite under one roof.

Debra and Bryce met in the parking lot of Dr. Buckley's office. Bryce walked up to Debra and squeezed her hand gently, reaffirming his commitment to their marriage. Debra was nervous but hopeful. She looked at the stunning architecture of the baby blue and white cottage house that had been converted into an office building, and inhaled her nervous feelings. It was a strange place to discuss Bryce's adultery and desertion because it reminded Debra of a happy abode.

They entered the building holding hands. Dr. Buckley's office was one of five suites in the building. Three psychologists and one social worker rented the other four suites from Dr. Buckley. The suites were soundproof to ensure privacy. Dr. Buckley's suite was located on the second level. It was the largest of the five, and had served as the master suite of the home before it had been renovated. As Debra inched up the stairs with Bryce, she felt embarrassed about talking to another stranger about her and Bryce's personal business. She would have been more comfortable talking to a minister, but Bryce was in control. Debra had met with Pastor Kelley already and shared her dilemma. He encouraged her to go to counseling with Bryce wherever he chose, so long as Bryce was serious about putting their marriage back on track.

Dr. Buckley stood at the top of the stairs greeting the couple with a smile. Debra stared hard at Dr. Buckley. He looked so young and handsome. He was not what she expected. He welcomed her and Bryce into his office and waited as they sat down. There was nothing spectacular about the room. It was a modest space with a tan colored couch, two leather arm chairs, and Dr. Buckley's expansive cherry wood desk. The color of the room was beige.

After the introductions, Dr. Buckley said, "Since Bryce initiated the call, I want to know what he hopes to gain from counseling."

Bryce looked at Debra lovingly, still holding onto her hand and said, "I want to gain Debra's trust back and get our marriage together."

"Bryce, I'm going to throw some tough stuff at you today, because I don't like to mess around when it comes to marriage counseling. Ground rules: behind these doors we have to be honest—lying doesn't help reestablish trust. Sometimes honesty hurts, but it works." He looked at Debra sympathetically. "Are we clear?" Both Bryce and Debra said "yes" in unison.

"What's wrong with the marriage?"

"Bryce had an affair." Debra blurted out.

"Why do you think he had an affair, Debra?"

"I'm not sure. I thought things were going pretty well between us. Maybe sex—having something different," Debra returned uncomfortably. She felt as if Dr. Buckley was blaming her.

"Have you ever asked him why he had an affair?"

"No—not specifically." Debra felt idiotic.

"Now is the perfect time, Debra. Look Bryce in the eyes and ask him why he cheated on you." Dr. Buckley seemed overly confrontational, like he was instigating a fight, but Debra conceded.

"Bryce, why did you cheat on me?"

"I don't know . . . I mean, I can't explain it."

Dr. Buckley penetrated Bryce with a stare. "Oh, yes you can. 'I don't know' is a cop out! Was it sex? Boredom? Tired of being married?" His voice was loud and jagged, cutting into Bryce.

"It was sex and excitement," Bryce answered reluctantly.

A tear rolled down Debra's cheek. She felt stupid for being here. She looked at Bryce and rolled her eyes disdainfully. *You walked all over my heart for sex and excitement?*

"So, Debra's not sexually exciting to you?"

"Yes," Bryce answered. *I thought this was Christian counseling.*

"So why did you need to go elsewhere, Bryce? If your wife gives you sex and excitement, why go out for sex and excitement? It's like owning a car and buying another one just like it. Debra doesn't please you in bed?" This Christian counseling felt more like military interrogation to Bryce. He had no idea that Dr. Buckley was going to come at him this way. He was not prepared. Debra looked offended, waiting for Bryce to answer. Dr. Buckley smiled. "*Honesty*, Bryce."

Bryce felt nervous. "It's not that she doesn't *please* me. It's just that when I ran into *Zee*, she was up in my space—on me—very provocative—teasing. It turned me on . . . that's how it started."

"So the reason why you cheated on Debra was because you were not getting the excitement that you need to be *charged*," Dr. Buckley clarified.

"Essentially, I think that had a lot to do with it. Zee was an old girlfriend of mine from the past, and she just lit a fire in me the night I saw her with the way she was acting toward me."

"Debra, how do you feel about that?"

Debra's voice cracked. "I think it's stupid. It makes me feel cheap, like I don't matter—like I can just be replaced. That the sacredness of our union boils down to sex and excitement . . . I took my vows seriously." She looked at Bryce and said, "If you think I've been *excited* by you every single day, you are dead wrong—but did I go out and sleep with someone else? NO!"

Bryce could see how much he was hurting her, how what he'd done had broken her spirit. Honest tears filled his eyes. He put his head down and sniffed in deeply before looking back up at her. "Deb, I'm so sorry. I could have come to you with this—before Zee and I happened."

"Yes, you could have, Bryce. I would have tried to please you—do anything you wanted me to—because of the *sacredness* of my love for you," Debra cried. She covered her face and wept. Bryce put his arm around her. Dr. Buckley gave them a moment before he got back on his confrontational horse.

"What are you going to do about it, Debra?"

She didn't look up. "I don't know..."

"That's not acceptable. What are you going to do now?"

Debra looked up at the ceiling. "I'm here. I'm trying to get past this so that I can save my marriage."

"So you want to stay in the marriage with Bryce even though he cheated on you?"

"Yes . . . I love him." She felt weak and wimpy for saying those words but they were true. She did still love him. Bryce stood up and pulled Debra to her feet. He pulled her into him and caressed her in a loving hold that made her believe in him.

"I love you so much, Deb" He said crying. "I'm so sorry for what I've done. I will never hurt you this way again, as long as I live—I swear it." Bryce was sobbing hard. Dr. Buckley gave them time to share their emotions. He felt that it was a good sign that they could make it. Bryce was genuine. Dr. Buckley could tell when people came in with an ulterior motive—like shutting up their spouse. He could see that Bryce genuinely loved Debra. His tears were not a façade. Dr. Buckley was pleased with their first session. He scheduled them for another appointment the following week.

13

Strong as Death

ebra sat on the sofa in Bryce's apartment waiting for him to finish the meal he'd cooked for her. They'd planned this evening at the suggestion of Dr. Buckley. He said that "dating" again would help them to reestablish communication, and renew their interest in one another. Debra had finally gotten used to Dr. Buckley's *interesting* style of therapy, and felt comfortable with him. It wasn't as bad as she'd thought it was going to be in the beginning—even the exercises he had them do, like write letters to one another to express how they felt, and find out things that they didn't know about each other by guessing one another's response to a questionnaire. Dr. Buckley was over-the-top confrontational, but he knew his stuff. He was a consummate professional. He was good at what he did. Debra believed that she and Bryce were making progress.

Their assignment tonight was to have dinner together, read the

Song of Solomon, and discuss one another's interpretation of the romantic biblical account of true love between a man and a woman. They were instructed to take notes and be prepared to share them at their next session. Debra adjusted herself and laughed at the way her stomach was growling. "Bryce, my stomach is saying, 'Please hurry up!'" she said into the kitchen.

"I'm coming. Hold your horses," Bryce laughed.

Debra rose and went into his master bath to wash her hands. On the way out, she stopped as she passed Bryce's bed. Frozen, Debra stared at it, wondering how many nights Suzette had spent lying there with Bryce while he'd been away from home. She could see the two of them together giggling—loving one another. It made her stomach sick.

"I thought you were, hun—" Bryce started as he walked into the bedroom. "Deb, what's wrong?" he asked. But he knew. A tear hid in the corner of her eye. He wrapped his arms around her. "Debbie, baby, I love you. Please help me to help us make it through this. Sorry is no consolation, baby, but I am. Look at me," Bryce prompted, softly cupping Debra's face. "The Word of God says that love is as strong as death, and if a man would give all the wealth of his house for love, it would be utterly despised. That's how I feel about you, Debbie. There's nothing in my life stronger than this," he said, taking her hand and placing it over his heart.

"I'm trying hard . . . it just hurts so bad on the inside, Bryce," Debra said tearfully.

"I'm gonna turn this thing around, Debbie. I'm gonna make you believe in me again. I'm gonna love you the way God desires me to love you. I promise." Gently, Bryce touched his lips to hers. Then he explored her mouth when she allowed him. He wanted her. He needed to show his wife the depth of his love without words. They were useless right now. Debra could feel his urgency.

She wanted to submit to him, but she couldn't. She broke away from his kiss.

"I'm sorry. I'm not ready for that yet. I can't handle it right now—emotionally I mean."

Bryce retreated. "I'm sorry, Deb. I wasn't trying to push you. The man in me just rises up when I'm near you. Take your time, baby. I want you to be comfortable with me again. I want you to love me the way you used to."

Debra nodded. "I will."

The two of them had dinner and discussed the Song of Solomon as Dr. Buckley had instructed, and Bryce didn't think it was such a good choice on a night like tonight when he was pumped full of testosterone. He didn't know the Bible had such sensual descriptions in it. He had never read the Song of Solomon before—not like this. They were dissecting it, pulling it apart, and applying it to their marriage. Bryce couldn't help but think of Debra in *that* way. But for now, he understood that she was off limits physically.

In an individual session, Dr. Buckley had explained to Bryce that *not* having a physically intimate relationship with Debra would be par for the course until some trust had been regained. "Women are different," he'd said. "Their bodies have to catch up to their hearts—not the other way around." And Bryce understood that now more than ever. Right now, his body was doing the running and wasn't concerned how far behind his heart was lagging in the race. It wasn't that his heart wasn't there. His body just ran faster. He settled for just being close to Debra as she sat facing him on the sofa with her feet in his lap while he massaged them gently, as they talked about what had to be the most sensual love story he'd ever read.

"Man, I must *not* have been paying too much attention when we were in pre-marital counseling and reviewed this book. I didn't know Solomon had all this going on."

"Well, he certainly was no slacker. He had seven hundred wives," Debra chuckled.

"But this one—this Shulamite girl—she had his nose wide open. He said she was the fairest. And she was the only one who went down in biblical history."

"Good point." Debra smiled. She stretched closer and kissed Bryce gently on the lips. It was a soft, innocent "I love you" kiss—not exactly what Bryce would have preferred, but it demonstrated the kind of intimacy Dr. Buckley said would have to come first before Debra could give herself to him again, so Bryce welcomed it.

14
Thanksgiving

Every Thanksgiving, Chase on the River closed for regular business and instead cooked and transported meals all across the city to the corridors where homeless persons made their residences. Noni had asked to volunteer and Chase allowed her to. He was impressed by her selflessness and how polite and kind she was to the people they served. She wasn't apprehensive or afraid. It took training and coaching to even get some of his adult staff to present with the type of disposition Noni served with. She was extremely comfortable, and not put off by any of the recipients' appearances. She served them just as she would have served a guest in the restaurant, with the same courteousness and professionalism. She beamed as a gentleman thanked her. "You are very welcome, sir. May God bless you and all that you touch," Noni said smiling humbly. Chase could see the Lord in her life. He'd made an excellent choice in mentoring her. She was so excited to have her first real job, and seemed even more thrilled to be passing out meals.

It was Chase's idea to have Noni interviewed along with him by Channel Seven's up-and-coming newswoman, Ashley Todd. Ashley had gotten in touch with Mona about doing a feature on Chase for Thanksgiving Day. Mona encouraged a normally camera-shy Chase, saying it would be excellent PR for the restaurant. This time he let Mona have her way. Ashley Todd seemed impressed with Chase and his service to the community. She listened intently as he spoke highly of the importance of mentoring young people and being involved in the community by giving back. He said he felt proud to feed the less fortunate and even prouder to have a young person volunteering with him. Ashley Todd was all smiles. Her perfect white teeth, cinnamon skin and sharp Rihanna hair cut gave her star-quality flair. She had possessive black eyes, and a petite frame that was covered by a red trench-style cashmere coat, with black leather trim on the collar, cuffs, and pockets. Chase admired how beautiful she was. He knew she was single—or hoped she still was. At least she was when Hello Detroit magazine had done a story on Detroit's most eligible bachelors and bachelorettes last month. She was the reason he'd purchased the magazine in the first place. Her face on the cover made him do a double take as he was picking up items from a gourmet market he frequented. Now here she was, interviewing him. He'd decided that it wasn't such a bad idea after all. Maybe he could get to know Miss Ashley better over a nice dinner. He massaged the thought while he watched and listened as Noni responded to Ashley's questions about teens volunteering in their communities.

Chase was proud of Noni's responses to Ashley. She was such an articulate girl, and passionate about community service. Both Corey and Maya had texted her during her interview, while Jason

Lockmore was nearby passing out hot meals in foil trays. Noni's aunt was stricter than strict when it came to the opposite sex. The amount of time Noni could spend with Jason was limited. Jason took the opportunity to serve with Chase just so he could be close to Noni on this holiday. They'd been inseparable since the fall ball.

After the live interview, Ashley complained that she'd gone for hours without using the "ladies room." She'd covered several events and had been keeping warm with mocha lattes. Now the liquid was screaming to be released. Chase, being the consummate gentleman, offered her the use of the facilities in his RV, which he'd nicknamed WOW—for walk on water. It was a luxury RV that he used every Thanksgiving when the restaurant delivered meals. It gave him and his staff a nice clean place to rest and come out of the cold when a break was necessary, and he often let the neighboring kids take a tour. It was Chase's most coveted "toy." He loved road trips, and WOW made his various trips more comfortable. The RV had earned a great deal of cross country miles with Chase at the helm.

After a few minutes, Chase went in after Ashley to make sure she'd found everything okay and wasn't locked inside the restroom. People often found the double-step lock problematic. He remembered when one of his "road dates" had been locked in for almost thirty minutes while he was outside talking to an older gentleman who was enraptured by the sleek motor home that had a depiction of Jesus and Peter walking on water. He had gotten so wrapped up in the conversation with the gentleman that he had forgotten her, until he had invited the gentleman in and heard her screaming for him. He had to make it up to her with much shopping on that road trip.

The figure representing Jesus was cloaked in a sparkling white robe, while the figure representing Peter was donned in a beige robe. They were faceless figures with robes. Chase hated the way artists often drew pictures of Jesus to fit a particular ethnic group. He viewed Christ as a colorless God who reminds us that it is only the soul within us that matters. Artist DeAndre Morris had done a stellar job of creating a scene that brought the biblical event to life. Just looking at the images pulled a viewer out on the water with Jesus and Peter. It was definitely a conversation piece, and Chase loved to engage about it. It reminded him to keep a steadfast faith in Christ.

Chase walked up on Ashley while she was in the middle of a cell phone conversation, discussing what clubs she would hit that evening. Every other word that came out of her mouth was an expletive. Chase cringed. *So much for getting to know her better.* That wasn't the kind of woman he wanted to know more about. He hated "potty mouth" women. The foul, ungodly language was a stain on what otherwise was a physically beautiful woman. She was so busy laughing she didn't hear Chase enter.

"Excuse me, Ms. Todd, I was just checking on you."

Startled, she swung around. "Hey, let me call you right back," she said, ending her call. "I was just taking a call—getting my evening schedule together."

"Some of my guests have had trouble with the lock in the restroom."

"It tried to give me a problem, but my granddad has one of these things, and I remembered how to work it," she smiled.

"Well, okay. Take your time," Chase said turning to leave. "It's pretty cold out there."

She waited for a moment for Chase to say something—anything to let her know that he was *feeling* her in some way. There had been an unmistakable attraction between them earlier. She hoped he would ask her out, or at least for her phone number. She already had a card prepared. She kept plain white business cards with the studio contact information, and personalized lilac colored cards that were strictly for "personal business." The lilac cards even stated as much on the back. *This is a personal communication card. Please **do not** share these numbers or email addresses with others.* She had come up with the idea of having different cards so that she never got the two of them mixed up. In her line of work, it was imperative that she was able to respond to someone quickly without making too much of a scene. She could always slip her personal card to someone in a moment's notice, and they would know immediately that her interest was "personal." She hoped to give Chase one right now. Unfortunately, Chase had crossed her off his list as quickly as he had put her on.

When he didn't offer further conversation she thought of something. "This is a wonderful RV. I've never been in one *this* luxurious."

"Thank you, I'm glad you like it. Hope my facilities met your standards," he said smiling.

"Oh, yes. Definitely. Just like being in a hotel, actually."

"Good." With that, Chase was gone, leaving Ashley to wonder if she had misinterpreted his interest.

"Probably has a girlfriend," she mumbled to herself. "She is one lucky chic."

Mona eyed Chase strangely as he exited. She'd been trying to hook him up—hoping to "help" her big brother find Ms. Right. She'd always wanted a sister. Chase picked up on Mona's conniving little grin and smiled, shaking his head in the negative.

Mona pouted quizzically. She raised her eyebrows. Chase could hear his sister's silent question. *What's wrong with her?*

Chase walked up to his sister and whispered "potty mouth."

"She's pretty."

"God looks on the heart."

There was no denying that. Chase was even pickier than his little sister when it came to dating. Mona feared she'd never get a sister at the rate Chase was going. Add all his religious convictions, and her chances were looking slimmer and slimmer. Chase's little princess daughter, Savannah, was nearby with Noni passing out meals from one of the meal trucks. Jason had walked around the block with a couple of men carrying boxes of meals and blankets to give to anyone on the streets who might have been in a makeshift home in an alleyway, or under a bridge.

Noni exited from the back of the meal truck looking a bit frazzled.

"You okay?" Chase asked.

"Just need a break."

"Hey, go on in the RV and take a sit-down rest."

Noni just nodded blankly. She'd been up since 4:00 a.m. helping the Chase on the River staff pack the meal trucks with food that they'd practically stayed up all night cooking. Chase figured she was probably just exhausted from the effort it took to pull off today's event. She'd been working like a Hebrew slave since last evening. Chase mingled with his workers and volunteers. He thanked everyone as he waited for the "street crew" to come back. This was their last stop. They could all wrap up and go home. It would be dark in less than an hour. Chase wanted to rest his feet, too. When Jason and the street crew returned empty handed, Chase knew that the mission was accomplished. He praised God in his heart for the work he'd been able to do today. Chase noticed the puzzled look on Jason's face when he didn't see Noni.

"She's taking a rest in the RV," Chase said. Jason, being a respectable young man, stood still waiting for Chase to give him the okay to go inside the RV. It took Chase a moment to catch on.

"You can go on in for a few minutes," Chase said. He checked his watch. It was exactly five minutes after four. He figured five minutes would be plenty of time for the two of them to talk or whatever. He didn't give Jason a time limit. Chase kept that to himself. He planned to come on board unannounced. Jason was an upright Christian young man, but he was seventeen, and Noni was sixteen. Chase was definitely going to keep an eye on him and Noni. There would be no mayhem or hanky-panky on his watch. He didn't trust teenagers that much. He knew better—he used to be one himself. And Noni *was* a beautiful girl. Chase liked Jason a lot, because he truly was a good kid who was pretty well grounded for his age. Chase thought that if he ever had a son, he would want him to be like Jason. Ironically, he and Jason shared the same middle name of *Arman*. Chase knew that because Noni had a tendency to say Jason's whole name like he was some sort of super star. *Jason Arman Lockmore*.

Chase had lost track of time while talking to a couple of employees about what they were going to do for the rest of the day. He looked down at his watch and his face contorted.

"What's the matter, boss?" L.J., one of his busboys asked.

"I forgot something in the RV," Chase said in a voice that was nowhere near his normally cool, laid back tone. "What was I thinking?" Chase chided himself, walking swiftly over to the RV. Twenty minutes had gone by. "That's plenty enough time to get into some kind of *trouble*," Chase said aloud. Elaine Hudson would take his head off with a butcher's knife if he allowed anything to happen to Noni while she was in his care. He could bet on that. And Debra Myles would burn the rest of his body at the stake. "Lord knows how much she loves Noni," Chase said to himself.

Chase snatched the RV door open. The scene on the sofa before him stopped him dead in his tracks. He was stunned by what he saw. Jason looked up at him with concerned eyes but didn't stop stroking Noni's long thick hair that she'd blow-dried straight in or-der to fit her knitted hat over it. Noni was unaware of Chase's pres-ence. She was consumed by her own state. She lay across Jason's lap bawling profusely. Her body shook violently as she wailed. Tears brimmed in Jason's eyes until he gave them up unasham-edly. He rocked gently with Noni's head in his lap, continuing to stroke her hair while he sat silently. He didn't wipe his tears.

It was touching. Chase had to bite back his own emotion. He understood Jason's plight. He couldn't have left Noni to let any-one know that there was a problem. He had to stay right there and let her know that he was *right there* for her. Mona had walked up behind Chase, bumping into him. Chase turned around and hushed her with a finger over his lips. Mona was carrying an exhausted Savannah, who had fallen asleep in one of the meal trucks. He al-lowed Mona to pass him. Gingerly she laid Savannah down on the sofa across from Jason and Noni. Savannah was in a deep sleep and was undisturbed by Noni's cries. Mona motioned toward Noni and Chase gently grabbed her arm, pulling her to the front cabin. He whispered to her. "A man has to learn gentleness alongside of strength. Jason is an athlete. He knows how to be tough and ag-gressive. He demonstrates that every time he's on the court—ev-ery day as a young black man. This is where a man learns the gen-tleness and compassion of Christ. Leave him alone. We're right here. Nothing inappropriate is going on."

Mona nodded in agreement with her older brother. "That's got to be rough for her, Chase. This is her first Thanksgiving without her parents. *Both* of them. You think it was too much for her to volunteer with us today? She told me that most of the holidays she and her parents volunteered at the shelters and soup kitchens. Maybe this—"

Chase shook his head in disagreement. "I prayed about it, and she wanted to. I think this made her feel like she was doing what her parents would have wanted her to do—what they've always taught her about the human condition. It was her *responsibility* to carry on in their absence. She just misses them dearly. Poor thing. I can only imagine the pain and loneliness she's feeling right now."

"I like Jason. I'm proud of him," Mona said.

"Yeah, he's a good guy. Real strong." Chase paused when he heard Jason praying. He and Mona bowed in silence. The loud crying had turned into soft whimpers and sniffles. Savannah remained asleep.

* * *

Bryce hung the photos of him and Debra on the Christmas tree. It was their tradition to trim their tree every Thanksgiving evening. Debra had gotten an arts and crafts idea from an HGTV show. She and Bryce had made picture frames out of colorful popsicle sticks. They glued the sticks onto the pictures, punched holes in the tops, and hung them with colorful yarn. It was a beautiful sight seeing Bryce use scissors and glue—making projects. It reminded her of the love they used to share a long time ago. Debra watched with admiration, dreaming of a time when their love would be strong again. Certainly Bryce had made her feel that he was working hard to win her back. They'd spent almost every evening together. The intimacy—except for love making—was being restored.

They'd picked out the tree the night before. It was a blue spruce—Debra's favorite. She loved the soft-prickle leaves. It was about seven feet tall. Debra always had a real Christmas tree growing up. It used to be the highlight of her evening to go shopping for a Christmas tree with her daddy. Daniel let her have whichever one she wanted—regardless of size or cost. His only requirement was that she watered and fed it the "food" it needed to stay nice and moist until Christmas.

Debra watched Bryce's strong muscular arms reach up and hang ornaments. The blinking white lights were so beautiful. This moment just felt right. This was how it was supposed to be, her and her husband together, sharing special moments with one another. Debra missed him dearly. She missed the comfort of sleeping next to him at night. She missed the strength of his arms holding her, loving her. She missed cooking for him. She took pleasure in serving him today. He'd been so good to her lately, and therapy was going well. Bryce was more thoughtful than he'd been during their pre-marital courtship. He'd picked up Debra's sinus and asthma medication from the pharmacy without her asking. He'd taken her car keys and had her car detailed. He'd even installed the new dining room chandelier Debra had purchased. Bryce called her periodically during the day while she was at work just to confess that he loved her and that she was the only person that ever mattered to him. Her heart felt the same for him.

Debra had decided not to attend dinner at her parents'. She'd made the commitment to work on her marriage, and it was too uncertain a situation right now—they were in a fragile state. She wanted to keep her plans with Bryce between them until everything was sorted out. Daniel respected her independence, but he didn't necessarily like it. Bryce could go jump in a river and drown as far as he was concerned. And as for Sheila, well, she had no opinion. It wasn't the worst thing in the world. After all, couples went through this sort of thing all the time. That indifferent attitude got up under Daniel's skin more than Sheila could ever understand.

So here Bryce and Debra were, celebrating the holiday together—away from everyone else and their opinions. The only opinion that mattered to Debra was God's, and she felt she was being led by Him to give her marriage her all—to pour herself out like a cup—to love and forgive her husband as the Lord loves and forgives. No one else mattered at this moment.

"How are we looking, baby?" Bryce asked surveying his work.

"The tree looks gorgeous, baby," Debra beamed.

Bryce stared at her silently with his eyes glossing over. She'd called him "baby." It was a sign of affection he hadn't heard her speak in a while. He missed the sound of her voice calling him, *"baby."* God had blessed him with such a beautiful woman. He didn't know how he'd ever strayed on her. "I love you, Deb—with everything that's in me. I love you, woman." His serious voice was deep and penetrating. It reverberated through Debra and gripped her heart. He walked towards her with open arms, and Debra walked into the strength of him.

"I love you, Bryce. I love you. I want us to work," she cried.

"We're gonna work," Bryce said hugging her. "We're gonna make it, baby. Stay with me." His tears mixed with Debra's own as he held Debra's face against his. "I'm so sorry . . . I'm so sorry I ever hurt you, mama," He said using the moniker he used for Debra when he was tender. He squeezed her to him and caressed her, kissing her forehead gently. He kissed Debra's tears. "I love you. You mean everything to me, baby," he said so sweetly, Debra cried even harder.

Their tender moment was interrupted by Debra's cell ringing. At first, Bryce looked around thinking it might be his, but then he remembered he had turned his off. They'd turned the ringer off on the house phone so that they wouldn't be disturbed. He looked at Debra curiously before both of them began searching for the thing. They had so many boxes opened with ornaments and such spread across the floor, it couldn't be easily located. They began laughing at their frantic treasure hunt.

Bryce stuck his hand in the craft box. "I got it."

Debra was on the other side of the tree on her knees. "Answer it."

"Hello. Happy Thanksgiving," Bryce said.

Chase sounded puzzled for a moment, taken aback by the male voice. "Happy Thanksgiving. May I speak to Debra, please?"

"Sure. Hold on a sec," Bryce responded, and handed Debra the phone. He wondered who the man was. Had Debra met someone during their separation? No. Not his Debra. Maybe this man didn't know that her husband was back—working things out. Whoever the fool was, he could take a hike.

"Hello."

"Hey Debra, it's Chase."

"Oh hi, Chase. Happy Thanksgiving."

"Same to you. Sorry to call you on the holiday, but we had a bit of a situation with Noni, today. First, she kinda had a breakown while we were distributing meals—but I think just being reminded of her parents caused that. We got through that pretty well. Jason was there and he just let her cry. I think she needed it."

"Certainly," Debra said listening intently.

"But then, when Mona and I dropped her off at Ms. Hudson's, we discovered a neighbor had left a note that she had rushed Ms. Hudson to the hospital. Apparently, the neighbor had come over to bring Ms. Hudson a cake, and Ms. Hudson fainted while the neighbor was there—and good thing she was there. When Noni saw that note she freaked out—totally hysterical. I think she believed that she was going to lose someone else close to her."

"Mona, Jason, and I checked the nearest hospital and were able to locate her aunt. We took Noni to the hospital, but they are going to keep Ms. Hudson overnight for observation, so Noni is going to stay over at Corey's tonight. The doctor said that Ms. Hudson's pressure was near stroke level. Turns out that Ms. Hudson hadn't taken her blood pressure medicine in a few days. I dropped Jason off at home after Noni got settled at Corey's house. That boy did not want to leave his 'boo,'" Chase said chuckling. "You might need to call and talk with her tonight. I've *never* seen anyone react that way—but she's only sixteen. She's doing the best she can under the circumstances, I suppose."

"You're right. I'll check on her right now."

"I have the phone number for Corey's mom. I can give it to you. She seemed to be a really nice lady."

"Thanks, but I know that one by heart," Debra said with a sly smile on her face.

"Okay. Well, I'll see you later."

"Thanks, Chase. I really appreciate you calling me."

"Who are you kidding? I know that Noni is your 'baby'."

Debra laughed. "Yes. All of them are—but she's extra-special. See you later."

"Bye."

"What's going on, baby?" Bryce asked, concerned about the matter and the messenger.

"Oh, one of my students had a rough time today. Both her parents were murdered this year. This is her first Thanksgiving without them."

"Wow. That's got to be one of the worst things that could happen to a person."

"Yeah. She's resilient, but she's human, too."

"Who was that on the phone?" Bryce asked, trying to sound nonchalant. Debra was kneeling down in order to pick up some of the items that were strewn over the floor.

"Oh, that was Chase. He's mentoring my student and he runs culinary workshops at the school twice a year."

"Oh," was all Bryce said. He couldn't help but wonder if that was the extent of the relationship. He was jealous. He hid it well. "You ready for that Riesling?"

"As a matter of fact, I am," Debra smiled. "Just let me check on my baby first."

"Okay. I'll get the wine glasses."

Debra went into her office and called Mrs. Hunt, she spoke with her for a while before speaking to Noni. Thank goodness Noni was okay. She sounded like she was exhausted. They talked for almost twenty minutes before Debra concluded the call. "God loves you, sweetie. And He's right here with you, and so am I. You have my cell if you need to call me. See you later," Debra encouraged. She could have cared less about the "therapy rules" and "client boundaries" right now. This was a child of God in need of some support.

Bryce was lounging on the sofa waiting for Debra. There were two wine glasses on the cocktail table in front of him. He patted the sofa cushion. "Come sit." Debra scooted next to him, snuggled up and laid her head on his chest. "Everything okay with your student, baby?"

"Yes. She's fine. Just a bit shaken. She's still grieving." Debra sat up and took a sip of her wine.

Bryce grabbed his glass, and clinked the two together. "To us. I love you."

"I love you," Debra said. It was getting late. She wanted Bryce to stay, but she didn't want to end up in bed with him. Physically, she was feeling the need to connect with him, but emotionally, she knew she still wasn't quite ready.

By the time Debra was on her second glass of wine, Bryce

was still nursing his first. "That's all you're having? This tastes great."

"I've got to drive. One glass is enough for me."

Debra hesitated before saying, "Bryce, I don't mind if you stay, so long as we don't . . . you know."

"Deb, I was serious when I told you that I wanted you to take your time. I want you to trust me, baby. I want you to be comfortable with me. I want you to *want* to be with me. There's no pressure on my end, honestly."

"Thank you," Debra said planting a soft kiss on his lips. He kissed her gently, and then pulled back. Debra slept the night on the sofa in her husband's arms where she knew she always belonged.

15

Group

Noni and Corey had become the best of friends—adding Maya McIntyre to their strange mix. It was a good outlet for Maya to have some friends who were genuine and not befriending her for some ulterior motive. Debra's schedule was so packed that she ended up seeing the three of them for group first thing in the morning. Debra enjoyed them so immensely she didn't mind getting to work an hour earlier to see them. She still saw them in individual sessions. The group process seemed more beneficial for the girls because they served as a support network for one another. It helped to keep them focused when they weren't in therapy. Sometimes, on days like today, Debra would bring in breakfast for them, and they'd just have a pow-wow session.

"Okay. I want to share something that I am very proud of," Maya said after swallowing a mouthful of pancakes.

"Go ahead. What you waitin' on, Christmas?" Noni teased.

"Noni, hush," Debra chided. "Do you know what she is going to say?"

"Nope. We don't talk about *everything* before we get to therapy, Mrs. Myles. What on earth would we need you for?" Noni joked.

"Very funny, little girl." Debra said giving Noni the "look."

Maya tilted her head. "Well, I am proud to say that I have been celibate since the beginning of August, and it is now December. That gives me four whole months!"

Noni and Corey cheered and clapped ridiculously.

Debra wasn't sure she was going to be able to handle their energy this morning. "What did you guys do, eat candy on the way to school this morning?"

"No, we're just excited about the progress of our fellow group member," Corey said seriously.

"Yeah, Mrs. Myles, you're the one who told us that self-respect was the next step to healing after *acknowledging* a problem. Maya *not* sharing her body with anyone is showing that she is respecting herself—getting to know herself—and not seeking acceptance through sexual relationships," Noni said almost mimicking Debra.

"Oh, listen to you, Oprah," Maya teased.

They all laughed—including Debra. Then she went back into therapy mode. "Maya, how do you feel about your abstinence? What do you think you've gained from it?"

"Well, I feel really proud, actually. This is the first time I've ever viewed abstaining from sex as *self-improvement*, but it really is. I feel in control—like I don't need to have sex to feel better about myself—or make a guy like me. I feel better about myself over all. Noni's been talking to me about praying and stuff. I'm not into church stuff really, but I do believe there is a higher power that I can lean on."

"His name is Jesus!" Noni interjected with a twang, sounding like a country evangelist.

"Yeah. That "higher power" stuff sounds spooky to me," Corey said.

Noni was serious. "That's why we should call him by his name—Jesus. He is the *only* power."

"Well, anyway, I'm growing mentally, physically, and spiritually, Mrs. Myles," Maya said.

"Good for you." Debra was content with the progress that was being made in each one of their lives. She was grateful to be their facilitator. She thanked the Lord for them, and for using her to touch their lives in some way.

"I've got something I want to share," Noni said, batting her eyes playfully. Somehow Debra knew exactly what Noni was going to say. "I think—no, I *know* I'm in love."

That confession triggered "Oohs" from the peanut gallery. Debra was still processing the statement, thinking about how she was going to deal with it from a therapeutic standpoint. Negating or minimizing a teen's feelings could be alienating, but not helping them to set parameters could be even worse. "Okay . . . " Debra said allowing Noni to continue if she wished.

"I know what you're thinking, Mrs. Myles. I'm only a junior—just sixteen and not mature enough to know what real love is . . . blah, blah, blah . . . "

"Did I say any of those things, Noni?"

"No."

"So why are you on the defense?"

"I'm not. I just know how adults think, like what we feel doesn't matter—or isn't real."

"Do you feel that you're mature enough to understand what real love is?" Debra asked. Corey and Maya remained silent with bulging eyes waiting for their comrade to answer the million-dollar question.

"Yes, I do. And I know that I have it."

"Okay . . . why don't you tell us what love is."

Noni accepted Debra's challenge. "Real true love is commitment, Mrs. Myles. It's sacrificing your needs and wants for the good of someone else. It's loving someone with a godly love— no matter what they do—or what flaws they have, you still love them and want the best for them. It's not just the sexual, romantic stuff—I mean my man is cute and all, but it's not about that."

Both Corey and Maya wore *"I guess she told you"* looks on their faces.

"You're absolutely right, Noni," Debra said with a challenge of her own. "And in addition, real love has *parameters*. It's not selfish. It waits until the appropriate time. It's pure and it's honorable." In her mind she was thinking about 1 Corinthians 13:4-8. *Love suffers long and is kind; love does not envy; love does not parade itself, is not puffed up; does not behave rudely, does not seek its own, is not provoked, thinks no evil; does not rejoice in iniquity, but rejoices in the truth; bears all things, believes all things, hopes all things, endures all things.*

"Right, just like it says in 1 Corinthians 13," Noni said.

This girl was something else. A force to be reckoned with. "You're right, Noni, but I don't want to get into a religious discussion here," Debra said. Although the girls were free to discuss their personal faith openly in group, legal and ethical guidelines prevented Debra from doing so. As a result, she chose her words carefully in situations like these when a student brought up Scripture, so that she could never be accused of imposing her faith on a student.

"It's cool with us," the peanut gallery said in unison.

"It's not for her," Noni said. "The school rule says that it's inappropriate for her as a *professional* to discuss religion with us while we are at school," Noni said bending bunny rabbit fingers in the air, making imaginary making quotation marks. Debra smiled at Noni with knowing eyes.

"Thank you, Miss Noni. Let's get back to the love thing."

"Well, I don't want to take up too much of group time, but dealing with what happened to my parents has been a major low for me." Noni paused and took a deep breath. "Don't get me wrong, my aunt Elaine is one of the sweetest people on the planet. I love her so much. I appreciate her taking me in, but its different," Noni said with tears falling. "She's not my mother—she's not my daddy. It's just that I can't talk to her about *everything* like I used to do with Daddy. I miss us holding hands, hugging, and talking about boys. Aunt Elaine is super strict. Shoot, she barely lets Jay come over . . . which brings me to the love thing. I *knew* I cared for Jason deeper than I've ever felt in my life outside of what I felt for my parents, but on Thanksgiving when I just lost it, he didn't say 'it's gonna be okay . . . stop crying . . . calm down.' He just said, 'I love you. And I'm right here.' And even though I was hurting so bad at the moment, I felt something warm on the inside. He *prayed* for me. I knew it was love. I'm in love," Noni said resolutely, wiping her tears with the back of her hand. She smiled to let them know she was okay.

Debra had to digress. She planned to talk to Noni later—alone and make sure that she and Jason weren't moving too quickly down the wrong path. Noni was in a delicate state. Debra knew that grief could transform into a totally different monster if the right circumstance presented itself. Jason had a good head on his shoulders and a relationship with the Lord. He was a Bible believing young man of God, but Debra couldn't help but think of what happened to Adam when Eve stepped to him looking all good with that piece of fruit in her hand.

"Okay, I don't have anything good to share, really. Actually, mine is terrible. My Todd isn't even *talking* to his dad now—because of me. I feel horrible about that. Todd's dad told him that our relationship was *unacceptable*, and Todd told his dad that *he* was the one who was unacceptable," Corey said with frustration. "Todd's talking about moving out. It's a mess. I've been so stressed out that I flunked my last physics test."

"Not the doctor! We got to fix this problem," Noni said, knowing that Corey had her heart set on being an emergency surgeon like her mother.

Maya looked at Corey incredulously. "For real. You're the one who helped me pass my last test."

Debra was less concerned about the last physics test than she was about the statement that had made her red flag shoot straight up in the air. "What do you mean *move out*? Where would he go? How would he support himself? He can't make it on his own with just a high school education—barely. He doesn't even graduate 'till June. You have to encourage Todd to start thinking rationally, Corey."

Corey let out a breath. "Mrs. Myles, this is group, right? So what I say in here is confidential, providing I'm not planning to kill myself or someone else right?"

"Yes. Those are the ground rules," Debra said.

Corey eyed Maya and Noni for their confirmation of silence.

Noni eyed Corey. "You know better, Corey. Don't play me like that. You know I wouldn't say anything."

"Me either," Maya said innocently, sounding somewhat offended.

"I'm sorry guys, it's just a touchy situation. Todd's grandfather—his dad's father, left Todd a trust fund instead of his dad. When he turns eighteen in January, he'll have partial control over it. It's like five hundred thousand dollars. His dad can't even touch it—he's not even the executor. It's some law firm guy."

Noni's eyes bucked wide. "Whoa! Now that's some *cheese*."

Debra's mind raced with all kinds of thoughts about Todd living on his own, having his own space, and uninterrupted access to Corey. She could hear Dr. Phil saying in that Texas drawl, *"How's that working for you?"* Debra massaged her temples. This session was slowly becoming a prelude to a nightmare. "That's *not* working for me, Corey."

"I know. I don't think it's a good idea either, but Todd is adamant. He says he's not going to be controlled by his dad like that. He called him a *racist*. Todd says he's been praying about it, but I think his mind is made up already."

"Okay. We've got some serious work to do, girls. Corey, I know you and Todd are an item, but try not to take on too many of his family problems okay? It will just complicate things for you. I want you to think of some positive things you can do right now that can help you to focus on *you* more. Family issues can get out of hand, and sometimes you have to just let those that are *in* the family work them out."

"In the meantime, try not to break any rules that Todd's father lays down—it will keep the peace. If he doesn't want you to visit Todd at his home, don't do it. You got that?"

"Yes."

The bell rang and Debra could say that she was glad. Their issues were serious. Debra never understood why adults just assumed that teens' issues were no big deal—especially at sixteen and seventeen. Their problems were major. They just weren't that old. "Guys we'll continue this on Friday. Do what I said, Corey.

See you guys later."

They sauntered out with their book bags, expensive purses, and "attitude." Debra smiled, thinking that she should get paid extra just for working with these three.

16

Crazy

After eight weeks of counseling, Bryce moved back in on a Saturday morning, less than a week before Christmas. The day was beautiful. They'd had dinner at Sinbad's and had gone to a jazz concert at the Fox Theatre.

"Wow. That was absolutely fantastic! Ooh, I was feelin' that one guy on 'I Go Crazy'. *Outta my mind when I look in your eyes* . . . " Debra sang as she and Bryce entered the kitchen. She laid her purse on the counter, kicked off her shoes, and leaned against the counter.

Bryce put the car keys in the drawer nearest the door. "Yeah, that brother had it goin' on for sure. He ain't Will Downing, but he had all the women in there mesmerized—including my wife." The word *wife* sounded foreign. He kissed Debra on the lips. She was stiff, her body rigid. Bryce sang softly off-key in her ear. *"Crazy* . . . " His eyes sank into her soul, wanting. Quietly he said, "I still go crazy, Deb." He traced the outline of her face with his fingers. "Are you still my wife, baby?"

"Yes," she said, but she wasn't ready to be his wife in that way tonight. Debra was still unsure what that would mean for her emotionally, or if she could even handle that level of intimacy. She needed them to take it slowly even though they'd decided that Bryce should move back in. She didn't want to be intimate with him before they had re-built a foundation. The old one was cracked like a dam that was barely holding back rushing waters.

"Be my wife tonight, Deb. I've been trying baby . . . trying hard to show you that I'm changing. I'm learning. I've been taking our counseling seriously, baby. You know that, Deb. Be my wife tonight . . . please." Determined, Bryce kissed Debra softly until she warmed to his touch, until her body responded with magnetic reciprocity.

Bryce's kiss was like the sweetness of some rare but unforgettable nectar that Debra savored greedily with the gliding of his lips over hers, his tongue taunting, then satisfying. She melted into him as he caressed her soft skin. Bryce loved his wife with a passion he had reserved for this moment. He wrapped Debra in a sweet lulling melody and she floated freely on musical notes. She let go of herself and welcomed her husband's love again.

Will Downing's voice was still filling their bedroom, crooning through the speaker of Bryce's iPod dock when Debra felt him move. Sleepily, she wrapped her arms around him. He squeezed her to his body before he reached over on the nightstand and silenced his cell phone. Debra coiled around him.

He patted her on the behind and said, "If I had any energy left, I would love you some more."

"In the morning," she mumbled before falling back to sleep. Bryce held her to his chest until his cell phone rang again. This time he turned it off. Debra was in a deep sleep. She breathed softly, undisturbed by his movement. A half-hour passed before Bryce thought to listen to Suzette's messages. She'd called *seven* times. He got up and went into the bathroom to listen. He'd been ignoring her calls since he and Debra had decided to work things out two months ago. Suzette had established a pattern of calling a couple times a week, but never at this time. It was almost four o'clock in the morning.

Her voice was frantic *"Bryce . . . my daddy . . . he's gone. He's gone. Oh, God help me . . . Bryce, please. I need you right now . . . please. If you ever loved me, I need you right now. My father is gone . . . I need you . . . please."*

Bryce's heart sprinted. He laid the cell phone on top of the sink and splashed cold water on his face. What was he going to do? He vacillated from anger to frustration to confusion. He couldn't just leave Debra in the middle of the night. They were trying to work things out. He wanted his marriage. But how could he just ignore Suzette at a time like this, after all that he'd done to her. He'd gotten her hopes up, and then had gone back to his wife, leaving Suzette broken.

Now Suzette's father, John Peters, was dead. Bryce couldn't just act like he hadn't given Suzette false hope. He pounded his fists into the sides of his head and let out an expletive. He snatched the cell phone off the sink and dialed Suzette's cell phone slowly and reluctantly, like he was punching in the code that would unlock a nuclear missile and send him into World War III. She answered on the first ring.

"Oh, Bryce . . . help me. Oh, God . . . my daddy is gone . . . "

Bryce tried to whisper. "What happened, Zee?"

"I don't know. Mommy said he complained about chest pains earlier. She woke up to check on him and he was gone . . . " Suzette cried into the phone.

"Zee, where are you? Are you at the hospital?" He could barely hear himself think over her sobbing.

"No, we left. I'm with Mommy. She's so cold. She just took something to help her sleep and locked herself in her room. You know how she is . . . I need you, Bryce. I need you . . . please."

"Zee . . . I'm at home with Debra. I can't . . . " Sweat trickled from his brow. He wiped it and closed his eyes. *This can't be happening.*

Suzette's cries were harder. "Bryce, please don't do this to me right now. You said you *loved* me. If she has you forever, then why can't you be with me right now! Please, don't do me like this right now, Bryce. I need you . . . please . . . "

Bryce sighed hard. His chest was tight like an over-inflated balloon that was seconds from popping. He knew his life would disappear with that popping sound. "I'll be there in forty-five minutes," he said. He pressed the "end-call" button and glowered at the fool in the mirror. How did he get himself in this mess? He was angry with Suzette. Angry with John Peters for dying on a night like this—the night he'd just made love to his wife after they'd officially ended their separation. A night that was supposed to be the start of him earning Debra's trust back. Why was his life this screwed up?

He opened the door and Debra was standing there looking like a ghost in a sheer white robe. Bryce froze. Hot angry tears were already streaming down Debra's face. "Were you talking to *her*?"

He didn't want to lie to her. He couldn't. "Yeah, Deb. That was Suzette. Her father just died, baby. That's it. There is nothing going on. I swear."

"What does that have to do with you, Bryce?"

"She called to tell me that, baby. She's just really upset right now."

"So."

"Deb, I'm not lying to you. I meant everything I said tonight. This is a new start for us, baby." Bryce was flustered. His color was leaving him.

Debra wiped her tears. "If you're back home to stay, come back to bed, Bryce." She turned and walked back into the bedroom. Bryce walked into the bedroom and slid on his pants. Debra whipped around. "What are you doing?" she asked, but she knew.

"Debbie, baby . . . I just can't leave her alone right now—"

"No!" Debra screamed. "You're here or you're there—make a decision right now!"

"Debbie, her father just died . . . I'm coming right back."

Debra didn't hear anymore. She was a locomotive. She ran into Bryce with a loud shrill. Swinging wildly, she pounded her fists into his face and chest. The contact sounded like ringside at a boxing match. There was no calming her fury.

"Debbie! Stop . . . Debbie!" He grabbed her arms and then she kicked wildly. He felt a pain at the base of his spine as she kneed him in the groin. He struggled with her until both of them fell on the bed. Debra was still kicking and screaming. Bryce rolled off the bed and then backed against the wall trying to shake off the dizzying caused by her kick. He inched up the wall slowly. "Debbie, it's the right thing to do. Please, try to understand. I just can't abandon her right now."

"Get out! Get out!" Debra hurled the glass clock on the nightstand at him. Bryce ducked and it crashed into the wall inches from where his head had been. He left the room walking hurriedly. Consumed by an animal rage, Debra ran into their closet, snatching down everything she and Bryce had worked hours to hang and organize earlier. She scooped up piles of his clothes and shoes, ran into the hallway, and threw them over the banister. She ran down the stairs and scooped the items up again. She rushed out to the garage and threw them on top of Bryce's car as he backed out.

17
It Is What It Is

Bryce hadn't intended to *be* with Suzette. It was all a blur. As soon as he had arrived at Suzette's parents' home, she'd asked him to take her home to her condo. He had only planned to stay with her for a little while, but before he knew it, he had made the second biggest mistake of his life. Bryce didn't have an excuse. He had no business being with her again. He felt overwhelmingly guilty afterward. He was human—a man, flawed—just like he'd told Debra. He loved them both.

Bryce knew his marriage was over now. It was in Debra's eyes when he left. He knew there'd be no coming back. Yet, he was drawn to Suzette. Suzette's cries had pulled every heart-string he possessed. He couldn't have just left her that way. His head still pounded from confusion.

* * *

Bryce was showering when Suzette awakened. The water blasting from the shower head was unable to ease the tension he felt. He thought of holding Debra just last night and how he'd been so glad to connect with her intimately. He'd felt as if they could give their marriage another try. He was positive it could work with Suzette out of the picture, but he couldn't cut Suzette out of the picture. She was as much a part of him as Debra was, whether he admitted it to himself or not. He stood in the steam contemplating for twenty-minutes before dressing. He walked back into Suzette's bedroom and stood over her. Her back was turned toward him.

"Zee, I have to go. I'll see you later," Bryce said stroking her hair.

She turned and looked up at him, searching his eyes for the unsaid words.

"I need to go to the barber shop and go pick up some things from the house." He kissed her forehead. "I'll come back later and help you do whatever needs to be done."

"Okay...what are you going to do?"

"I'm going to get an apartment again."

"What about us?"

"Zee, I've got to sort this out. But I *do* love you."

Suzette settled under the covers and looked up at the ceiling. Her face was blank but tears slid from her eyes that were black as coals. "That first night we had dinner together, and we made love, afterward you told me that you loved me—that the love had never left."

"It never did, Zee. Be back later," he said turning to walk out of the room.

"Wait," Suzette called out. She reached over, opened the nightstand drawer, and pulled out the key that Bryce had given back to her a few months ago. She crawled across the bed and handed it to him. She pressed it into his palm and held it there before squeezing him to her. She cried, hoping that when he went home to get his things nothing would keep him from returning to her.

Bryce caressed her delicately. "Zee, I'm coming back, baby. I swear." He kissed the key and tapped her forehead with it. He was telling the truth. Suzette's heart fluttered. She smiled. "Call and check on your mom. I'll be back," he said.

Greg's Barber Shop West was packed with brothers waiting to get their urban groom on. Some were talking sports, some about women, some telling lies. Others were simply laughing at the lies that were being told. It was already 10:30 a.m. Bryce took a seat and grabbed the latest ESPN magazine. Greg motioned that there were three ahead of him by putting up three fingers. Bryce nodded back. His headache had him squinting. He rubbed his temples. He'd have to get his things from Debra right after this. He didn't want to face her today. He didn't want to face her again. Why had he hurt her so badly? He hadn't meant to. What happened to him last night? Just touching Suzette again brought back all those feelings he thought he could just wash away and ignore. Bryce's thoughts were derailed by the sound of a voice he didn't want to hear at the moment.

"Oh, today must be my lucky day," Tyler said sarcastically as he strutted through the door and made eye contact with Bryce. His gait was determined. His tall broad statuesque stand was authoritative.

"Man, I'm *not* in the mood right now," Bryce quipped.

"I don't care what kind of mood you're in!" The shop quieted. Tyler was standing over Bryce like he was ready to pounce on him at any given moment, looking like a 230 pound grizzly bear.

"Fellas, take that in the back," Greg warned with a stern but quiet voice, knowing how far the two friends went back. It wasn't uncommon for brothers to have spats from time to time.

"No need, Greg. Ty and I are through talkin.'"

Normally Tyler was the calm one, a gentle giant. Today he wasn't. "Oh, I'm NOT through. You sittin' around here all smug while your wife is sitting at home crying, tore up over your worthless behind! And you are so foolish, you can't even see that you're about to throw away your marriage for some sleaze!"

Bryce shot up like a canon meeting Tyler's stare. "Zee, is no sleaze. Watch yourself!" They had the attention of every man in the shop, including the young charismatic Pastor Corey Perry of Greater Christian Center. He and Debra had gone to college together. He was positive that Bryce was Debra's husband. He said a prayer for Debra in his heart.

"Look at you defending her, like you made vows to her instead of Debbie!"

Every eye was on Bryce and Tyler. Greg put his clippers down, leaving old man Johnson in his chair. He walked over to the two and pushed both of them to the back of the shop where there was an empty room. Greg called it the "discussion room." Greg shut the door behind them, and went dutifully back to old man Johnson as if nothing had happened. Another round of gossip started that rivaled any beauty shop in the city on a Saturday morning.

"What in the world is wrong with you, Bryce? It's like I don't even know you anymore. How could you do that to Debbie, man?" Ty demanded, standing in the center of the room that was empty aside from two chairs.

"Ty, this is none of your business!"

"You are my business! We're brothers, right? Debbie doesn't deserve this, man. What kind of woman is Suzette to just go off and play house with somebody else's husband like it's nothing?"

"Ty, I told you . . . back off of Zee!" There was a spitfire in Bryce's eyes, warning. If Ty said one more derogatory thing about Suzette, Bryce was going to hit him, and just deal with whatever the big bear was going to dish out afterward.

"Why did you even go back home if you were going to do Debbie like this? Have you seen her this morning, man? *My wife* is over there right now, trying to calm her down. That girl looks like she belongs in a mental hospital somewhere. You're not right, Bryce."

"Man, you don't even understand."

"Understand what? You are a *married* man."

"I love Zee."

"It's just *sex*, man. You need to reel it on in, Bryce," simulating fishing rod movements with his hands. Tyler couldn't believe how the enemy had distorted his friend's thinking.

"See, that's where you wrong, Ty. My relationship with Zee is not about sex. I love her. I've always loved her."

Tyler sighed in disgust. "Bryce, man, you should have thought about that *before* you married Deb. You are killing her!"

The fire in Bryce singed the room. "You wanted to talk, I'm talking!

Tyler calmed himself and said rather quietly, "Man, you are about to make the biggest mistake of your life."

"It is what it is."

"Bryce, this is called a *fling*. Don't destroy your marriage over it. The Word of God says—"

"Ty, I don't want to hear about the Bible right now." Bryce wasn't sure what he believed anymore. "I know what the Word says. Just me and you—man to man."

Tyler blew out a hard defeated breath. He didn't have anything else to correct Bryce with. Morals and values didn't matter in a case like this, since it was obvious that Bryce and Suzette had created their own. "Man, are you ready to lose everything? Because that is what's going to happen."

Bryce sat down in one of two chairs that were in the room. "Man, all I know is that I thought I was ready to work things out with Debbie—go back home and be with her. Then Zee called and told me that her dad had passed. I knew I needed to be there with her. I *wanted* to be there with her. I can't get her out of my system. It was taking every ounce of my being to keep from calling her when Debbie and I started going to counseling. It's far beyond a fling."

"I mean, Debbie is a good girl, she's loving, accommodating, she's a good housekeeper—she's the kind of woman that will bring you breakfast in bed—pack your lunch, leave little love notes and stuff. It's just that . . . I don't know . . . we don't gel as much. She's at church 24/7. I have to suggest things for us to do. When we go out dancing it's like she's embarrassed that I got my hands on her. And I'm like, 'You're my wife, Deb.' It's just the little stuff. She waits for me to make love to her. I can count the times on my hands in the five years we've been married that Debbie has initiated sex . . . and when she did, it was when she was taking her temperature trying to get pregnant. Then it was like, 'Bryce, my temperature is up.'"

Tyler listened with an objective ear. The Word of God in the book of James came to his remembrance. *So then, my beloved brethren let every man be swift to hear, slow to speak, slow to wrath, for the wrath of man does not produce the righteousness of God.* He forced himself into a placid disposition. "I mean, you just got back together. You haven't given her time to change. You don't even know if she has changed already—or is willing to. Bryce, why can't you just tell Debbie what you need, man? It just seems so simple to me."

"Because I want her to do things naturally, man. Another man probably wouldn't have any complaints. It's not like she's a terrible wife. Most men would be crazy about a woman like Debbie, but I'm not most men. I feel like Deb is what I needed five years ago, but my needs are different now. Who I am is different now."

"You came to this conclusion *after* sleeping with Suzette? What about everything you promised Debbie all throughout counseling, Bryce? Give the girl a break. What do you want her to do—not bring you breakfast in bed? And if sex is an issue why don't you tell her what you want—tell her you need her to initiate?"

"Ty, you're not going to like my answer to that."

"Man to man, say what you need to say."

"*Everything* I need as a man, I get from *Zee*."

Tyler sighed hard shaking his head.

"You said you wanted to talk, I'm being honest, Ty. It's like, why put the effort in over here, when I got what I need over there? Zee and I are soul mates. If I wasn't sure before, I was sure last night."

"Bryce, it's *wrong*. It's in direct opposition to the Word of God—you know that," Ty pleaded.

Bryce stood and walked toward the door. "It is what it is," he said before walking out. He was worse off than Tyler thought. He had a heavy spirit all around him—confining him to foolishness. Tyler knew that this was a prayer job. Bryce's mind was gone—his soul sold to the devil.

18
Telling Secrets

Noni knocked quietly on Chase's restaurant office door feeling sneaky. He called for her to come in as he reviewed the financial records. Mona had insisted he do it before he left for home. They were still in the black. He was glad about that.

Noni entered unassumingly. Nervousness sequestered her usual smile. "Chef Chase, can I talk to you about somethin'?"

"Sure. What is it?"

"If a person overhears somethin' about somebody they care about—that they're not supposed to overhear, but what they overheard is somethin' that needs to be told to somebody else, so that the somebody that's cared about can get some help, is it wrong for the person that overheard to tell what they overheard?"

Chase looked baffled. Lines appeared on his smooth forehead. He scratched the top of his head. "Let me get this straight. Person

A overheard something about person B—that they shouldn't have heard. But the information needs to be shared with person C, so that person B can get some help?"

Now Noni looked baffled. "Uh . . . yeah. I think that's what I'm trying to say."

"Is Maya or Corey doing drugs or something—or pregnant?"

"No it's not that. It's an adult."

"Is something wrong with your aunt?"

"Unh-Uh."

"Well, what did you hear?"

"It's Mrs. Myles. She hasn't been doing too well lately. See, her husband cheated on her with some tra—lady, but Mrs. Myles forgave him and they got back together. But then he cheated on her again—with the same lady. Now they're probably going to get a divorce. But I don't think she wants a divorce. She was crying really hard—I overheard her talkin' to nurse Carlton."

Chase sensed that he was stepping into dangerous territory considering the fact that if he was honest with himself, he'd admit that Debra Prince-Myles was one woman he was extremely attracted to. "How do you think I can help, Noni?"

"I don't know. Maybe talk to her. Cheer her up or something. I don't know. It seems like you two get along really well—like friends. And I just like her a lot. I thought you needed to know. I feel bad for her."

"That sounds pretty serious, Noni. I'll see what I can do to lend support without letting her know what you just told me—I think it would be embarrassing."

"Mrs. Myles should just drop that fool. She can do better than that. My daddy told me that a man who cheats on his wife is showing a lack of respect for God. He told me he never cheated on my mother—that she was the love of his life. Mrs. Myles deserves somebody like that."

"Your father was a smart man."

"I think you're smart too, Chef Chase."

"Thanks, Noni. Now get on outta here. Mona's going to drop you off at home. I promise to do whatever I can for Mrs. Myles."

"Thanks. This is just between me and you, right, Chef Chase?"

"Certainly."

"Good. See you later."

Chase's heart was warmed by Noni's concern for Debra. She was a little woman wrapped in a teenager's body. Wow. Chase would never have thought it was that bad between Debra and her husband. When he'd answered the phone on Thanksgiving Day, Chase assumed the two had worked everything out. It was a shame this was happening to Debra right before Christmas. She seemed like a genuinely good woman.

19
This Christmas

ebra's father knew something was up. He was trying to respect Debra's privacy—her marital decisions, but he knew something was wrong the minute she'd told her mother she had "other plans" for Christmas. Like it or not, he was going to stop by and see what was going on for himself if she hadn't returned a call by evening.

Debra sat on the floor in the family room and leaned against the sofa looking at the lights on the Christmas tree that lied every time they blinked. They looked celebratory and festive, when there was only emptiness and a broken heart in her home. She and Bryce had decorated the tree together on Thanksgiving. The handcrafted picture frames that she and Bryce had made together were a hideous mockery. She stared at the different ornaments and the glass bulbs and wished it all away. She reached over and poured herself another glass of wine to ease the aching she felt in her soul.

She reflected on her life with Bryce and the moments flashed before her as memories would at the time a person took their last breath. She squeezed her eyes together and the burning was unbearable. Through glossy blurred eyes, she focused on the tree that should have symbolized blessedness and joy. She felt neither of those things. Yes, she heard what her pastor had said—that you could still have joy even if things in your life weren't good—even if you experienced the loss of a loved one—or a financial setback—the loss of a job. Sure, it was true. Debra just didn't *feel* it. Was she an unbeliever because she couldn't tap into the joy at this moment? Was she a terrible Christian because she couldn't think of the goodness of God at this moment—only the broken heart that made every breath she took laborious? Now here she sat alone on Christmas hating every part of her life.

She couldn't stand to be around her mother tonight. She couldn't take the prodding. Their relationship was strained enough as it was. One derisive comment would send her over the edge. She crawled underneath the tree to retrieve the present that Bryce had placed there just two weeks ago—the same Saturday he'd moved in, and subsequently deserted her for the second time. She opened it hurriedly, driven by some mad frenzied haunting. It was a diamond wedding band that fit into her wedding ring. The inscription read: *B and D forever*. How that made her ache and boil inside.

"Liar!" She screamed so loudly the words tore at her throat, scorching her vocal chords. She tossed it into the fireplace. She scrambled to her feet and tore every ornament off the tree, every stupid lying picture of them. She pulled and snatched until the deceitful symbol had toppled over. She heard the noise when it hit the floor. In her mind it was a faint echo that was drowned out by her own screams. She felt the destruction of the delicate glass bulbs under her feet. "I hate you! I hate you!" she shouted.

The water from the tree stand spilled out over the expensive hand-woven rug Bryce had purchased. Debra's head spun violently, her equilibrium disrupted by chaos. She couldn't keep herself balanced. Down she went, fainting. Her body plopped onto the floor like a rag doll.

* * *

"Debra Ann! Debra Ann!" Daniel shook her. His heart thumped turbulently. What in the world had happened? Had she and Bryce fought? Surely he would kill him. The family room was in utter chaos—broken glass, torn pictures. He noticed the blood on the cream-colored rug and looked down at Debra's delicate feet, which had been cut by the glass. He could see pieces of it still stuck in her skin.

Sheila stood by nervously and began to cry. She cried for the pitiful state her only child was in, and for the fact that they weren't close enough for Debra to come to her and talk about whatever was happening in her life. "I'm going to call an ambulance."

Daniel cradled the upper part of Debra's limp body in his arms, slapping her face gently. After a few seconds she opened her eyes and mumbled something unintelligible. The sound of her voice stopped Sheila in her tracks.

"She's okay," Daniel said moving Debra's hair from her eyes. "What happened in here, Princess? It looks like a tornado has been through this room." He looked over at the half-empty bottle of wine.

"My God, she's drunk!"

"Sheila, get out of here right now if you're going to start up! Do you see this place? Obviously there's something more going on!" Daniel snapped. "Princess, what's going on? You can tell me anything, you know that," Daniel pleaded in a calm, quiet voice.

Debra flung her arms around her father's neck and cried. "Oh, Daddy. Help me, please . . . " she cried hard on him.

"I'm right here," Daniel said patting her. She wasn't his thirty-five-year-old daughter. She was his little girl. The one who crawled up on his lap when no one else understood her. He lifted her onto the couch. Debra was sweating profusely. "Go get a cold rag and some water," he said to Sheila. Debra held onto Daniel for dear life. Her grip around his neck was so tight that Daniel couldn't wiggle out of her grip if he'd wanted to. She loosened her grip on him when she remembered what day it was.

"I'm so sorry to ruin your Christmas, Daddy."

"You haven't ruined anything. I was just concerned about you, that's all." He wiped her face as soon as Sheila had returned with the rag, and then placed the cold rag across her forehead. "What happened in here?"

"He left me, Daddy—for Suzette. He moved back in two weeks ago, and that same night she called him . . . he just left me," she cried again.

Daniel could have strangled that fool. "Don't you worry about it. You're here with me, Debra Ann. It's going to be alright. I'm here for you." He turned and looked at Sheila who was pacing the floor. "Your mother and I love you. We just want you to be okay." Sheila nodded in agreement with Daniel's words. Daniel propped a pillow under Debra's head and stretched her feet out. He propped them up to get a closer look at the tiny shards of glass that were stuck in them. He sent Sheila out to the car to get his tweezers out of the glove compartment. "You got peroxide?"

"Upstairs in the medicine cabinet," Debra said groggily.

"I'm going to get this glass out of your feet. It may hurt a little."

"Okay," Debra said sounding like a compliant child.

Daniel took great care until he had extracted every bit of the tiny pieces of glass that had gotten stuck underneath the skin of her feet. "All set," he said. He'd sent Sheila up to draw a bath for her. "Daddy's going to get this mess cleaned up," he said standing. He walked over to the tree and set it upright.

"Daddy, I don't want it in here. Can you please just throw it out?"

Daniel looked perplexed. "Sure, baby, if that's what you want me to do. Do you have one of those tree bags to cover it?"

"In the kitchen underneath the sink where the other trash bags are."

"Okay. I'll have it out in a few minutes."

Sheila walked back into the family room. "The bath is ready," she said to Daniel.

"Princess, go on up and get in the tub. I'll bring some tea up to you when you're done." He gave Sheila a warning look. She knew exactly what it meant. *Don't upset his little girl.* By the look in his eyes, Sheila knew there would be some talking done to her tonight if she didn't obey. She rolled her eyes.

"I mean it," Daniel said aloud as if he had actually voiced his first warning instead of glaring.

"I hear you," Sheila said nonchalantly. She didn't ask Debra one question as she helped her into the tub. She made no comments about her drinking half a bottle of wine. Nothing about her slurring. Nothing about her marriage. She didn't want to set Daniel off. Sheila knew what he was thinking about—something that had happened years ago, but that he'd never really let go of. She had felt the tension in the room as Debra explained what happened between her and Bryce.

Sheila put fresh linens on the bed while Debra took her bath.

She left the door to the bathroom cracked so that she could hear what was going on in there. Debra was thirty-five years old. Certainly she didn't need Sheila to wash her, too. Daniel was doting on her like she was a injured little girl. Sheila fluffed Debra's pillows and a half-hour later a weary Debra eased into bed.

"I'm going to go down and get your tea. Be right back," Sheila said. Debra only nodded back. The telephone rang and Sheila picked it up.

"Hello."

Chase didn't know the voice. "Merry Christmas, may I speak to Debra please?"

"Who's calling please?"

"This is Chef Chase from Peace Valley, he said formally."

"Hello, *Chef Chase*, this is Debra's mom, Mrs. Prince," she said looking at Debra. Debra shook her head in the negative. She didn't want Chase to see her like this.

"Debra's not feeling too well. May I take a message for her?"

"Yes. Actually, I just wanted to drop off some Christmas presents from some of the students and me. I promised I'd get them to her today. I don't have to come in. I could just leave them with you if that's fine."

"You just want to drop off some gifts from some students?" Sheila repeated, questioning Debra with her eyes. This time Debra nodded in the affirmative. "I think that will be fine. Either her Dad or myself will be here to receive them."

"Thanks, I'm still making gift drop-offs. I should be there in an hour."

"Okay, see you then."

Sheila didn't ask about Chase. She didn't say one word to Debra aside from questions she needed to ask, like if she was comfortable or if she wanted the television on. She went downstairs.

Daniel had taken the tree out, cleaned up the mess, and had made a hot cup of tea that was now warm.

"How's she doing?" he asked as soon as Sheila walked into the room

"She's fine. I'll take the tea up," Sheila said removing the tea bag and putting the mug in the microwave.

"Good."

"How do you think this happened?"

"If I know my little girl, she probably got angry and tore the thing down. This is Christmas. It's a hurting time when someone has walked out on you—cheated and humiliated you."

Sheila heard unspoken words. "I suppose," she said quietly. "A co-worker of Debra's is going to drop off some gifts from the kids at school. He said he'd be here in an hour."

"Okay. I think I'm going to spend the night here with Princess.

Sheila rolled her eyes. "Daniel, she's going to be asleep in a few minutes, there's really no need to babysit her like that."

"Sheila, if you want to go home, you can. Either you can pick me up in the morning or Debra can drop me off," Daniel said with finality.

"For heaven's sake, Daniel, it's Christmas!"

"That's exactly why I'm going to stay here with my little girl. She needs somebody here. You saw how she looked."

"It was probably more of the wine than anything else."

"How would you know?" Daniel cut into her. He tried not to go there with Sheila tonight. He wished she had stayed at home when he decided to check on Debra. Her cavalier attitude about the whole situation had brought up old memories of the Christmas that he would probably never forget, although he'd convinced himself that he had forgiven Sheila a long time ago.

"Fine. We'll stay here." Sheila didn't want to go into battle with her husband right now. She wanted to get away from Daniel. Debra was sound asleep when Sheila made it upstairs. *She probably needs to sleep off that wine*, Sheila thought to herself. She turned off the television and turned out the lights. Sheila brought the tea back down stairs and drank it herself.

"She's asleep" she said to Daniel.

"Good. We can sleep in the guest room after her co-worker gets here." There was agitation in his eyes. He tried to mask it, but Sheila understood.

"Is there something you want to say, Daniel?" she asked knowingly.

"No," he said quickly. He didn't want to discuss it. He was wrong. He knew it. He'd let those feelings resurface again. It had been years, still he hadn't let go—hadn't fully forgiven.

"I think you need to say whatever it is that's on your mind, Daniel Prince."

"I said I don't have anything to say, Sheila. Leave it alone, please."

Sheila was impatient with him. How long was he going to badger her about *it*? She knew the moment Debra cried on him, telling him that Bryce had had an affair, it would bring up his old feelings. From time to time, Sheila would catch Daniel staring at her, despising her. She'd inevitably ask him what was wrong. His answer was always the same: "Nothing." Debra was grown now. Sheila wondered why Daniel had stayed, if he still hated her.

"I'm hoping that any problems we've had are forgiven and forgotten," Sheila said, opening the trunk where Debra kept extra blankets. She took out an afghan and wrapped it around her body before sitting in the oversize lazy boy. Sheila reclined back, and her feet elevated on the built-in ottoman. Daniel sat on the couch and turned on the television with the remote. He said nothing to her. "Daniel?"

"Sheila, please. It's Christmas."

She conceded, but she was irked. She sipped the chamomile tea and tried to forget about what Daniel was thinking and what Debra was feeling. Life happened sometimes, and that was that. One had to move on—let go, if you will. Sheila closed her eyes and fell into a comfortable nap until the doorbell rang. She let her feet down, and walked into the foyer and opened the door.

His handsomeness was captivating. "Hello. You must be Chef Chase," Sheila said.

"Yes. Merry Christmas, Mrs. Prince. It's nice to meet you." Chase was toting two large gift bags. He handed the heavier one to Sheila first, and shook her hand firmly. "This is for Debra—just a couple of things from a few students and me. Sheila hadn't expected the bag to be so heavy. She got a tighter grip on it and smiled. This one has food in it that needs to be refrigerated," he said handing the second bag to Sheila.

Sheila searched his eyes. She wondered why a *female* teacher hadn't brought the gifts over. Immediately she was curious as to what type of *relationship* Debra shared with the nice looking man with the deep black eyes. Men were apt at moving in on another man's territory quickly. It was no doubt that this 'Chef Chase' knew that Debra and Bryce were not together. After all, why was he so adamant about dropping off her gifts *tonight*?

"Would you like to come in for some tea, Chase?" Sheila asked, wanting to launch a thorough investigation. Chase sensed something in the tone of her voice.

"Well, no. I don't want to bother you. I just wanted to make sure Debra got her gifts. I have to get back to my sister's place—my daughter is there waiting for me."

"Oh, well, don't let me keep you—"

"Hi, I'm Daniel—Debra's father," Daniel said. He'd walked up as quietly as a housecat.

"Nice to meet you, Mr. Prince. I'm Chase Martin."

Daniel looked at him with a certain familiarity. "You own the restaurant, *Chase on the River*, right?"

"Yes, that's right, Mr. Prince."

"Shucks, call me Daniel. You volunteer at the school in the culinary department too, right?"

"Sure do," Chase said beaming.

"Princess told me about your restaurant. I hear you've got quite a place downtown. I'm going to have to come down there. I've been told the food is delicious."

"Thank you. We'd love to have you. Maybe you and Mrs. Prince could come down one day this week. I promise to take good care of you."

"I think we will. Hey, Princess is sleeping, but you can come in and have some tea or hot chocolate, if you want."

"No thanks. I left my little princess back at my sister's so I could drop off a few things. I'm going to get back to her before she starts calling me on my cell phone. You know how little women are."

"Little women? Big ones too. Debra and her mother hunt me down all the time."

Chase chuckled. "Well, it was so nice to meet you. Tell Debra I hope she feels better."

"Will do. I'll see you later," Daniel said shaking Chase's hand firmly. He smiled and nodded. He liked the vibe he got from Chase. He closed the door behind Chase and took the heavy bag from Sheila. "Why don't you put that food in the refrigerator, Princess might be hungry when she wakes up." His demeanor had softened. He kissed Sheila on the neck and patted her behind.

"Are you hungry?" she asked.

"What's in that bag you brought Debra from the house?"

"Dressing and ham—everything."

"Well, shoot, she and I can share. Plus, Chase brought her over something to eat, too. She can't possibly eat all of that food."

"Okay. I'll fix you a plate."

"Thank you, baby," Daniel tried hard to keep the peace with Shiela.

She wondered what had gotten into him all of a sudden, but she didn't say anything about it. It was Christmas. "You're welcome, Mr. Prince."

Debra slept soundly until 12:30 a.m. Daniel and Sheila didn't hear her because they were too busy watching a movie, and arguing about which movie the main actor had starred in before. They were sitting across from each other on different sofas.

"Time-out," Debra said making the sign with her hands, ending their discussion.

"That's your mother, trying to prove me wrong as usual," Daniel said. "How are you feeling?"

"I'm hungry."

"Well, there is plenty in there to eat. And *Chase* brought over some food too," Sheila said insinuating.

The first thing Debra did was search in the refrigerator to see what Chase had brought over. The food was packed in his restaurant take-home containers. He had told Debra that his family didn't do the traditional "holiday dinner" every holiday. This Christmas they'd mixed it up. He'd brought stuffed red snapper, lobster bisque, grilled duck, wild mushroom rice, and homemade rolls. For desert he'd made her a lemon meringue pie and had brought along several of the mini sweet potato delights.

Both Sheila and Daniel watched her as she opened each container. It was all presented nicely as if it were going to be served at a table, not like carry-out. Debra smiled.

"You've got gifts too," Sheila said. Daniel went to retrieve the bag. Both of them were curious. The first package was from Noni—it was a hand-knitted bolero. Debra tried it on. "That is beautiful," Sheila nodded.

"She made it herself," Debra said proudly. She reached into the bag and there was a leather rainbow journal from Noni as well. Debra's eyes welled up with tears. There were several other gifts in the bag from Maya and Corey—slippers, a gourmet tea bag set, a novel, and gift certificates from Noni's aunt. A medium size package had Chase's name on it. Debra opened it slowly. It was a figurine by Annie Lee called Love Song. A faceless couple sat tenderly together listening to an old phonograph. Sheila eyed Daniel as Debra opened the Christmas card that had a hand written message from Chase. *May the peace of God, that surpasses all understanding guard your heart and mind through Christ Jesus.* There was a gift certificate inside. Debra took it out of its envelope. "Whoa!"

"What's that?"

"A full spa day at Butterfly Day Spa!"

Sheila elbowed Daniel. She mouthed the words *four hundred dollars.* Daniel looked strange. Maybe Sheila *was* on to something. Maybe there was some sort of *relationship* going on. That didn't sound like his little girl at all, though. But that didn't mean that Chase wasn't "slow-walking" Debra down. He'd ask her about it when the opportunity presented itself.

"I'm going to finish the movie," Sheila said.

"I'll be right in, baby."

"I see she found something else to argue about," Debra whispered to her father as soon as Sheila had left the room.

"I try not to pay her too much attention when she does that," Daniel whispered, winking.

Debra hugged Daniel close. "I love you, Daddy."

"I love you too, Princess." He pulled back. "You change the locks?"

"Yes. For the second time."

"Doesn't matter. I want you to be safe. A man is either at home, or he's not. Don't allow him to come back and forth. You are better than that. And it's too much going on out there with AIDS and stuff."

"I know, Daddy."

"Alright."

20
Baby

It was six weeks into the new year and Debra did not look forward to what this year would bring, nor did she reminisce about the year that had slipped away with her whole world following. She sat at her desk trying to complete a report, but her thoughts kept returning to Bryce. Did he love her at all? Deep down somewhere inside, despite everything, she wanted her marriage. She wanted him. She wondered if he was really in love with Suzette, or just enjoying the thrill of something new. Maybe they could overcome this. Maybe she and Bryce could still work it out.

A thought popped in her head. It tugged at her. She told herself, *no*. She wouldn't do it. What would it solve? She still knew the retrieval code to check Bryce's cell phone messages. They had listened to, and laughed about some silly message one of Bryce's former employees had left him one day. She never forgot that code. She had tucked it in the back of her mind. Surely he had changed it by now. He'd told her that there was no need for them to have secrets. That his love was real. That she'd never have to worry about him being unfaithful again.

She picked up the phone and dialed the voice mail number for Bryce's cell. When prompted, she punched in the pass code anxiously—dreadfully afraid of what she might hear. She listened to each message carefully. It was like Bryce lived in another world, apart from her. Debra's stomach churned when she heard a woman's voice. She listened quietly as the room spun around her.

"Hey, babee," Suzette said with the word baby drawn out irritatingly long. *"Oh, you were so right... and the home kit too. Dr. York says we are definitely pregnant! Six weeks. I'm so excited! I'm going shopping for baby clothes! Love you.*

Debra hung up and dialed Bryce. The message she left was hot and indignant. "If you can pull yourself away from your tramp for a few moments, I'd like a call back." Here she was suspended. How was she supposed to tell her father about this? Why did Bryce lie so much? Less than two minutes later, her cell phone rang. She answered it quickly.

"That message you left was unnecessary, Deb," Bryce rebuked her as soon as he heard her voice.

"So! Are you going to file or do you want me to do it?"

"File for what?"

"A divorce—then you and Suzette can go ahead and have your happy little family—the way you want it!"

"Deb, I've never said anything about a divorce. I was trying to work things out!"

"Does working it out mean having a *baby* with someone else?" Debra was inflamed.

"That was something that just happened, Deb. It's not like I planned it." He didn't bother to ask her how she knew. He had planned to tell her about it when he had to.

"Well that's what happens when you're layin' up with somebody!"

"Look, I'm at work. I can't get into this with you right now, Deb. If you want to meet somewhere in about an hour, let me know."

"Meet for what, Bryce? I want out. I want out!!" Debra screamed before slamming the phone down.

Bryce called right back. "I'll meet you at the house in an hour."

"If you show up at my house, I swear I will have you arrested. I mean it!" Down the phone went again.

Debra calculated the time in her mind. Could it be that Bryce had gotten Suzette pregnant on the same night he'd moved back in—the night he and Debra had supposedly started over? It had to have been. Debra closed her eyes. *Another woman is having my husband's baby.* She rose from her desk and walked toward the window. Her legs felt like jelly. Her stomach had knotted so tight and felt so sick that she was gagging. Debra felt as if she was dying. She bent over the garbage can and vomited. Her face was drenched with perspiration. She pushed her hair away from her face and continued to vomit until she felt her insides were depleted.

Virginia walked in bouncing cheerfully. "Debbie, you want to step out and get some lun—Debbie, are you okay?" Virginia asked rushing over to where Debra sat on the floor in front of the garbage can. Virginia bent down beside her.

Debra was too weak to respond. Her body jerked as she continued to vomit. Some of it missed the basket. Virginia stood and pressed the intercom button. "We need a custodian in the health wing right away!" Virginia lifted Debra and walked her into the nurse's station and shut the door. Debra cried loudly. She walked over to the sink and splashed water on her face and rinsed her mouth. She took the mouth wash from the sink counter and swished it around, as she cried. Virginia waited until she had gathered herself. "Debbie, what happened?" Virginia asked. She knew the vomiting was an emotional response. She saw that through the tears.

Debra sat on the examining table. "She's pregnant . . . they're having a baby."

Virginia knew exactly what Debra was talking about. "Did Bryce tell you that, Debbie?"

"No. I checked his cell phone messages. She was so excited . . . she said that he'd told her she was pregnant already. I guess he's happy about it. I can't believe this is happening to me."

Virginia let out a sigh. "Oh, my dear, I'm so sorry. I wish there were words I could say, sweetheart." She'd known all about how Debra and Bryce had been trying to get pregnant—the doctor's visits and the temperature taking they'd done before they had separated the *first* time. This was crushing. Debra unbuttoned her stained shirt carefully. Virginia opened one of the drawers and took out a plastic bag for Debra to put her shirt in. She opened another drawer and pulled out a T-shirt. She handed it to Debra.

Debra slipped the T-shirt over her head. "I feel like God just doesn't love me right now, Virginia. What have I done wrong to have to hurt like this? What did I ever do to Bryce? I don't get it." Debra shook hard.

Virginia encircled her in an embrace. "God loves you—has always loved you. You'll get through, sweetie," was all Virginia said. At times like this, it was best to say as least as possible. Virginia didn't have the answers. What else could she possibly say to a woman in Debra's predicament?

A knock came at Virginia's door. She walked over to answer

it, opening it only enough to speak. It was Noni.

"Nurse Carlton have you seen Mrs. Myles? I have a session appointment this hour. I see Mr. Stokes in her office mopping . . . "

"Yes, dear, but she's ill. She's going to go home early today, alright? Why don't you go and write yourself a pass and I'll sign it," Virginia said handing her a blank pass. She shut the door back softly.

Noni backed slowly away from the door, not convinced. It took her only a few seconds to scribble out a pass and knock on the door again.

This time Debra answered the door. "Hello, Miss Noni." She had straightened herself up as much as she could.

Noni's light brown eyes examined Debra. "Mrs. Myles, are you alright?"

Debra knew that Noni was probably processing a hundred and one thoughts right now. She'd lost her parents for goodness sake. "Noni, I feel really ill. Today is just not a good day. It's nothing to concern yourself with, sweetheart. I'm going to go home and get some rest. We'll have our session soon as I get back to work, okay?" Debra tried to reassure her.

Noni's face was marred with reticence. "Okay," she said.

21

This Ain't the Life I Ordered

Debra could hardly believe her new year had started off like this. Her husband was literally living with Suzette *and* expecting a baby, and yet, she wanted him. Her heart hurt for him. How much worse could it get? She'd called in sick today because she couldn't deal with anyone else's problems. There were too many of her own standing in line, blinking, waiting for her attention. It was three o'clock in the afternoon. She'd slept all day. She was still in her pajamas. She turned on the coffee machine and grabbed her coat out of the closet in the foyer. She stuffed her feet into some rubber boots and made it down the walkway to the mailbox. Just as soon as she opened it, a black Mountaineer pulled up alongside of her. A slender man wearing a big heavy coat got out.

"Debra Myles?"

For some reason, Debra thought he was some type of delivery man. He was holding a manila envelope that was extended towards her as he moved closer. Then her discernment prevailed. She felt like falling out in the middle of the snow like a child in the midst of a tantrum. She was weak all over. Her eyes became a solemn glossy pool that made the man look as if he were walking under water. "I don't want it," she said in a whispery, strained voice, slowly shaking her head from side to side. She could barely get the words out.

Normally, the gentleman would have repeated the same rote statement he made every time he did this. *"You've been served."* But he was a believer, so he spoke not of his own volition. "Debra, the Lord God is with you. *'I shall never leave nor forsake you,'"* he quoted, *"God is not a man that he should lie."* He switched the envelope from his right hand to his left and reached out for Debra's. Robotically, she met his hand with hers and he held it firmly but tenderly. *"All things work together for good to them that love the Lord and are called according to His purpose.* Peace of the Lord be with you." He gave Debra the envelope and she held it to her chest, nodding—acknowledging his words, but the inside of her toppled over like a heap of rubble. The man backed away slowly and climbed back into his truck. Debra stood in that spot with her winter coat open, exposing her silk pajama covered body to the harsh cold she could no longer feel. Through tears, she watched the blur of the black vehicle turn off her block and out of the subdivision.

Debra shuffled back up the walkway in shock. She was a mindless, disoriented creature, trying to process her life—a life that had climaxed to the manila envelope she clutched to her chest. She'd left the rest of the mail in the box without thinking. Nothing else mattered right now. She likened her life to a fine piece of china that had shattered into a million pieces that could not be put back together—no way, no how.

She searched her mind for offenses against Bryce, but she couldn't recall any that would give him cause to treat her this cruelly. She remembered all of the therapy sessions with Dr. Buckley—every lie Bryce had told both of them. What had happened to her marriage? What had happened to her life? It was a lying, deceiving representation of "happily-ever-after." It wasn't fair. God wasn't fair. What about the family she and Bryce talked about having? Everything she'd ever hoped for in life had disintegrated.

Debra remembered Thanksgiving evening. She could still hear Bryce telling her that he loved her—that they were going to work. Now, she held a motion for the dissolution of her marriage—her life. She sat slumped on the floor leaning against the door in the foyer, not having enough energy to move. She couldn't have even crawled if she wanted to. She felt paralyzed. Her heart seemed to slow to a weak thump. Her thoughts scattered across her mind. She didn't know what day it was anymore. Why was she home? Why was she still in her pajamas? She knew nothing.

The strength of the Word that the server had given her just moments ago couldn't penetrate her heart right now. A cold icy frost barricaded it. Debra scurried somewhere in the corner of her mind where there was no feeling or existence—a space just as empty as her life aside from the jeering voices. Negative raging thoughts taunted her. *Look at you. Why would a man want you? Nothing about you is sexy. You are as plain as they come. You couldn't please your husband. He left you for another woman. Your life is over. You're pathetic!* A cruel sarcastic laughter inundated her head in that mind's corner, but Debra couldn't leave it. She didn't have the strength to walk or crawl out of that space.

Debra could no longer breathe. She was suffocating in that

corner. It was as if all the oxygen had been sucked out of that room. Frightened, she shivered forcefully until she was pulled out. "JESUS!" she screamed aloud gasping for air. Then she repeated that name. That calming, gentle name. Rocking back and forth with automation, Debra attempted to calm that inner, frightened child. "Okay, okay, okay . . . " she cried.

* * *

It was 7:00 p.m. when Debra awakened on the floor in the foyer. She had slept in a fetal position, curled into her winter coat for warmth. Wearily, she sat up. She gathered the envelope and clutched it to her chest again. She stood and walked into the kitchen, tossing the second "destroyer" of her marriage onto the kitchen table. She leaned against the counter and stared at it, letting go of her tears. Fifteen minutes passed before Debra plopped down in the chair directly across from the space where the envelope had landed, to end the dubious stand-off. Her outstretched hand barely touched the envelope as she pulled it to her. She opened it and read. Debra smiled a maniacal smile. She was strong. She would confront him for this. Surely he owed her some sort of explanation as to how they had arrived at this point after all he'd said—after all his lies. Debra scooted her chair back, wiped her face and rose from her seat. She stormed over to the telephone and punched-dialed Bryce's cell phone number. A relentless anger stirred inside of her as she listened to the stalling ring of his phone.

"Hello?" Suzette queried naturally, like she'd been given the right to answer *Debra's husband's* phone. Suzette's voice transformed Debra's anger into pain.

Debra tried hard to keep her voice steady, daring. "May I speak to Bryce?" It was a wimpy command.

Suzette's response was artificial. "Who's calling?" she asked caustically. Her cruelty disarmed Debra.

Debra's voice shattered. "His *wife!*" It was only moments before Bryce was on the line.

"How can I help you?" he said flat and unconcerned, as coolly as he would have responded to a nagging, unsatisfied customer.

"Why are you doing this to me?—I don't want a divorce, Bryce. You said . . . we were going to work . . . work things out. What about therapy and all of that?" Debra cried. Her vulnerability agitated him.

"Look, don't call me with this. You made a choice. This is what *you* wanted. You wanted me to leave, so now I'm gone." Bryce's indifference was chilling. Debra couldn't believe that this was the same man who had made love to her a week before Christmas. The same one who promised he would never hurt her again. The one who said that she meant everything to him.

Debra suppressed her pride and said the words her heart wanted to say. "Bryce, I'm still willing to work things out . . . if you just . . . come home."

Bryce let out a long, exasperated sigh before returning to that cold, smug man Debra had never known. "You know what, Deb? I am *home.* I'm right where I need to be—exactly where I want to be. Believe that. And if you need anything else from me, you need to talk to my attorney. I'll email you her information."

The dial tone brought a fresh new pain. Debra doubled over. "Oh, God. Oh, Jesus . . . Oh Jesus, please . . . "

22

Have a Heart

Valentine's Day. All Debra could think about was 'the Valentine's Day Massacre'. That's what Bryce had done to her heart—her love. Roses and candy? Whatever. Debra had watched the students walk around all day with teddy bears, balloons, and heart shaped boxes of chocolate. It made her want to puke. She felt like making up some excuse so she could go home and bury her head under a pillow, just so she wouldn't have to listen to all the oohs, ahs, and squeals of girls who had received some special token of love from their boyfriends. It was silly to be jealous of them. She knew that. They were just kids, but her heart couldn't tell the difference.

Another funky celebration is what she was angry about. Christmas. New Years. Valentine's Day. She wanted all the days to just vanish until her heart was in a place where it could withstand seeing someone else happy. She was glad that she had only an hour left before she could escape this place that was inundated with love and tokens that she could no longer relate to. Debra began to tidy up her office. She heard their voices in the wing before she saw their faces. As much as she loved them, she didn't want to see them right now. She just wanted to be alone in a place where she could just cry it all out. Noni knocked gently on the door wall since the door was opened. Maya was by her side. Two musketeers instead of three.

"Happy Valentine's Day, Mrs. Myles!" they both said looking innocent.

"Happy Valentine's Day, ladies," Debra said in a voice she masked to keep from sounding gloomy. It didn't make sense to rain on their parade. It wasn't their fault her life was a mess.

"You got any more students this afternoon?" Noni queried.

"No. Why? Is there a problem?" She hoped there wasn't because she didn't want to hear about it today.

"Nope. No problem. We just wanted to give you your Valentine's Day gift and show you how much we love you," Noni said sincerely.

Debra couldn't help but smile. They were truly the only bright spots in her life these days.

"You guys got me a Valentine's Day gift?"

"Yep. But it's around in the culinary class," Noni said smiling.

"Really?" Debra asked curiously. She wondered what they were up to, and where was their third partner in crime?

Maya looked like she was definitely up to something. "Yep. We've got something really special for you today."

"First of all, how did you all manage to get out of your last hour classes?"

"There are no last hour classes today, Mrs. Myles. Everyone is at the Valentine's Day dance in the gym," Noni answered.

Debra had completely forgotten about it. She wondered why it was so quiet on the floor. "Oh," Debra said.

Maya pulled Debra by the hand. "Come on Mrs. Myles, I think you're gonna love what we've planned."

"Okay," Debra said following them out of the office and around the corner to the culinary room. It looked like an industrial kitchen on one side with table seating in the middle, and a traditional looking classroom set-up on the other side. The girls had three helium balloons tied to a teddy bear in the center of one of the tables that was set for seven. Debra couldn't see any of this at the moment because they had led her there with her eyes closed. When Noni walked her to the table she told Debra she could open her eyes.

Debra beamed. "Ooh, I get an early dinner today?"

"Yes, ma'am complete with entertainment."

Jason Lockmore pulled out a chair for Debra and she scooted closer to the table. The aroma in the room was just as pleasing as she knew the food was going to taste. She looked into the kitchen area and saw Mrs. Humphrey, the culinary arts teacher, wearing an apron. Debra watched as she removed something from the oven. She waved. Mrs. Humphrey winked. Corey sat perched on top of a stool across from the table. Todd Bennett was seated right next to her on a lower stool with his keyboard in front. Todd was a gifted student who maintained a 4.0 average. He had a medium build with wild, shoulder-length blond hair that made him look scruffy. He looked more like a rocker than a young man who planned to be a surgeon. He had the most beautiful, humane, blue eyes that gazed upon Corey with adoration. She gave him a cue with a slight nod. Todd began lightly stroking the keys. A sweet sound filled the air that shocked and pleased Debra. The incredulous look on her face was evidence of the fact that she was amazed by Corey's voice which hummed a sweet melody. Corey was a bird singing with a human voice.

> *"From the first moment that I saw you . . .*
> *I knew this was different.*
> *My whole world stopped when you smiled.*
> *Could you hear my heart beating?*
> *Yeah . . .*
> *This love is real . . .*
> *No need to question*
> *The way I feel*
> *Ooh, I can tell you, I can tell you, I can tell you that . . .*
> *This love is real . . . "*

Todd blended his voice with Corey's on the chorus, singing the words he had penned for her. Debra thought she was going to fall out of her chair. Corey sang with such a heart-felt plea that Debra understood the words to the song more fully with each verse. *My goodness*, Debra thought to herself. *This girl has the voice of an angel.* Debra couldn't hold back her tears. They were happy ones. For that one hour, Debra forgot about herself and her problems as she had lunch with her babies. She forgot about her pain. She knew that God had put these girls in her life. They were ministering to her spirit as much as she was to theirs in therapy.

23
Snow Trauma

It was a Thursday evening. Debra had just come from the beauty shop. Her hair was laid, bouncy, and camera ready underneath the hat she wore to keep it from getting snowed on. She'd learned that morning that the snow blower was broken. Something was wrong with the motor. It couldn't have happened at a worse time. Daniel and her mother were in Las Vegas for a week to celebrate their anniversary. Mr. Craiggs and his wife had taken a trip to South Africa. The snow was falling furiously. It was coming down so plentifully and so fast, Debra didn't even find it beautiful. She remembered her father telling her not to let the snow pile up, so it wouldn't be too heavy if she had to shovel it. It had to be at least five inches now. The weather men were predicting at least another seven would fall by morning.

Debra brought her work bag inside and changed her clothes. She retrieved the shovel from the wall in the garage and started with the driveway. She wished she knew more of her neighbors, but a lot of them kept to themselves. Plus, they probably expected that Bryce would do it, not knowing he didn't live there anymore. He was living elsewhere.

Lifting the shovel seemed like fighting against gravity. Heavy snow flakes chilled her face as she worked her way up the driveway heaving snow to the left. She was bending her knees like Daniel had taught her, but she still felt like she was giving a two hundred pound man a horseback ride. By the time she made it up the drive way, Debra was crying hard. She hated Bryce. This was his job.

The confident woman who had convinced herself that she didn't need Bryce around to take care of these kinds of things was failing her on-the-job training course. "Lord it's not right! What did I do! What did I do!" Debra screamed. She could barely see in front of her as the snow flakes swished around in her face. She ran into the garage throwing the shovel against the wall, punching the button that let the garage door down. She swung the entrance door open and slammed it shut, before running through the kitchen and up the stairs like a scorned child. Afterward she plopped down into the tub of hot water she'd prepared before she'd gone out to shovel. It had cooled a bit but it was still hot. She sat in it and cried until her skin shriveled. The hair-do she'd just paid fifty dollars for was finished. Debra didn't care either. She didn't care about any-thing. She didn't even feel like praying. "What ever happened to, 'I'll never leave or forsake you?' I feel pretty forsaken right now!" she shouted at God. Her body jerked so hard from crying that her back ached even more. And where was her God?

Debra awakened to seven more inches of snow—just as the meteorologists had promised. Her back was still aching from last night's shoveling attempt. She needed to get that blower fixed. She didn't even know what shop Bryce took it to for service. She wouldn't dare call him. She had to grow up. This was the worst week possible for her father *and* Mr. Craiggs to be gone. Debra looked out of the window and wanted to cry all over again. She couldn't shovel today even if she wanted to. The sight of it was too overwhelming. Seven inches on top of the five metro Detroit had received yesterday afternoon, was too much to take on. It was 5:15 a.m. Debra prayed for strength, then washed her face and brushed her teeth.

She went down to the kitchen and made a cup of hot chocolate. She had just taken her first sip when she heard a motor running—a snow blower. She went to the front window in the living room and saw one lone ranger treading through the snow with a blower. She thought it was Bryce at first, but another careful look revealed the man's identity. It was Chase. Debra sighed a sigh of relief. "Lord, that was one of the quickest answers I've ever received. Now, if You can treat me like that with all the other stuff I've been praying about, I'll be set."

It took Chase forty-five minutes to clear the driveway, the walkway, and the sidewalk. She waited until he had finally made it to the porch. She heard the shovel scrapping against the stone pavers.

Debra opened the door. "Morning," she said awkwardly.

Chase was startled. "Whoa . . . morning," he returned, smiling, trying to keep his eyes on her delicate face, and not on the red long johns that caressed every curve she possessed.

"Would you like some coffee? I'm making breakfast too," Debra offered.

"Uh . . . sure. I'm just about finished. Just have to put the rock salt down when I'm done with the porch."

Ten minutes later, Chase rang the doorbell. Debra had changed into a pair of jeans and a white T-shirt, and as far as Chase was concerned, that outfit was just as venomous as the long johns. He was nervous on the inside. Second guessing himself. If her husband came home at this very minute what would he do? People could get out of hand in situations like these. His mind started wandering off to crazy scenarios. He unconsciously felt for the pistol he kept on him. He'd gotten his permit to carry a concealed weapon several years ago after he was robbed at gunpoint. It was always on him. He carried it for protection and hoped he'd never have to use it. Debra seemed to have read his mind.

"Chase, my husband filed for a divorce. He's living with someone—and expecting a baby. The locks and security codes have been changed. He definitely does not live here anymore."

"Oh, you didn't have to share any of that with me, Debra," he said, but he was glad that she had.

"I just wanted you to feel comfortable. You look a bit nervous."

"So do you," Chase said with a grin. They chuckled.

"I'm making omelets. What's your pleasure?"

"What do you have?"

Debra smiled. "Let's see, green peppers, red peppers, yellow peppers, onions, turkey, chicken, cheese, and tomatoes."

"Well I'm a garbage can omelet man. I'll take all of it."

Debra laughed. "A man after my own heart. That is just the way my daddy likes his too. Speaking of Daddy, he picked the worst week ever to take a vacation. I shoveled so much yesterday I feel like my back is broken."

"Glad I could help out."

"Are you always up this early?" Debra asked prying.

"Yes. I usually make it over to the restaurant at eight. We start serving lunch at eleven a.m. I figured it would take an hour or so to take care of you. Another forty-five minutes to an hour to get back home."

"I really appreciate you, Chase." Debra was as surprised as she was nervous. "I know you're really busy. Breakfast is the least I can do for you."

"You're quite welcome," Chase said. He was putting in every holy effort to keep his eyes from wandering all over Debra. Why was she so beautiful? He looked up at the ceiling "My, Lord," he whispered to himself.

Debra didn't hear him because she was rinsing off the knife she'd used to chop the veggies. A few minutes later, she brought Chase his omelet. She'd garnished the plate with orange slices and parsley.

"This looks very chef-like Chase teased."

"Well, when you're serving a chef, you gotta come correct."

"Ah, I see. You like cooking?"

"No," Debra said rather quickly. She chuckled. "I do it out of duty. My dad was a cook in the Marines. He taught me how to cook. My mom and I are spoiled by him. He did almost all of the cooking in the house. If I had a choice between cooking and cleaning, hand me a mop and a broom."

"Now see, we could be best buddies, because cooking I love; the cleaning is a different story. I have a housekeeper, and believe me, I have to pay her well. If it weren't for Mona, my office at the restaurant would be a disaster."

"Chase you can go ahead and eat. My omelet has got a minute or so to go."

"Oh, no, that's rather rude. I'll wait for you. I can't start eating without the chef."

"Okay," Debra said. Bryce had always started without her, sometimes taking his plate into another room.

Debra and Chase ate breakfast and talked about everything.

Chase had brought Debra a USA Today paper. Noni had told him that she liked to read it every day. It was six-thirty a.m. when Debra thought to turn on the television to see if schools would be open or not. She doubted they would. Chase had caused her to forget all about her daily routine.

Just as she flicked on the remote, she heard the announcer say, *"Once again, all Wayne, Oakland, and Macomb county schools are closed."* Debra shouted. "Yes! I can go right back to bed. Hallelujah! Thank you, Oakland county!"

Chase smiled at her bouncy, girl-like response to the report. "Well, life ain't so good for us restauranteurs. People still have to eat. The chef still has to cook."

"I'm so glad I bought five new books at Borders yesterday while I was waiting to get my hair done. I'm about to *chill!*" Then she remembered Bryce. Some days when she had these emergency school closings due to weather, Bryce would stay home with her. She'd bring him breakfast in bed, and then they'd make love afterward—on and off all day.

"Debra *Ann* . . . did you hear me?" Debra was distracted by her thoughts until Chase had called her name.

"Huh?" she said, reentering the conversation. Then it registered that he had called her *Debra Ann.* She smiled. "How did you know that was my middle name, Chase?"

"I didn't. It just seemed to fit."

"That's what my daddy calls me when he's trying to get my attention," she laughed.

Chase stood. "Listen, I've got to head out. Thanks for breakfast. The coffee was delicious. You saved me four dollars at Starbucks."

"Would you like some to go? I have millions of thermoses around here."

"Sure."

Debra searched the cabinet and found a brand new silver thermos. She filled it with coffee and screwed the lid on tightly. "Here you go," she said handing it to him. The moment seemed rather awkward. She usually handed Bryce his coffee before he left for the office.

"Thank you."

"You are very welcome. Thank you so much, Chase," Debra said. She hugged him and kissed him on the cheek. Chase couldn't tell if it was the heat from the hearth burning him so hotly or an internal heat that had ignited from holding Debra's body. He felt like he was melting. God's Word came. *Can a man hold fire to his bosom and not be burned?*

Chase let go of her perfect frame. "Thanks again, Ms. *Debra Ann.*"

Before he'd left, he'd gone to his truck to retrieve the treat he'd brought her. His own lobster bisque soup for lunch, and two of Noni's mini sweet potato pie delights. Debra smiled wide that he'd thought about her. Lately she'd been feeling forgotten. Unattractive. She got in bed and escaped into a book she'd bought. It was better than dealing with reality.

24

Spoons, Forks, and Knives

Debra and her attorney Helena Ortiz sat at a table across from Bryce and his attorney, Bailey McKinley, in a conference room at Helena's law office. The sleek modernistic office with mahogany paneled walls and expensive art paintings was filled with so much animosity that Helena could feel it crawling on her skin. Debra wondered how it had gotten so ugly between her and Bryce. It was like Bryce hated her now. Everything was an argument. Not only was Bryce demanding that they sell the house and Debra move out, now he wanted his deceased mother's antique silverware set back. He wanted the flat screens, most of the furniture and everything else *he* purchased for *their* home. Debra had picked out the furniture, but Bryce had actually purchased it. He still had the receipts and copies of the checks from his personal account. Debra couldn't believe it had come down to this.

Bryce had stopped depositing money into their joint account at the beginning of the year. Debra had been handling the mortgage and utilities by herself since then. Thirty-eight hundred square feet was a lot of house to heat in Michigan—not including the basement. And it was straining her. It seemed that Suzette had Bryce backing out of every promise he'd ever made to Debra. What had she ever done to Bryce to make him deal with her so treacherously?

Bryce wanted almost everything in the basement recreation room too—both the pinball machines, the pool table and all seven arcade games he'd bought for his Old School Row, which held all the old games that used to be at the neighborhood arcade when he was in high school.

"Bryce, if you hadn't just stopped paying the bills, I would have given you your mother's stuff already. You made a promise to keep that house up until this was over."

"Deb, I can't keep paying close to four thousand a month for mortgage and utilities on Crescent Drive and pay to live where I'm staying, too."

"If you weren't taking care of that *tramp*, maybe you'd have enough money to take care of what you promised!"

Bryce ignored Debra's comment about Suzette. "What about when the divorce is final, Deb? Then what are you going to do? You still expect me to pay all your bills?"

"They are not *my* bills—they belong to both of us!!!"

"Well, I don't live there anymore, so I don't think I should pay for you to stay there. I say we just sell it and split whatever profit we make. The house is in my name anyway."

Debra jumped up out of her chair and slammed her hands on the table so hard it scared Bailey. Debra was up in Bryce's face with a vengeance. She let out an expletive. "What does that mean?

It's *our* house! I don't care if the deed says Mickey Mouse on it!!!"

"Helena, get your client. Everyone needs to calm down," Bailey warned.

Helena gently pulled Debra back down into her chair. "Debra is entitled to a percentage of Bryce's 401k and the rental properties. Let's compare the figures and see what we can work out."

Debra and Bryce had already been there arguing almost two hours. Bailey and Helena were trying to keep their respective clients cool while they sorted out the details of their divorce, so it would be smooth sailing when they went to court. Bailey looked at her Blackberry. She had scheduled a lunch date with an old flame. "Can we take a ten minute break, then come back and look at the figures, so we can wrap up today?"

"Good idea," Helena said.

Hot, violent tears streamed down Debra's face. "I'm gonna take a break alright, and I'm NOT coming back in here to talk about spoons, forks, knives, and pinball machines!!!" Debra screamed. "Bryce, whatever you want you can have. It's *your* house. You can have it. I will move. I want nothing from you. Do you hear me! I'll move out by Good Friday. And I don't want to see you again until the day we make this thing final!" She looked Bailey in her eyes with a cold stare. "Does everybody in this room agree to that?"

"Debra, I don't think we should do it this way," Helena warned.

"No, this is exactly the way we need to do it," Debra countered. "I will move out by Good Friday, I don't want any of the rental properties or any of his 401K, and he gets none of mine." She cut Bryce a cold look. "I don't want any spousal support—nothing from you. You keep everything you got—including your name, as I will gladly take my daddy's name back! Just walk away like we never happened. That's what I want to do."

"I accept that offer," Bryce said quickly. Bailey nodded in agreement with her client.

"Give us a minute alone," Helena said pulling Debra into the hall. Debra grabbed her coat and purse. Helena had known Debra's father a long time. She didn't want to make Daniel think that she wasn't representing Debra to the best of her ability. "Debra, this is a bum deal for you. It's not fair or equitable."

"Helena, if you haven't noticed, life ain't fair!" Debra said, swallowing another painful lump in her throat.

"Debra, I think you're just operating out of emotion right now. You might wake up one day and regret this offer. Think about it some more, Debra—please."

"No. I don't need to think about it anymore, Helena. I hear so deeply in my spirit the Lord telling me to let go. *He* is my pro-vider—not Bryce. This is not an emotional offer, though my tears flow and my heart is broken—this is a spiritual release," Debra said heaving out the words. "Draw up whatever you need to. I'm going home to start packing my things. This part of my life is over."

For the first time in years, Helena wanted to cry with a client. Her eyes welled up and she fought back tears. She could feel the crushing of Debra's heart like it was her own. She hurt for her. Helena wondered how love could so easily vanish from people's hearts. How a man could one day love his wife, then turn around and leave her for another woman, and forget every vow he'd made. How he could so callously dispose of the wife he had promised God he would cherish until death did them part. Helena thanked God for the man she had at home.

* * *

Debra was a wreck. Where could she go? Who could she talk to? She'd been keeping everything under wraps from her mother so that Daniel wouldn't get involved. She was warned by Minister Calloway at church not to share the details of her marital business, for the simple fact that couples sometimes had problems and then worked them out. It wasn't so easy for parents or in-laws to move forward. It was best to keep them out of it as much as possible.

Debra drove around aimlessly for a while, but then, before she knew it, she was pulling up to *Chase on the River*. She tried to wipe her face some, but the tears kept coming anyway. She felt like she was going to burst open any minute if she didn't just cry and get it all out at once. She spotted Mona pulling up with a very handsome gentleman. The car stopped and the man got out and opened Mona's door. When Mona stepped out, the man hugged her close and whispered something in Mona's ear that made her smile. He deep kissed her right in the middle of the parking lot for what seemed like an eternity. Mona pulled away gently and wiped her lipstick off the man's lips with her thumbs. The man watched Mona as she walked toward the door. Debra got out of her car.

"Bye, baby. I can't wait to see you tonight—I love you," the gentleman called out. He was tall and chocolate, dressed in a black cashmere coat. He looked like a model.

"I love you too, Lamont Drake," Mona said, turning around and blowing a kiss at him. She saw Debra. "Hey, Debra . . . what are you doing here?" she said smiling. She noticed her face and said, "Is everything alright?"

"I came to see Chase, is he here?"

"Yeah, I'm sure he's still here. Come with me," Mona said locking her arm in Debra's, walking her to the front door. "Kevin, take Mrs. Myles back to Chase's office and hang my coat up for me please," Mona said to one of the young hosts as soon as they entered the restaurant.

Kevin gingerly placed Mona's mink coat over his arm and walked Debra back to the office as instructed. Chase's door was cracked open. Kevin tapped on it lightly.

"Come in," Chase called out.

"Chase, Mrs. Myles is here to see you," Kevin said.

Chase looked pleasingly surprised until he saw the look on Debra's face. Kevin had darted off down the hall to Mona's office to hang up her coat.

Bailey McKinley stepped out of Chase's bathroom. "Chase, I like what Mona's done with the place it looks very chic and—" She stopped mid-sentence looking just as puzzled as Debra did.

"Not you again," Debra said before turning to leave. She made it halfway down the hallway before Chase caught up with her.

"Wait, Debra! Don't leave. What's the matter? Tell me what's going on."

"I'm sorry . . . I didn't mean to come unannounced," Debra cried, "It's just that I don't have anybody to talk to, and I need somebody to tell me that everything is going to be alright because right now, nothing is alright!"

Instinctively, Chase pulled Debra into his arms and hugged her as she sobbed on him. "Shh . . . it's alright. It's gonna be alright, Debra Ann." Chase rubbed his hands over her back to calm her. It seemed to him that he could feel her pain through her heavy wool coat. What was he doing? If he didn't know any better, he'd swear he was falling in love with this woman he called *friend*.

Bailey had slipped into the hall and was looking on enviously, admiring the way Chase held Debra. How tender he was with her. How loving his embrace seemed. How powerfully protective his arms must have felt. She imagined the scent of Chase's skin. The brush of his lips against Debra's ear, telling her everything was alright. Bailey smiled regretfully.

Mona came strutting down the hallway at a quick pace. "Chase, they've got a problem in the kitchen, they need you right a—way." Mona said stunned, seeing Chase holding Debra while Bailey looked on. She didn't know Chase had Bailey there. *What is she doing here?* Mona thought to herself. Chase and Bailey had been over for years. Bailey's own fault. She'd done Chase wrong when he was struggling to pull the restaurant together. She'd wanted him to give up on his dream and do something else so that her parents would be satisfied that she was with someone who had a *future*. Bailey still regretted that decision.

"Debra Ann, I've got to see what's going on in the kitchen. Why don't you go back in my office and rest—put your feet up. Have you eaten?"

"No," Debra said weakly.

"Good. I'll bring us back some lunch, okay? Stay put . . . be right back," Chase said backing away. Chase looked at Bailey. "Today's not a good day for us to talk, Bailey. I'm sorry. Maybe some other time."

"No problem," Bailey said poker faced, ever the quintessential Queen of Cool.

Debra met Bailey's stare on the way back into Chase's office. The two women stood face to face in the hallway, each only half-way understanding the other.

"Debra, I'm sorry. I was just doing my job earlier. I hope you understand that," Bailey said sincerely. "But I want you to know something—woman to woman . . . if I were you, and I had *Chase Martin* holding me like *that,* I darn sure wouldn't be thinking about no fool named Bryce Myles—he's not even on Chase's level, baby. Chase is the cream of the crop, girl. *Desire what you deserve*, Debra," Bailey said before walking out of the back door.

Chase returned twenty minutes later with a fancy looking, gold rolling cart. The food was covered by decorative tin tops that had elaborate designs. Debra had calmed down enough to fall into a cat nap. "Hey, wake up in here, its lunch time," Chase said rolling the cart over to his table.

Debra sat up and rubbed her temples. Her head was pulsating. "I need some aspirin or something." She reached for her purse and searched the bottom for any straggling pills that may have been left behind. She was popping headache medicine like mints these days. She put one on her tongue and Chase handed her a glass of water. She threw her head back and gulped the water and the pill down. Chase smiled.

"What's for lunch?" she asked.

"You're favorite soup to start with."

"My lobster bisque? Boy, do I love you," Debra said chuckling.

"Yeah and I brought you a good ol' steak with my specially stuffed mashed potatoes."

"I'm gonna be fat when I leave here."

"No such thing. Come sit," Chase beckoned, pulling out a chair for her. She stood and walked towards him.

"Ooh, let me wash my hands first," Debra said trotting toward Chase's restroom. She came out a moment later and scooted up to the table.

Chase had set everything out. He took her hands in his and prayed. "Father, God, You are the Prince of Peace, the restorer of our souls, and our true source of strength. We ask, Dear Lord that you cloak us in your mercy, and give us refuge under your wings that we may be able to withstand the world. Thank You for the opportunity to fellowship over the meal that has been prepared for the nourishment of our physical bodies. Bless all the preparing hands, in our Savior, Jesus' name. Amen."

"Chase, I'm sorry about earlier. I didn't know you had company. It's not like me to just pop up on people. I just didn't know where else to go, you know?"

Somehow he knew what had happened already. "That was perfectly alright. That's what friends are for—the unexpected times."

"I didn't mean to interrupt your date with the *Wicked Witch of the West*."

Chase chuckled. "Believe me, it wasn't a date. Bailey and I go way back to my B.C. days—before Christ. She said she just wanted to come by and chit-chat about something. How do you two know each other?"

"She's Bryce's attorney."

"No."

"Yes, and she did a good job of making me want to slap all the make-up off her face this morning at that stupid meeting with Bryce. I was praying more for the two of them than I was for myself because I wanted to leap across the table and choke both of them to death. I had to keep repeating scriptures to myself like a Sunday school student," Debra said. She told Chase the whole story about Bryce's demands and her final offer. "So I have about a month to find someplace else to live—but enough about that. Let's change the subject. Are you and Bailey *special* friends or something? I really didn't mean to start anything today."

"No. Rest assured, there is *nothing* special about Bailey and me," Chase said shaking his head in the negative.

He and Bailey had met while he was working as a cook at a restaurant and taking culinary arts classes at a community college. She had just graduated from law school and was on her way up the socio-economic status ladder. He was twenty-eight and she was twenty-five. Chase had fallen in love with her, even though socially and economically, she was out of his league. He loved her sassiness and wit. He had done his best to be good to her, provide her with all the simple things he could afford, and he had given his heart totally—which was crazy to even him, because before then, he had been rotten when it came to women. He never intended to be tied down to just one. Bailey was the first woman besides Marva, his high school sweetheart and mother of his daughter, that he had ever considered marrying.

"I believe that Bailey loved me too," Chase said. "But I didn't fit the mold of what her parents wanted her to have. Her father, being a judge, thought that I was beneath his daughter, so Bailey turned her attention to somebody who met her family's approval—an up and coming prosecuting attorney named Desmond Williams. After about two years, Bailey started cooling us down. Whenever I tried to be with her she would say she was busy, needed space, and so on. I knew something was up. She had probably forgotten that she'd given me a key to her place. I used it one night and caught her in a very compromising situation with Desmond. And that was that."

"Wow—that's terrible."

"Actually, it was divine because I was so torn up over Bailey that it made me search for a meaning and a purpose for my life. Because of that, I came to know Christ, and Bailey, she learned a valuable lesson about love. She married Desmond that same year only to find that he was a wife-beating womanizer. They divorced three years later. The good thing is, she'll recognize *and* appreciate real love the next time it comes her way, and she won't let anyone or anything keep her from it," Chase said.

Mona chimed in over the intercom. "Chase, the mayor is here. He's at table six."

"I'm having lunch with Debra," Chase said toward the intercom, in his 'don't bother me anymore' voice.

Mona chuckled. "He's the mayor."

"Yeah. He runs the city, not me. He's getting a free lunch. That's good enough."

"I'll go greet him personally," Mona said defeated.

"Uh-huh."

Debra curled up on the inside. She had all of Chase's attention. "No more interruptions after this. Patrick Kelley and his wife are here too," Mona said over the intercom again.

Chase smiled devilishly. Patrick Kelley was a retired NFL player who owned a restaurant called Pat's Place that was just a few blocks from Chase on the River. "He's probably over here spying on me," Chase said laughing. "I'll be out to greet them before they leave. Bye, Mona."

"Okay. I get the message," Mona returned.

"Do you two go at it like that all the time?" Debra asked.

"Only when Mona tries to mold me into some social butterfly. I appreciate the VIP business, but every customer is essentially the same. You have to be fair. I can't get up and jump every time a VIP comes in. I wouldn't get anything done around here."

Debra looked into Chase's eyes. She wondered if he was all the man she felt that he was. If he was really this kind and gentle— this caring. She used to think of Bryce that way. Now he'd turned into some husband-monster who was trying to squeeze the life out of her and crush her spirit in the process.

Debra and Chase ate together and a weight lifted from Debra. Chase prayed for her before she left. Debra felt as if she could stay in Chase's arms forever and not face her life, but she went home and began packing her things.

Mona strolled into Chase's office when Debra left.

"I'm starting to think my big brother is *smitten*."

"What are you talking about, Mona?" Chase asked, smiling

knowingly.

"I think you are sooo deep into Debra, you can't see straight. You should have seen the look on Bailey's face when you were hugging Debra in the hallway."

"We're just friends, Mona. That's it. She's going through a rough patch right now. I'm just trying to lend some support."

"Well you looked more like somebody's man holding them, than somebody's friend. You're feelin' her aren't you? Cuz you dismissed Bailey like a cold case."

"Bailey is Bailey. We can't go backwards."

"Is that what she wanted?"

"I'm not sure. We didn't get a chance to talk, but I'm sure it was related. And with Debra, I feel the Lord is just using me to lend some support—that's what other Christians are for."

"Are you telling me that you don't *want* Debra? Because there was so much love and passion in your eyes, while you were holding her, I thought I was watching a love story."

"You were imagining things, little girl."

"So you're saying you *don't* want Debra?

"What do you mean *want* her?"

"Oh, come on Chase, I'm talking like, 'take to bed' want."

"I don't let my mind travel that road."

Mona sensed something telling in his eyes. "I thought you Christians weren't supposed to be liars."

Chase laughed. "I'm not saying that the thought has *never* crossed my mind—I just don't entertain it. Debra's married and going through a messy divorce, so as far as I'm concerned, she is *absolutely* off limits."

"So if she weren't married, you'd let yourself think about making love to her?"

"I'm sure it would be a more prevalent thought than it is now, but because of the vow I made to the Lord, I'd still have to can it, anyway. At this point in my life, I only date with the intentions of finding a wife. I ain't tryin' to be celibate for the rest of my life."

"See, that's why I think Christianity is confining. Sex is so natural."

"It's not confining, it's my *choice*. For three good years I've stayed the course, and I plan to keep staying the course, until I say 'I do'. That's God's way."

"Chase, not getting any for three years sounds like a prison sentence to me."

"I don't care what it sounds like. I love the Lord more than I love sex. Every command the Lord has given us is ultimately for our protection and growth—so that we become more like Jesus, Mona. Sex is something that the Bible clearly states should occur in marriage only. Look at the rate of broken families."

"Children out of wedlock. Women devastated after they find out some fool they've given their bodies to could care less about them. You've been there yourself, sis. People have sex without any regard for true commitment—I used to be one of them. You know how I was back in the day. But look at the situation with Marva and Savannah—look at all the hell I went through to get that girl out of that situation—all because of one night of pure lust. I knew Marva wasn't right and wasn't planning to be right. I just felt like, 'I'm gonna get my needs met this one time.' By God's grace, I don't have HIV or something else instead of a beautiful little girl. This time, I'm waiting on God."

"I admire you big brother, I'm just not there yet. I mean, don't you ever long to be caressed and kissed by a woman—to have a woman just surrender herself to you—giving you your very own personal playground?"

Mona's question sent Chase's mind someplace he didn't want

it to go. For a split second he burned in a flame of desire. He shut
the thought down. Chase shook his head. "Thanks for the visual,
Mona."

"Sorry," Mona chuckled.

"Seriously, the answer is *yes*, and to tell you the truth, all I can
do is pray about it. I watch what I listen to, what I talk about—
what I read. I believe that God—because He loves me, wants the
best for me, and I want the best for me. I believe if I do things
His way, instead of my way—which has been proven not to work,
mind you," Chase chuckled. "He will bless me with the desires of
my heart. Scripture says so. *Delight thyself in the Lord, also. And
He shall give you the desires of your heart.* My *wife's body* will
be my personal playground. I don't want to be outside of God's
will anymore. I want every blessing He's willing to give me. *Every
good and perfect gift comes from the Lord.*"

Mona considered everything that Chase said, but she honestly
wasn't there. Right now she just wanted to enjoy her life—by her
own rules. One thing was for sure, however, whether Chase knew
it or not, he was falling in love.

25
The Wanting

C hase lingered after church service, waiting for his best
friend Corey Perry, Assistant Pastor of Greater Christian
Center, to finish greeting his church members. His father,
Pastor Charles Perry was out of town, and Corey had preached the
message in his absence. He had fair skin with dark brown eyes that
were deep set and pensive looking. He sported a close-cut fade
and stood about six feet tall. He was handsome with a softness to
him that made him easily approachable. Even being a man of God,
he still had to fight the women off—churched and un-churched.

It had been a packed house in the large sanctuary that could fit
two thousand comfortably. The receiving line on Sunday morning
was like that of a concert. It was the members' time to connect
with their pastor and thank him for the message—thank him for
allowing God to use him to minister to the congregation. For some
members, like Monica Weathersby, who was one of the devil's

chief-influenced humans on the planet, it was a time to put temptation to action. Every week her dresses got shorter and her cleavage more exposed. Corey kept his comments to Monica as short as possible. He'd even secretly assigned one of the elder sisters of the church watch dog duty just to monitor Monica and keep her at bay. If Sister Montgomery saw Monica doing any devilment, i.e. hugging too long, batting her beautiful hazel eyes, or speaking in a tone that wasn't fit to be spoken in a sanctuary, she'd walk over and move Monica graciously past pastor saying, "You're not the only one who wants a few words with Pastor Corey on Sunday."

When the line finally fanned out, Chase walked up to Corey and said, "You must be scared I'm going to ask you for a re-match on the basketball court." Corey had killed him during their last one on one.

"Scared of you? Only if Jesus is playing with you." The two of them laughed.

The two old friends went back a long way—in the days before both of them even knew Jesus. They'd been best friends since elementary school. Although Corey's father was a minister, Corey rebelled against that upbringing and his calling until he realized that his arms *were* too short to box with God. Their lives had changed so drastically for the better. Corey was just thirty-five years old, but his love for God and The Word surpassed his age. What he lacked in age, he had in heart for God. Chase was one of his biggest supporters.

"I just need to bounce something off you, if you got a minute," Chase whispered.

"You better come on back to my office before Mother Harris gets over here." Corey said.

Chase turned his head slightly to the left and noticed the healthy woman sporting a big green hat and matching dress. She seemed to be marching their way. Her bowlegged gait reminded Chase of John Wayne. The two of them laughed again. Mother Harris was a staunch critic. She had something to say about every sermon—every happening at Greater Christian Center, and usually her rant went on way past the time Corey's ears could bear. They made a mad dash to Corey's office. Settled in, Corey took off his robe. Chase sat down in the chair across from Corey's desk and sighed. His mind wandered off to her again.

"Chase, what's on your mind?"

"Man, I'm all twisted up."

"Is it Savannah? Are you having problems with Marva again?"

"No. I wish it were that easy. It's a woman—a married woman."

Corey's eyes bucked wide. "Come on, Chase. I *know* you know better than that!" Corey admonished.

"She's separated and going through a divorce. I didn't know any of that when I met her though. Corey looked at Chase seriously. "I'm not involved with her sexually or anything. I met her while volunteering with the culinary program at Peace Valley High. She's the school social worker. Like I said, she's in the middle of a nasty divorce. You know that kind of situation has always been off limits to me. I've just been a friend. I call her maybe once a week just to check on her. I've shoveled her snow a couple of times. Nothing intimate or flirty, Corey."

Corey let out a sigh of relief. "Okay, so far so good, buddy."

"The problem is: I have some very strong feelings for her. I didn't realize it until the day she showed up at the restaurant in tears after returning from a meeting with her husband and their lawyers. She was in bad shape, so I was just trying to comfort her you know, so I held her in my arms, and man, it was like I was holding on to a part of me—it's crazy I know. We've never been on a date—had a kiss—nothing, but I felt like she was mine. "I've never experienced anything like that before. Not with Marva. Not with Bailey. Not anyone. And before you say it—it's not sexual. Yes. She is beautiful. She has a beautiful figure, but it wasn't that. Everything about her just moves me. I feel like I love her. I want to care for her, protect her."

Corey sat patiently meditating on Chase's words before he offered his advice. "I'm telling you this as your assistant *pastor* and your *best* friend, leave it *alone*, Chase. Everything you feel is probably as real as this desk right here," Corey said knocking his knuckles against the cherry wood desk. "But I believe that God still honors marriage, even when it's raggedy, even when the people in it are separated. As long as that covenant is there, you are in dangerous territory, my friend. And you know it's easy in situations like that for emotions to get out of control."

"Yeah, I know. Her spirit is so broken right now. Her husband had an affair and left her for the woman—and he and the woman are expecting a baby. Maybe that's the reason I feel the need to protect Debra—I don't know. I feel like I'm in love with her.

"Debra?"

"Yeah, Debra. Debra Prince-Myles."

Corey revved back in his chair. "Whoa . . . whoa . . . whoa . . . . *whoa!*"

"What?"

"*That* Debra Prince."

"What do you mean, *that* Debra Prince?"

"I know her from college." Corey and Chase had parted ways after high school. Corey had gone on to college at Alabama State and Chase had stayed home running the streets. "Debra is a sweet girl. She wasn't like the rest of the girls at school. From what I hear, she saved herself for marriage. It's really interesting that you brought this up. I was in the barbershop a while back, and Debra's husband was there. I'd met him a few years ago at one of our homecoming games and I was sure that was him. Anyway, a friend of his came in yelling at him about leaving Debra to go be with another woman. The two of them had caused a scene, and I was sure it was going to get out of hand until the owner made them go in the back room. He left shortly afterward and so did his friend. I was sitting there thinking how terrible it was for a woman like Debra to get stuck with someone like him, so I just prayed for her right then and there."

Chase shook his head. "Wow. Small world."

"Yes, my friend, it is. Oh, and I can see how you could have feelings for a woman like her, but these situations are fragile, Chase. I've seen it right here at this church. A husband and wife are separated for whatever reason, and sometimes one of them is even with someone else. Then, one day, they both decide that their marriage is worth saving, and poof! Out goes the outside lover. I've counseled both the husband and wife, *and* the outside lovers, Chase. It's a no-win situation for the outsider. Let Debra go through on her own—with God. You can't afford the consequences, natural or spiritual."

Chase took in everything Corey said as a pastor and his best friend since elementary. He knew he was right. He'd learned with his ex-girlfriend Marva what it was like to be in a no-win situation. Five years ago, he had allowed Marva to change his life in one night. Although Chase had been walking righteously before the Lord, he still had feelings for Marva. He always had. In the days when he was running the streets, being a menace, Chase had many women. He met his match in Marva. She had that same nonchalant attitude about being tied down to one man. It made Chase love and want her more. They had dated on and off until Bailey came along.

Chase had given himself to the Lord after Bailey, but Marva was still stuck in the same life she'd had years ago. She still desired that glamorous street life—a life free of responsibility. A life where she could be with any man she wanted, when she wanted and just walk away afterward. She'd called Chase late one night talking about old times—intimate times. He allowed those images to seep into his head and invade his thoughts until he had the strong desire to relive them. He knew it was wrong, but for that moment, he wanted his manly needs met. He put what God wanted aside for the sake of the flesh.

Nine months later, he had a beautiful daughter, but Marva didn't slow her lifestyle down for Savannah. Most often, she left Savannah with relatives, or others—sometimes in unsafe situations. When Savannah was just one year old, she'd somehow gotten burned while in Marva's care. That incident had gotten child protective services involved. The most serious accusation was the one that Chase still pained over, and the one that sent him to court fighting for full custody of Savannah. Reflecting on that, Chase decided to just back away from Debra. He'd already learned a lesson the hard way.

26
The Asking

Chase couldn't shake the thought of Debra. He'd slept fit-fully for three hours before finally giving up on getting any sleep. Thoughts of her curled around his conscience and wove throughout his mind like an ivy vine, until they had taken over. He got up out of bed and went into the living room and looked out of his high-rise window where he had a view of the Detroit River. He leaned his arm against the floor-to-ceiling window. Shirtless, his muscular back and arms looked divinely powerful as the moon cast light on his solid frame. His riverfront condo was a modern safe haven for him, but it lacked something he'd wanted for a couple of years—a wife.

He wanted the kind of woman he could grow old with. Someone he could trust with every secret. Someone who could be the mother of his children. A woman he could be vulnerable with, and yet be strong for. Someone he could protect, but give in to.

A woman who could fill him with passion and stay on his mind. Every time he thought of a wife, he thought of Debra. But she was no more available to him than a figment of a person's imagination. She belonged to someone else—no matter what the circumstances were. Nevertheless, he knew he could love her totally. If given the chance, he would.

Chase plopped down on his brown suede sectional and continued to stare out the window at the amazing stars that decorated the night sky. He reveled in God's awesomeness that was manifested in the ebb and flow of the river. Then he prayed. "Have my needs been long forgotten, Oh, Lord? Have I not been faithful to your Word, Father? Your Word says, *Let us therefore come boldly to the throne of grace, that we may obtain mercy and find grace to help in the time of need.* Father God, here I am—Your son, coming humbly, asking for that which I desire—a wife that is a woman after your heart Oh, Lord. It is my desire to please You with my lifestyle, Oh, God. Please continue to give me the strength to walk in Your way. Amen."

Chase rose and walked into Savannah's room. He looked around the extravagant little princess's quarters and beamed with pride. Her color-blocked, lavender and pink room was the perfect expression of femininity. Her white, four-poster, Victorian inspired canopy bed was fit for her royal majesty. Mona had decked it out elegantly in a Cinderella and Princess theme. A glass slipper sat atop her white dresser and reflected in the mirror amidst the soft white night lights on either side of the mirror. In the corner on her shelves were hundreds of dolls that resembled all nationalities and all manner of fashion.

Across from the bed was a shelf filled with adventure stories and fairy-tales that Chase never denied reading to her at bedtime— or whenever she begged. She had a secret chest by the window where her "dress up clothes" were kept—the ones "Auntie Mo" had given her to play in. Chase watched her peacefully sleeping body rise and fall gently with each breath she inhaled and exhaled. She was dressed in pink girlie pajamas that had red lips all over them. Chase smiled. One of Mona's gifts.

Chase eased himself onto Savannah's bed and kissed her cheek. Her caramel skin was as soft as it was when she was a newborn. Her thick wavy hair was untamed and splayed across the pillow like a separate entity. She wore a satin eye mask that was partially covering her cute little face. The sight of her looking like a little Mona caused Chase to chuckle. Underneath that eye mask were the most gorgeous, slightly slanted black eyes that could still hypnotize her daddy into doing anything. Chase took her hand and brought it to his lips. He kissed it gently and pulled the covers up to her chin. He wondered how Marva could have neglected someone so precious. He felt ashamed that he had once thought about marrying her. She cared more for her men and her lifestyle than the little princess that looked just like her. One thing was for certain, Chase would never allow Savannah to be in a situation where she would be hurt again.

He still remembered the day that he was giving Savannah a bath and she said those words. "Chris touched my private, Daddy. I told him I don't like it when he washes me." She was three years old at the time. Chase had almost toppled over into the tub of water he'd just pulled Savannah out of. He questioned her repeatedly, sometimes asking the same question in a different manner to make sure he had heard her story correctly. His anger burned hot against Marva that night. He was so enraged that his anger was dizzying. His head beat like giant war drums. He could have killed that night. It took all of the godliness in him not to go over to Marva's and shake her senseless, then kill whoever the person was that had touched his little girl.

Chase had immediately taken Savannah to Children's Hospital and called protective services himself. The doctor found no signs that she'd been harmed physically, but that didn't mean that Savannah hadn't been fondled like Chase suspected. He felt like a failure that he hadn't been there to protect her. Half of the time, he had no idea where Savannah was. He was lucky to see her two times a month. Marva's addresses and numbers changed so frequently—but those child-support checks were directly deposited into her account. Whether Chase saw Savannah or not, Marva still had the child support money. That was more important to her than ensuring that Chase could build a relationship with his little girl.

Marva was a strikingly beautiful woman, and subsequently never found it difficult to find a man who was willing and able to take care of her financially. Upon questioning Marva, Chase discovered that "Chris" was the fourteen-year-old son of Marva's newest lover. Chase filed an emergency petition to have Savannah removed immediately. And the fighting began. Now, two years later, he finally had full custody of Savannah. Marva had given up her rights. Chase suspected that the fading beauty was on drugs—cocaine. She had no room for Savannah in her life.

His little girl was still going to therapy, making the adjustment of living with Chase and not seeing her mother anymore. With much prayer, she was doing fine. She was a glowing kindergartener. Chase couldn't have been happier. Maybe one day, he'd have a wife who could step in and be a mother to Savannah. It was nice to have Mona, but Savannah needed a mother of her own. More than that, her daddy imagined someone he could come home to every day. He had to admit celibacy had stretched him farther than he ever thought he could be stretched.

He walked into the kitchen and filled a glass of water. He

gulped it down and searched the cabinet for something to munch on. He smiled when he found a bag of tortilla chips. He opened the refrigerator and hunted for salsa. His hand roamed all over the cold inside until he found his treasure. He checked the bin for shredded cheese. Bingo! He put his tortillas in a bowl, heaped salsa on top, and crowned it with cheese. He nuked it in the microwave and returned to the living room. He hit the remote and the flat screen rose out of a cabinet. He turned it to the cartoon channel. Savannah had him hooked. He was lucky that an old-school cartoon was on—Scooby Do, one of his favorites. He reclined on the large sectional fluffing a few of the aqua and brown stripped decorative pillows behind his back. It was 1:00 a.m. He adjusted himself and decided he'd camp out right here until the sleepy bug bit him again—if it bit him again. If it didn't, it was Saturday. He could sleep in longer. Chef Stevens had been holding things down at the restaurant on the weekends since Savannah had come to stay with her dad. Chase reserved the weekends for his favorite girl.

Chase's phone rang a half-ring then ceased. He looked curiously at it from across the room as if it could reveal the answer to the question he'd just asked in his mind. *Who was that?* More than likely someone had realized that they'd dialed the wrong number before he had a chance to answer. Curious, he got up and picked up the phone, pressing the back button on the caller ID. The phone number and the name Myles stared back at him. Maybe something was wrong. He hit the dial button.

"Hello?" Debra answered sounding caught.

"Hey, this is Chase. What's going on?"

"Uh . . . nothing. I'm sorry if my calling so late woke you. I wasn't thinking. I'm sorry."

"Don't worry about it. Is something wrong?"

"Not really, I just couldn't sleep, Chase. Sorry for being a pest," Debra said, exasperated.

Chase could hear the anguish in her voice. She'd been crying. "Well actually, I was up having a midnight snack—so you didn't wake me, and you're definitely not a pest."

"Oh," was all that Debra could say. She felt stupid. "How was work today?" she asked, chiding herself. She felt more ridiculous.

"Today was good. Savannah didn't have school because of Teacher Planning Day, so she hung out with me at the restaurant. She's wonderful. Mona trained her in the art of being a good hostess," Chase chuckled. "I think she enjoyed herself."

"Good for her. I used to love to hang out with my dad, too. Those are the special times I always remember about Daddy. I wanted kids so badly at one time so I could do things like that with them."

The past tense word *wanted* alarmed Chase. "You don't want kids anymore?"

"Chase, I'm thirty-five—soon-to-be thirty-six, and soon to be divorced. I've sort of let go of that dream right along with the 'happily-ever-after,' know what I mean?"

"Never give up on your dreams, Debra Ann. It's not too late. Women are having children later in life nowadays. You have no idea what God has in store for you. If we don't have hope, what is there to live for?"

"Sometimes Chase, I don't know. As much as I know God, the more I don't know Him. I feel like I'm out in the middle of a tossing sea with just a raft and God is just watching me suffer."

"I can understand that you may *feel* that way Debra, but that's not biblical. That's just you thinking with your human mind. God never leaves or forsakes us. He's right here helping you to get through," Chase said with so much sensitivity.

"I don't feel like it. Let's not talk about it anymore, Chase. I'm

sorry that I called. Thanks for calling me back. Talk to you later."
With that, she hung up the phone. Chase hit himself in the head.
What was he thinking? What ever happened to just *listening* without offering advice? How many times had Mona told him that's
what women needed most—to be listened to—not a man to solve
all their problems. Chase had blown it.

"Darnit!" he said aloud, angry with himself for the clumsy
response. *Stick to cooking Chase, not counseling.* Quickly he re-
dialed Debra. When she answered he said, "I know it's late, but
I just want to pray for you Debra Ann." She couldn't say no to
that—whether she felt like it or not. Afterward, she did feel better.
What was so powerful about Chase's prayers for her that soothed
her anxiety and helped to restore her peace? She drifted back to
sleep wondering.

27
The Judas Level

"Okay, how are we looking upstairs?" Daniel asked Tyler after he and Chase had just loaded the last of Debra's large items into the moving truck.

"Pretty good. We can probably fit Debra's chest and small stuff into the truck. She and Tammy are up there getting all the clothes out of the closet," Tyler replied.

Chase was glad for that report because his stomach was growling. "That's good. It shouldn't take us longer than a couple of hours to get all the stuff moved into the condo. And then we can eat. I'm starvin'."

"Son, you must have read my mind," Daniel said grinning at Chase.

Thanks to the three of them, and help from Tyler's wife, Tammy, Debra was leaving this part of her life behind. Her new condo was just a few blocks away, still close enough for her to get to work on time every day.

Debra stood on a foot-stool checking the top shelf of her walk-in closet for scarves or small items that may have been diffi-cult to spot. She found a pair of Bryce's old blue jeans. She tossed them into the trash can. She stepped down off the stool and moved it so that she could roll up the rug that covered the hard wood floor. Tammy was busy putting Debra's shoes in clear plastic shoe boxes.

"You need help with that, Debbie?" Tammy asked tightening her ponytail.

"Nah, I got it." Debra rolled the rug up and noticed a piece of paper stuck in the corner. She retrieved it and sat on her knees reading. It was a letter. One that had been forgotten and had ended up under the rug accidentally. She read it curiously.

> *Dear Bryce,*
>
> *I have so many feelings about us being together last weekend.*
>
> *I don't know what got into me. Of course, I didn't plan it. And I know you were just stopping by to see Ty. There was no way you could have known that his trip had been extended and he had to stay in Minnesota three more days. He had just called and told me that before you rang the bell. You and I have been attracted to each other since we met. I guess we've just never acted on it until last weekend. A part of me regrets what happened between us. But the other part of me doesn't. It was something that was destined to happen sooner or later. I think the curiosity was killing both of us. It made me*

think that maybe when you brushed up against me in the
kitchen during the Super Bowl party earlier this year, it
wasn't an accident. Now, I find myself longing for you.
And I don't know what we are going to do about Debra
and Tyler. I guess it's business as usual with them. But
for you and me, you are always welcome.

Tammy

The letter was dated three years ago. Debra felt an angry blaze of fire. The deception was still mounting, even with Bryce gone. Debra walked over to Tammy without a word. She held that letter shakily in her left hand. The betrayal gripped her tightly around the neck until she felt like she was being choked. Her hand flung out as quickly as a sling shot, hitting Tammy across the face so hard it knocked her off balance. Debra lunged at her swinging like she was in a street brawl. Every blow connected. She was beating Bryce. She was beating Suzette. She was beating Tammy. She was beating life itself for cheating her out of what was supposed to have been a "happily-ever-after." She hit Tammy for every dinner she'd sat and ate at her table over the last three years. For every trip the two of them had taken to various shopping malls. Every girls' night out. Debra punched her for the web of deception she and Bryce had spun and hidden for three years.

The ruckus and rumbling sent Daniel, Tyler, and Chase running up the stairs, thinking that perhaps the women had accidentally knocked over Debra's huge Shaker chest trying to move it. Chase had beat Daniel and Tyler up the stairs, but Tyler followed closely behind. The walk-in closet is where the ruckus was coming from. For a moment, Chase was stunned, still trying to make

sense of the scene. He couldn't grasp or believe what he was seeing. Debra was on top of Tammy beating her.

"Debra Ann!" Daniel and Chase shouted simultaneously. Chase
ran toward the women grabbing Debra from behind, lifting her
off her feet with his arms locked underneath hers, restraining her
with the skill of a seasoned police officer. He pulled her out of the
closet.

Tyler went for Tammy and walked her out into the bedroom.
Debra bucked and kicked at Tammy like a wild stallion. "You
filthy, disgusting piece of trash, get out!" Debra screamed.

"What the—what is going on in here!" Tyler yelled at Debra.

Debra twisted and squirmed in Chase's restraint, trying to
fight herself loose. Her efforts were tiring him. He had no idea the
slender, delicate butterfly was a powerhouse *this* strong. He had a
strange desire to laugh almost.

"Get the letter!" Debra shouted. "Did you know that she and
Bryce slept together, Tyler? Huh?"

Tyler was dumbfounded, unbelieving. Tammy's huge black
eyes opened an inch wider. She lunged on the floor toward the
balled up white piece of paper that held her fate. Tyler pushed
her out of the way, snatching the piece of paper off the floor. His
hands shook nervously as he read. His caramel complexion was
flushed with embarrassment and heart break. He shook his head in
a crazed, maniacal gaze. "What is this, Tammy? This is your hand-
writing, baby. Tell me something, huh!" Tyler demanded. Tammy
stood silently with guilty tears that told the story in the absence of
her voice. "You slept with Bryce—my best friend? In my house—
in *my bed*? My, God, what kind of *devil* are you?" His breathing
was laborious, intimidating.

Chase had loosened his grip on Debra, just enough so that he
wasn't hurting her. He and Daniel made eye contact. They were

thinking the same thing. It looked as if Tyler might attack Tammy. It would take both of them to take the big bear down. Chase would have to turn Debra loose for sure.

"How could you disrespect me like this, Tammy!" Tyler shouted inching closer to the woman who wasn't even brave enough to look him in the eyes.

Her response was a weak, cowardly confession. "I'm sorry."

"You're sorry! You ruin our marriage—our whole lives and you're sorry!" Tyler was standing over Tammy. The bear was shaking uncontrollably.

Chase spoke softly to Debra. "*Debra Ann*," was all he said. It was a plea that she understood when he released her. He walked over to Tyler. Daniel stood on the other side.

"I've given you everything, and what do I have, Tammy? I could kill you right now!"

Daniel moved in front of Tammy. There was no sense in taking any chances. The bear could grab and choke the life out of the woman before he or Chase had the opportunity to free her. "Tyler, let her be. Go on home now," Daniel pleaded in a quiet, fatherly tone.

"Tyler, I'm so sorry, I brought you into this." Debra said touching his arm gently. "I would never hurt you purposely. I love you like a brother. You've been good to me." Tears poured from Debra's eyes—empathy tears. She felt Tyler's pain and humiliation like her own. Tyler took his gaze off the woman that stood before him and looked at Debra. Her eyes were sincere. He left hurriedly. Debra feared he would go looking for Bryce.

"Get out of my house before I do what Tyler is too much of a man to do!"

Debra's crimson handprint was painted across the spot where she had slapped Tammy, and a purple bruise had formed on Tammy's

right eye. Her nose had started to bleed and both her lips were gro-
tesquely swollen. She didn't look at all like the beautiful woman
who had arrived to help pack just hours earlier. She wasn't the
sexy vixen who'd had slept with Debra's husband. She was a pile
of trash.

Tammy scurried past Debra and Chase looking dazed and
disoriented. Daniel followed after to see if she needed cab fare.
He still didn't think it at all proper for a woman to be walking
the street without a way to get someplace safe. Debra didn't care.
And Chase wasn't leaving Debra's side. Debra wiped her tears
with the back of her sleeve and resumed putting the shoes in the
plastic containers as if the last few moments hadn't happened. She
couldn't break down right now. She needed the energy to finish
getting the things on the truck. Today she was moving into her
new place—starting over.

"Why are you just standing there, Chase? See if Daddy needs
help with something," Debra said without looking at him. Chase
moved without a rebuttal. He was still in shock from what he'd
seen, feeling sorry for Debra. She was still going through. He
could tell that she was breaking. Her soft brown eyes were glis-
tening with tears. She was taking deep breaths trying to stifle what
was brewing on the inside of her, but her resolve was strong.

Chase had made it to the landing when he had the unction
to go back to Debra. He followed his mind and there Debra sat
on her heels with her face buried in her hands crying out the betrayal. It was a hard, shaking cry. Chase kneeled down next to her
and pulled her across his lap. Debra's head lay in his lap. Chase
touched her head and prayed. "Father, God you are King of kings.
Lord of lords. Surely you feel the pain of the weak and broken.
Surely you can heal every hurt. Give peace where there is none.
Provide a covering of mercy. Give Debra a sound mind and heart

that is fixed on You even at this moment. We know Oh, Lord, what seems like destruction to us is sometimes your rebuilding process. We honor and love You, Lord Jesus for being an amazing Savior who cares about the things that concern us Oh, God. And bless Tyler right now, give him peace and a sound mind—and Tammy as well. Give us the physical strength that we need to complete what has to be done today—and the spiritual maturity to praise You through every challenge. In the name of Jesus. Amen."

Daniel had stood at the doorway bowed in prayer with them. His "Amen" caused both Debra and Chase to look in his direction. Debra got up and ran into his arms, laying her head on his shoulder.

"It's okay. Cry and get it out Princess. It's alright," he said comforting Debra. She cried on him for minutes before he said, "Hey, let's take a break for a while and get something to eat, huh?"

"Daddy, we've got to get everything over to the condo, today. I can't stay in this house another day."

"We need a break, Debra."

"Daddy . . . "

"*Debra Ann*," Daniel said lifting Debra's chin, "you need a break."

Chase emerged from the walk-in closet where he'd gone to make a phone call and to give Debra and her father some privacy.

"A friend of mine owes me a favor. He's on his way with some more guys who can get the rest of this stuff moved into the condo. We can take a break. Matter of fact, it's enough of them to have everything moved. And Debra, don't worry. Everything will be safe with them—all the furniture is tagged according to rooms, so it shouldn't be a problem."

"Sounds like a plan to me, Chase. What do you say, Princess?"

"Okay," Debra said reluctantly.

"Everything will be moved in tonight. I promise. We'll kiss this place good-bye," Daniel said.

Debra nodded. Daniel went across the street to get Mr. Craiggs to help him and Chase get Debra's chest downstairs, even with a dolly it was a tough job. Afterward, Debra, Chase and Daniel headed to a nearby restaurant for pizza. They'd left the keys with Mr. Craiggs and his wife. Daniel, Debra, and Chase sat and talked for more than an hour after they'd eaten. Then Debra made them take her to at least three stores to pick up odds and ends she needed for her new place. By the time she was done with them, they were more exhausted than they'd been from lifting and moving furniture.

It was six-thirty in the evening when they pulled up to Debra's new home. A black church van with the words *Greater Christian Center* printed in white letters was out front.

Debra was amazed when she walked in. Mr. Craiggs' wife, Leona, was in the kitchen. She'd cleaned out all of the cabinets and put away most of Debra's dishes. The kitchen was the only room in the house that didn't look like Debra had just moved in. There were at least six men Debra didn't know in her home busying themselves, putting away last minute items.

"Well, nice of you to join us hard working men, Chase Martin," Corey said teasing.

"You're welcome, *Pastor* Corey," Chase chuckled.

"And hello, Debra. How are you?"

"I'm fine. Thank you. It's nice to see you. You look good," Debra said to Corey.

"So do you."

Debra was grateful for everyone. "Wow. Hey, Mrs. Craiggs thank you so much. You didn't have to do this."

"It was my pleasure, sweetheart. Anytime."

Debra was impressed. "You guys have done an outstanding job. I really appreciate it. Really."

"Luckily we had Good Friday service earlier and most of these brothers don't know when to go home, so they got sucked into service," Corey said.

"It was our pleasure, Pastor Corey," one of the men said.

"Well, we're going to get out of here and get something to eat. I've got to feed these brothers."

"I'll take care of it," Chase said going into his wallet.

"It's on me. I got it this time. It was my pleasure," Corey said nodding to Debra.

Chase walked outside with him. The other men crowded into the church van while Chase and Corey stood on the sidewalk talking.

"Where you guys headed?" Chase asked.

"The steak house around the corner."

"I'm glad you offered to pay," Chase laughed.

"Oh, don't worry. There are plenty of things going on around the church that need your money." The two men embraced each other patting each other firmly on the backs. "How's it going with Debra? You ain't been in no trouble, right?" Corey inquired.

"No, Sir. I don't see her unless I'm at the school—which is not often. I've been doing a good job staying away aside from helping her move in today."

"She is one beautiful woman," Corey said smiling."

"You telling me?" Chase laughed.

"You watch your back, man. Fine as she is, the devil gon' be ridin' you hard to get you to break down."

"She's not that type."

"Her spirit is broken—women seek out love and affection—that translates to sex for us men. Be careful. Don't let your guard down. I'll be praying for you."

"Thanks. How are you coming along?"

"That date didn't work out. She was looking for a meal ticket—and I'm looking for a for real woman. At least celibacy is a little easier when you ain't got nobody to do it with, or who you want to do it with."

"I know that's right," Chase said standing closer to Corey. "I try not to even look at Debra hard. I can hear that old devil talking, sayin' 'Wouldn't you like to have her?'" Chase squeezed his eyes together tightly feigning pain, "And I'm like, 'I love Jesus, I love Jesus!'" he shouted.

"You crazy!" Corey laughed. "And I *know* you telling the truth because that is one beautiful woman—inside and out. Brothers today are just raggedy. She messed around and married an idiot."

"No doubt. She is sweet as honey. Good upbringing. Virtuous. It seems like she was a devoted wife to her ex-husband."

"Not-quite ex. Don't forget that, man. Anything can happen. Stay prayed up—better yet, stay away from her," he smiled.

"I hear you," Chase nodded.

"Alright, see you on Sunday. Wear your good suit—it's Easter," Corey joked.

"Later."

* * *

Daniel looked at his watch. It was a quarter 'til nine. "Princess, let me get on home, before your mother calls me again."

"Okay, Daddy. Tell Mama I'll be by for Sunday dinner."

"Will do." He kissed her on the forehead and gave her a good night hug. "Chase, come on out to the car with me," he said unexpectedly.

Chase looked strange. "Okay . . . sure."

"I want to thank you for helping Princess out today—even praying for her. This has been really hard on her. I've never seen her so broken in all her life. She's a strong girl. And I . . . she's just weak right now. I know you're an upstanding man of God. I can tell that by your conversation—the way you handle yourself. I just have this ability to discern things, and I get really good vibes from you," Daniel said stroking his goatee. "And with Debra Ann, I can tell that she thinks you're special. Her eyes sort of light up when she talks about you or whenever you're around," Daniel said smiling. "I know what kind of woman I raised. I'm pretty sure that Bryce is the only man Debra's ever been with. I just don't want her to do something rash because of what's going on." Daniel cleared his throat. "I don't know if I'm making myself clear or not, Chase. I realize that you two are grown. I just want Debra Ann to be righteous even when the world doesn't treat her that way, you know what I mean?"

"Daniel, I'd be a liar if I told you that I'm not attracted to Debra beyond a friendship . . . but I haven't pursued her that way. In fact, I try to stay *away* from her because of my attraction to her," Chase chuckled. "Debra is the kind of woman men like me pray for. I know that she's virtuous—I don't have any intentions of undermining that. As beautiful as Debra is, she is still married as far as I'm concerned. I don't ever want to be in a love triangle. That's not me. My intentions with her are noble, Daniel. I'm *not* going to put us in a situation that she or I will regret if things work out with her and her husband," Chase admitted.

Daniel wanted to tell Chase that if he had anything to do with it, Bryce didn't stand a snowball's chance in the fifth level of hell to get back with his little girl after all he'd put her through. The two men stood on the sidewalk eye to eye, revealing the depths of their personalities and their concern for the woman they loved in common. Daniel nodded. "Very well, Chase. I'll see you in the future. Thanks for all your help today—especially with Debra Ann. She whooped Tammy something good," Daniel chuckled. "I know she was torn up about it afterward because she felt like she muddied her witness for the Lord, but everyone has a breaking point. I told her ask God for forgiveness and let it go."

"Absolutely. She's strong, too. I thought she was going to get away from me for second. I'd like to think I'm in pretty good shape, but she was tiring me out," Chase smiled.

"Shoot. That girl is something else. She's got a strong heart too," Daniel said patting his fist to his chest. She's going to be alright."

"Yes, she will. God takes care of His own."

"Good night, Chase."

"Was Daddy out there harassing you?" Debra queried as soon as Chase stepped inside. Her soft face looked more relaxed. She had pulled her hair on top of her head in a high ponytail and wrapped a bandanna around the front. She looked like a cute housewife.

Chase smiled. "Na. He was just thanking me for helping out today."

Debra smiled unbelieving. "Uh-huh."

"What?"

"Chase, I know my daddy like the back of my hand."

"*Debra Ann*, your father and I just had a very good talk—he wasn't harassing me. Actually, I like him a lot." Chase said smiling, looking at her with those eyes that made Debra blush on the inside.

"If you say so. How about a movie?" she asked holding up a DVD.

"What's that?"

"Comedy. I need a laugh. *Let's Do It Again* with Bill Cosby and Sidney Poitier."

"Woman after my own heart. That's my favorite."

"Good."

They sat on Debra's Victorian sofa and watched television until it watched them. Chase had fallen asleep in his sitting position, with his head flopped back against the top of the sofa. His neck was a bit cramped from sleeping that way for almost two hours. Debra was stretched across the sofa with her head in his lap. Her soft, light-brown face was serene. He wondered what she was dreaming about. He looked down at her admiring all that she was. He stretched his hand out slowly without making any quick movements and stroked her face as lightly as he would have touched a butterfly's wing. His fingers barely grazed the surface of her skin. Debra didn't stir. She lay in some protective, cocooned wonderland, shielded from all that she'd been combating for the last few months.

Chase thought about the day's happenings, and how embarrassed and humiliated Debra must have felt when she'd found that letter. He'd watched her and Tammy earlier, hugging one another and referring to each other as "Sis," giggling like two school girls as they packed and organized Debra's things, talking about the various shopping trips and girls' nights they'd shared. Tammy having slept with Debra's husband was a Judas-level betrayal, and it probably occurred more than the time mentioned in the letter. Still, Debra had pressed on. Chase admired that about her.

She'd had her moment of breaking, but she was resilient. Her strength as a woman was just as prevalent as her softness. His heart longed to kiss her. He took her hand gently in his and planted the softest kiss he could on it, one that had been reserved for a moment like this, where he could hear the sound of his own heart beating and he was certain that he was in love. He closed his eyes, holding her hand to his lips before placing it back across her stomach. It was time for him to go home. If he stayed, he'd drive himself completely mad thinking about loving her—not just in the physical, but *really* loving her. He thought about how it would be to take afternoon naps with her and be the man she came home to at the end of the day. He thought about loving her to sleep at night and waking up with her in his arms in the mornings. Something on the inside forced him to erase those thoughts. He shook her gently. "Debra . . . Debra Ann."

It took a minute before Debra even showed signs of life. Slowly she twisted until Chase's gentle shakes pulled her out of her sleeping paradise. "I'm sorry. I must have fallen asleep," she said.

"We *both* fell asleep. It's time for me to get home."

Debra sat up. "Is Savannah coming home tonight?"

"No way. She is *not* thinking about her daddy this weekend. She and Mona are having their little girls' time this weekend. They're going shopping in the morning. She'll be back tomorrow evening. We'll worship together on Sunday."

"That's good. I promised Daddy I'd go to church with him and Mama." Debra stood up and took their glasses into the kitchen and put them in the dishwasher. Chase picked up the popcorn bowl and followed her. He handed it to her and watched as she loaded it into the dishwasher as well. *She's everything I've prayed for. Why is this happening this way?* Chase questioned himself. Debra did something to him he couldn't explain. He walked to the entryway and retrieved his heavy leather jacket from the closet. Debra helped him put it on. It seemed to Chase that the two of them had done this routine a million times before. Why did everything feel so *natural* with her?

"Thanks Chase. I appreciate all your help—especially the extra help from Corey and the rest of the guys. That was really nice. You didn't have to do that."

"It was no problem," Chase said. Debra hugged him and Chase held her to him for moments longer than he should have. Debra didn't pull away either. She let herself lean against him, soaking up his strength. She knew that when he left, she'd have to deal with what it meant to live alone. It was Chase who let go first. "I'll call you tomorrow and see how you're coming along."

"Okay. Good night, Chase."

"Good night, Debra."

28
The Other Side of the Couch

Debra sat slouched in a chair in front of Dr. Buckley's desk. His receptionist had let her in the office. She'd mentioned that Dr. Buckley had stepped out for a moment and would be right back. Debra was ten minutes earlier than her scheduled appointment time so she just let her head hang back as far as she could, looking up at the ceiling—trying to prepare herself for the tangent Dr. Buckley was sure to be on. She'd cancelled every appointment she'd made with him up until today. Dr. Buckley had called her himself to encourage her to stay committed to therapy.

Debra looked around Dr. Buckley's office and decided it needed some sprucing up. It was clean and orderly—but had no life. It was too plain. She thought of ways she could spice it up and make it look, well, more chic. A nice brown leather sofa—or maybe a deep red. And maybe some art would help. The beige was getting on her nerves—then again, everything seemed to get on her nerves these days—even the kids at work she lived and breathed for.

Debra wasn't sure she could handle Dr. Buckley's confrontational style today. She was definitely falling apart—had fallen apart. She needed something to help put herself back together. She was ashamed to admit that she was questioning God. Didn't He *know* Bryce was going to do this on the day they married? Why didn't He just tell her not to marry Bryce?

"How are you doing today, Debra?" Dr. Buckley asked startling her and kicking her out of extreme office make-over mode.

She felt caught. "Hi, Dr. Buckley," she smiled.

"It's been quite a while. I thought maybe you moved to another country or something," he joked.

"Humph. I feel like moving off the planet."

Dr. Buckley perched himself on the corner of his desk. "What else do you feel?"

Debra could hear the horses galloping. *Here we go.* "I hate Bryce and I'm sort of mad at God."

"Sort of?" he asked ignoring her comment about Bryce altogether.

Debra sat up. She hesitated before saying, "Okay, I'm mad. *I'm mad.* There. I said it."

"What does God have to do with Bryce leaving you and divorcing you, Debra?"

"What do you mean, what does He have to do with it?"

"What does He have to do with it? We have something called free-will, you know?"

"I know that. But I feel like I should have been warned or something."

"Would you have listened? The way you described your courtship with Bryce, it sounded like you were head over heels about him. I don't think you would have listened—maybe you would have—I don't know. Is it God's fault that your marriage failed?"

"No," Debra said reluctantly. She felt uneasy as if Dr. Buckley was going to attack her for what she'd just shared. After all, he *asked*.

"Okay, so tell me then, why are you mad at God?"

Debra was defensive. "I said, 'sort of'."

Dr. Buckley rounded his desk and took a seat in his chair, an action which made Debra feel less intimidated.

"Mad is mad. *Sort of* doesn't cut it with me, Debra. You know that. If you're angry, you're angry."

"Dr. B-u-c-k-l-e-y," Debra said noticeably agitated. "I don't have an explanation, it's just how I feel. I know that God doesn't go around making people do the things they should unless they want to. I just feel like I've been duped—can you understand that?!"

"Certainly. You've given me the answer. You feel like you've been duped and Bryce is the reason—he is the one who duped you. He sat here week after week talking about what needed to happened to make your marriage work—promised he was going to do those things, and then the first chance he got, he ran right back to Suzette."

"Thanks for the recap."

"I'm going somewhere with this, Debra, be patient. You know something? I feel duped too. I thought that everything that Bryce said was genuine. I thought he was genuine in his love for you. I prayed for you both. I asked God to bless your union. And you know what? Maybe Bryce was genuine about how he felt about you and your marriage—in fact, I believe he was, Debra."

Debra looked at Dr. Buckley with an incredulously hot stare.

"Here me out, Debra. It is very possible that Bryce was telling the truth about how he felt about *you.*

"What he obviously *didn't* tell the truth about was his feelings for *Suzette*, Debra. We didn't address the issue of Suzette because Bryce chalked it up to some sort of fling. I had no reason to think that he was in love with Suzette also, which would have taken us in a totally different direction in treatment. In essence, I wasn't even able to do my job properly, because Bryce lied to me."

"Yeah, well, that makes two of us."

"So now, we've both been duped by Bryce, and God didn't give either one of us a heads up."

"What is your point, Dr. Buckley?"

Dr. Buckley chuckled a bit. He'd never seen the meek little Debra this aggressive. "My point is that we are not going to know everything that is going to happen to us—we aren't mind readers, or heart readers—that would make us miniature gods—of which there is no such thing. So as Christians, this is where we accept God's divine providence and ask for further direction, healing, and strength. Have you done that, Debra?"

"Right now, I'm just trying to make it to work every day. I have insomnia and I'm depressed, and praying doesn't seem to be helping." She dared a rebuttal from Dr. Buckley by holding her glare on him.

"You may not think it's helping but it is."

"Yeah, well that's your opinion."

"Do you have any thoughts of harming yourself, Debra?"

"No, I'm not suicidal if that's what you're asking me."

"That's what I'm asking."

"No."

"How are you handling the pain?"

"I cry mostly and don't eat. I've lost ten pounds already."

"I noticed. Starving yourself is a self-destructive act, Debra—

you know that."

"It's not intentional, Dr. Buckley. My nerves are so bad, I just don't feel like eating most of the time—I don't have an appetite."

"Eat anyway, Debra. Preserve yourself as much as you can."

Debra burst into tears. "This is hard," she spoke in a shaking voice, "I've never felt this bad in my entire life. I feel like someone has just ripped me in two." Debra looked pathetic. Her eyes were hollow caves that led to nowhere. Dr. Buckley felt the intensity of her cry.

"I need you to 'Do you' as they say, Debra. I need you to take care of *you* right now. If you need something to help you sleep at night, or something for the depression—temporarily, I can refer you to another colleague of mine for a script, but I need to continue to see you once a week until we pull through this."

Debra just nodded. For the next few minutes, Dr. Buckley explained to Debra the assignment he expected her to do in preparation for their next session. She was to write down every negative thought she felt about herself and find a scripture that combated it. *Why did he feel that "assignments" were necessary?* Debra didn't feel like doing some stupid assignment. She just wanted to go live up under a rock. She nodded and promised to keep her appointment, but if she had the power to evaporate into thin air she would have.

29

Snitches

Debra had the worse attendance that she'd ever had since working at Peace Valley. She left early often and called in sick more frequently. She felt guilty about it, but it was the only way she could cope. It was either be at work crashing or at home crashing—the latter always won. It wasn't a life that she was used to at all. She was trying to fortify herself with prayer and wondered if those prayers were going any farther than the ceiling because her heart was still broken.

She had crying spells and had lost interest in almost everything. No more belly dancing class—which she had taken as a way to spice things up with Bryce, anyway. No more swimming every Wednesday at the YMCA. She just didn't feel like doing anything these days. Dr. Buckley practically cornered her into resuming her Pilates class. He swore it would help with the stress. Debra knew for certain that she was clinically depressed, but *knowing* was only

229

half the battle. The only bright spots in her life were the three mus-keteers, better known as Noni, Corey, and Maya.

Debra stood inside of her school office checking her make-up and face in the mirror inside her coat closet. She'd bought a new suit and new make-up to try and make herself feel better. It was a weak camouflage. She'd had another one of those mini break-downs as soon as she entered her office. She wanted to get rid of any signs of it before the girls came. The little women were so intuitive. They picked up on everything—especially Noni. She was like an old grandmother. Debra reapplied some foundation, blotting where she'd cried it off underneath her eyes. She dolled up her eyes with more frosty gray shadow and jet-black mascara. Debra gave up a smile as she thought of her babies. She smoothed her red Tahari suit that consisted of a waist length jacket and pen-cil skirt. She had been a little daring and worn a pair of sexy, black patent leather, Kate Spade shoes with a three-inch, chunky heel. She looked like an undercover vixen—really impressive for a quarter after seven in the morning.

She heard the girls' laughter in the corridor. Corey was the most animated today. It had been their idea to keep this "breakfast club" group session thing going. It was working, so Debra didn't have many complaints—except for the fact that she had to get to work early in order to accommodate the trio, but it was a good way to start off the day.

"Whew. Good Morning Ms. Myles," Noni said, entering first, eyeing Debra's outfit with admiration. "You must have a lunch date with Chef Chase or something cuz you are looking fly, fly, fly!" Corey and Maya laughed in chorus.

"Excuse me?"

Noni realized that in her teasing she had over-stepped her boundaries. "I'm sorry Mrs. Myles, you really look nice today."

"Really." Corey and Maya chorused again.

"Thank you. And why would I have a lunch date with Chef Chase, Ms. Noni?" Debra questioned sternly.

Noni was undone. "I'm sorry I was just trippin'. It's just that he sort of looks at you in a . . . cakey kind of way. I'm sorry."

"Listen up, Mrs. Myles is *married*. Chef Chase and I are co-workers—that's it. Talk of *anything else* is inappropriate, Noni."

Noni felt the seriousness of Debra's tone as if it were her own mother speaking to her. "Yes ma'am."

Debra started with Corey first. "Corey, how are we coming?"

"It's still going pretty well. My mother and I are talking more. I think the sessions we've been having with you have helped a lot. My dad tries to be at home more and you know . . . act like a family man. It's cool."

"What about Todd?" Debra asked. All of their eyes were huge as saucers.

Debra panicked. "Corey?" she asked nervously, afraid that she might just find out something she didn't necessarily want to hear right now.

"Well it's going . . . uh . . . okay. But it's challenging at times."

"*What* is challenging?"

"The living situation."

"What living *situation*?"

Corey exhaled. "Mrs. Myles, Todd moved out three weeks ago. He has an apartment near the new theater complex. He's on a month to month lease. He was accepted to the University of Michigan with a full scholarship so he's just going to stay there until he starts at U of M."

"Do your parents know that Todd has his own place right now?"

"No." Corey said ashamed.

"What happened to honesty, Corey?"

"Things have been going so well . . . I just didn't want to get into a fight with my mother. I'm not going to stop seeing Todd, and I didn't want her putting me on some prison work-release schedule telling me when I can see him—or barring me from going over to his place. I can handle myself."

"I never said you *couldn't* handle yourself. I believe you are strong in your faith Corey. It's just not wise to spend a lot of unsupervised time with someone of the opposite sex who you are really attracted to."

"We haven't done anything but kiss—that's it."

"But you've been lying to your mother. When you tell her you are going over Todd's, she doesn't know that he has his own place now. I'm sure she's thinking an adult is there—correct?"

"I told you, you should just tell her," Noni interjected.

"I'm not the one who almost had sex, smarty pants," Corey said eyeing Noni.

"Uh-oh," Maya said twisting her lips.

"Back up! Somebody better get to talkin' right now," Debra said eyeing Noni.

Noni was angry with Corey. "You big, BIG MOUTH! We were talking about *You* and Todd, not me and Jason!"

"Spill it!" Debra said.

"It's nothing—nothing happened."

"Spill it!"

Corey looked remorseful that she had blurted that out.

"Jason and I were kissing and it got a little heated, but we stopped. That's it."

"Heated—how heated?"

"No clothes came off—it just got heated."

Debra let go of her breath. "Where did this take place?"

"At my house. Aunt Lane was gone shopping."

"Does she know about this?"

"No. Jason wasn't supposed to be there. I called him over. I just wanted to see him—we didn't do anything."

"Sounds like you need a little honesty in your life too, Miss Noni," Debra said. "Ladies, I know everyone is sixteen or seventeen—juniors who will graduate next year and go off to college. But there are a lot of things you don't understand or don't know. I need you to take my advice and don't put yourselves in a bad position where you may compromise your purity. Save that for someone who is going to commit to you for the rest of their lives." As soon as Debra said the words, she felt like a hypocrite. She'd saved herself for Bryce and where did that get her? It surely wasn't a guarantee that he'd be committed to her for the rest of his life. He was already gone from her life.

Debra had used the word *purity* instead of virginity because she knew that some of the girls she dealt with were no longer virgins. To her, virginity was a scientific word—that was an "is" or "isn't," marking someone as damaged goods if they were no longer a virgin, while purity was something a young woman gained each day she respected herself or set herself aside physically and emotionally. A young woman could actually practice *purity*. That's what she wanted them to focus on. She waited on Maya to spill on her status, but she'd already heard part of her story through the school grapevine. Then she decided that time was running short.

"I'm sorry," Corey said sincerely to Noni, interrupting Debra's processing of how she was going to handle Maya.

"We're straight," Noni said just as sincerely. "You're still my girl, but in the hood, there's this sayin' . . . 'Snitches get stitches,'" Noni said pushing her fist into Corey's nose playfully.

Debra rolled her eyes before saying, "Maya, I already know that you've been seeing Devin Carter—on the football team. And what I want to say is . . . he has a reputation. I want you to tread very lightly. In fact, that is not someone I would recommend for you. You've been doing very well with your health and your emotional status. Devin is a little *different*." What Debra wanted to say is that Devin had probably slept with half the female senior class. Alexandria Cortez's experience ended tragically at an abortion clinic. She didn't want to see anything like that happen to Maya.

"Dang, she just put you on *blast* like a mug!" Noni laughed along with Corey. Maya wore a "busted" smirk on her face.

'Like a mug?' Are they saying that again? Debra mused. "Maya do you understand where I'm coming from? I'm not you guys' parents, but therapeutically, I need you to stay focused on things that are going to build you up instead of tearing you down."

"We've already had this conversation with her. But some of us are a little *hard headed*," Noni said. Corey nodded her head in agreement.

"Mrs. Myles, I'm listening to everything you're saying. My dad doesn't even like Devin, but he really is a cool guy. Sometimes you just have to get to know people. Some people around here didn't like me for whatever reason, but once they got to know me it was different."

Debra knew it was a no-win situation with Maya. Even though she'd made some significant strides with her self-esteem, she still had a long way to go. Being friends with two level headed girls like Noni and Corey helped a lot, but it was the spiritual emptiness that frightened Debra about Maya. Debra understood Maya's need to date Devin. It was affirming for her, even though Debra thought it disastrous.

"Maybe nobody liked you because you run around grippin' that little Toyota Prius hybrid like you are Miss Snooty Tootie,"

Corey teased.

"You're the one driving a new BMW!" Maya said.

"I'm walkin'! Aunt Lane ain't even thinking about letting me get a new car right now. She says it would be *distracting*, but it sure can't be as distracting as Jason Arman Lockmore!!"

They all laughed. Debra gladly put them out at the sound of the eight fifteen bell. She sat back in her chair chuckling. *"'Snitches get stitches.'* If they aren't careful, I'm gonna be the one causing stitches around here," Debra said to herself. She stood up and went over to the window. It looked peaceful outside this April morning. The campus was so pristine and neatly manicured. She couldn't wait until they put the flowers out next month—if it still wasn't too cold. May meant nothing in Michigan.

Debra started thinking heavy thoughts. What was she going to do with the rest of her life? Now that she had moved, what other changes would she make? She'd already lost a close friend in Tammy. She gritted her teeth when she thought about that. Gwen, her best friend in the whole world, had passed when they were just teens from a rare form of cancer. Debra never made that many female friends after Gwen. She knew that she would never have the type of friendship she had with Gwen, with anyone else. Tammy was the second woman she'd shared a close friendship with. Now it was just Debra and God. "I need you to love on me, Lord God. Please, love on me." Debra said exasperated.

"Good Morning," Chase said to prevent himself from studying Debra's backside view any further. He took in her heels and the pencil skirt that fit her like it had been made just for her. *Ooh wee.*

Startled momentarily, Debra turned. "Good Morning," she said cheerfully. She took Chase in with his navy slacks, blue and white pinstriped button-up, and casual loafers. He looked handsome. "What are you doing here? I thought your program ended."

"It did. I just came by to bring Mrs. Daughtry a gift. I finally made it into an inner-city high school—their set-up is not as nice, but it'll work. Just thought I'd drop by and say hello."

"Well, it's always a pleasant surprise." She hadn't talked to or seen Chase since the day after he had helped move her into her new condo a couple of weeks ago.

"You look exceptionally nice today—something special going on?" Chase pried.

"No. Just felt like spicing it up a little. Actually, you're the second or maybe should I say *fourth* person to compliment me today—I saw the Three Musketeers earlier. I'm starting to wonder how I've *been* looking," Debra laughed.

"You're always beautiful. Today is a little more . . . sexy." He regretted saying that. He hoped he didn't sound too forward or inappropriate. Why had he used the word *sexy*? Surely he could have kept that to himself.

"Sexy, huh?" Debra smiled.

"I mean—what I meant is that you look a little more . . . edgy."

Debra laughed at Chase's foot-in-mouth. "Nope. Too late. I'll take sexy, thank you." Debra's telephoned rang. She walked over to her desk and answered it. A moment later she walked toward the bookshelf and raked her fingers across the books on the second shelf. "Yes, I have it. Sure you can borrow it. No problem."

Chase was in some kind of trance looking at Debra. He wanted to scoop her up in his arms and . . . by gosh, he wanted to kiss her. He let himself look freely while Debra's back was turned toward him. He shook his head in awe and admiration of all that Debra was.

"She is rather fly today, ain't she?" Noni queried.

Chase was busted. "Oh . . . hey, good morning, Noni"

Noni had a silly little "I caught you" look on her face. Debra ended her call and turned.

She looked embarrassed to have Chase in her office after what she'd said to Noni this morning. But she had been truthful in what she'd told Noni. She had no interest in Chase. "Yes, what can I do for you, Ms. Noni?"

"Forgot my Spanish notebook," Noni said reaching over and bending down on the floor where she'd laid it earlier.

"Alright. You need a pass?"

"Nope. I'm good," Noni said slyly, eyeing Debra and Chase with her lips twisted.

When she passed Chase on the way out he whispered, "Snitches get stitches."

Noni burst into laughter. "Right!" she said, smiling knowingly. "Have a great day Mrs. Myles—you too, Chef Chase," she giggled.

Chase stifled his laugh and his grin with a pretend cough. He'd been busted alright.

"You have to excuse her. She has a pretty wild imagination, Chase."

"She's a one of a kind."

"A one of a kind *pain*."

Chase laughed an easy, lighthearted laugh. He didn't want to overstay his welcome. "Well, I just came by to say hello—see how you've been doing."

"Thanks, I appreciate it . . . and you know I'm just a phone call away."

Chase felt guilty behind that statement. He had only called her once since helping her move out. After that evening watching her sleep, he knew most certainly that he was in love. Since their relationship at this point could only lead to a dead-end street, he retreated. It seemed like his withdrawal made the situation worse, because the more he stayed away from Debra, the more thoughts of her infiltrated his mind. *What was she doing? How was she feeling? Was she okay? How was she holding up emotionally? Did she need anything?* He chided himself for not calling more often. "I'm sorry. I should have called to check on you more. I've been uh . . . "

"Busy?"

"Uh . . . yeah—sort of. I'll do better."

"It's okay. I understand. The world doesn't revolve around Debra Ann."

My world does. "I just haven't been a good friend, lately. I'm going to change that."

"Chase, I'm okay, really. I don't want you to feel like our friend-ship is an obligation. Lord knows no one needs another obligation on their plate."

"Debra, you're not an obligation. Please don't feel that way. That is the absolute furthest thing from the truth." *I'm just mad crazy in love with you and don't know what to do about it.* "Hey, you know the high school cook-off competition is next week in Birmingham. Did Noni tell you?"

"Only a hundred times. I'll be there. She better be glad it's not the week after," Debra laughed.

"Why, do you have something special planned?"

"Actually, I'm going to Cancun. I need to get away."

"With anyone special?" Chase pried.

"Just a couple of real nice women in my Pilates class. They practically coerced me into going, and Daddy agreed to pay for it. So you know I gave up on resisting."

He was relieved she didn't say that she and her husband were going to rekindle their relationship. It was a selfish but honest thought. He hadn't forgotten what his best friend said about separated couples going through divorces. "Well, you deserve it."

"I've been trying to convince myself of that, but we just came back from spring break," Debra chuckled.

"Sometimes you have to do what you have to do. You need the rest."

"Thanks for the encouragement, now I don't feel as bad," Debra smiled.

"Glad to help clear your conscience, Debra Ann. So I'll see you at the cook-off?"

"Yes. Maybe you could stop by my place for a little while afterward—I miss having a little company."

"Sounds like a plan." *Chase, don't start none. And it won't be none.*

"Okay, see you next Saturday."

"Bye," Chase said before leaving. He could have stayed in her office all day long just looking at her. What in the world was happening to him? This was just crazy.

30

Hot Lips

The high school cook-off competition was extraordinary. Debra had no idea that there were so many young people who could cook so well. She had sampled so many delicacies, she felt stuffed when the evening was over. Chase stopped by for coffee as he had promised. Debra was looking so lovely in her Merlot colored dress, Chase wondered if he should have taken his behind straight home, instead. She was like some kind of human magnet, pulling him to her with an overpowering energy. They were having a great conversation until Debra broke down and told Chase about her bout with depression.

"Chase, I just feel so scared right now. I feel worthless . . . ugly . . . ashamed. What did I do wrong?"

Chase sat next to Debra on the sofa in the living room listening intently. He placed his coffee cup on the marble-topped cocktail table beside him. "Debra, no. Don't allow Satan to take you there. You didn't do anything wrong. You can't control another person. You can't make someone love you or be good to you. You just can't. Just know that you are a *beautiful* woman. You have nothing to feel ashamed about."

"He just left me. He's *divorcing* me. I couldn't *keep* my husband," Debra cried.

"Debra, you shouldn't have to *keep* anyone. Bryce should have *wanted* to stay with you. If his mind is made up, what can you do?"

Debra began to cry harder. "My God, life wasn't supposed to be this cruel . . . "

"Come on, don't . . . " Chase said hugging Debra close to him. He released her enough to look at her. "Debra, you are a beautiful woman. Don't ever think otherwise. A real man would be glad to have you." He wiped her tears and Debra cried on him. Chase patted her back with his strong hands as if he were comforting his sister. He felt the jerking of Debra's body as she cried hard on him. He squeezed her more tightly. He felt a danger in doing that after a minute or so. The warmth of her fragile body next to his heightened all of his male senses. Yet, she was not his to hold. Legally, she still belonged to Bryce. In God's eyes, she still belonged to Bryce. The divorce wasn't final yet. All of Chase's good common sense warned him not to get too attached.

Even after she and Bryce divorced, Debra had a lot of healing to do. She couldn't be ready for anything other than a friendship. Yet, at the moment, Chase envisioned more. He tried to steer his thoughts in some other direction, but holding Debra the way he was, comforting her, brought a sense of comfort to him as well. It felt natural to have her in his arms that way. The danger Chase had felt moments before, returned with persuasive heat as Debra scaled her hands across his back. He tried to reason the touches, but his heart knew what kind they were. They were too soft and too deliberate to be mistaken for anything else but sensual, seducing touches.

Chase heard the warning bells as if he were inside of a fire station. He froze, paralyzed by a myriad of forbidden thoughts. He stood between walls of reason and release. Then he separated himself from her, tugging her arms gently. He held her hands in his to keep Debra from putting another spell on him. "Debra Ann, I need to go home. I'll call and check on you in the morning," he said huskily, sinking into the eyes that were spilling over with pain. He stood. Debra stood also.

Chase put more space between him and Debra. Afraid he would abandon her, Debra leaned in to persuade him with her lips. Chase let Debra's kiss rest softly on his lips. She lingered, holding the sweet seducing flame to his mouth. Debra had no idea how long it had been since he had held a woman—enjoyed a woman. He was tempted with thoughts that he worked hard to keep at bay. There they were gnawing at him. *This is the perfect opportunity. She wants you, Chase. Look how long you've waited. If God cared, he would have sent you a woman by now. Take her.* Every ounce of wisdom reminded him that making love to Debra wasn't worth another whipping from God. Savannah's mother was a constant reminder of the consequences of his disobedience. It had taken Chase over two years to get custody of his daughter. Would God bless an unholy union? Something taken without right? A body stolen? *Wait on the Lord. He will perfect those things which concern you.*

Chase backed up a step. "I can't go there, Debra," Chase said in a husky, longing timbre that was evidence of how much Debra's touches and kiss had affected him. "I'm sorry. Call you tomorrow," Chase said. He didn't wait for her to respond. He didn't trust himself enough to listen to anything Debra had to say right now. He left without another word and Debra cried herself to sleep afterward, feeling embarrassed *and* abandoned by God.

* * *

Debra's eyes were swollen shut the next morning. She put a cold rag across them to reduce the swelling. She looked at herself in the mirror. It looked as though she'd had an allergic reaction to something. "Chase wouldn't think I was so beautiful now," she said aloud. She stared at her image. Sorrowful eyes made Debra cry again. "I'm an idiot. Lord, God, I am so sorry for what I did last night. I have no excuse, Lord. I was wrong. I just wanted to be held and touched. I wanted to feel loved." *Love on Me,* Debra heard in her spirit. "Please forgive me. It's so hard, Father. I didn't ask for this. I feel like You're punishing me. I tried to be good to Bryce." Debra went into her room and sat on the bed. She read her Bible and sat quietly until the phone rang. She looked at the caller ID. It was Chase. She didn't want to answer it. She was thoroughly embarrassed.

"Good Morning," Debra greeted anyway.

"Good Morning. How are you doing?" Chase asked. His tone was light and cheerful.

"Besides feeling like a total idiot, pretty good."

"Debra, I called to talk to you about last night. I—"

"Chase, I'm really sorry," Debra said before Chase could finish his sentence. I hope you don't think I go around throwing myself on men. I was out of my element last night. I don't know what got into me. Please don't let what happened paint a picture that's not really representative of me—of God."

"Listen, last night was *all* my fault, Debra. Honestly, the Lord had warned me before I got there. We probably should have stopped for coffee at a restaurant or coffee shop. But no, Mr. 'I can handle myself' over here, came over anyway. The Lord had given me a plan. I turned a curve," he chuckled. "But I just want to get something straight with you, *Ms. Debra Ann.* I'm not gay, on the down-low, bi-sexual—or confused. I am one hundred percent *man*, which means that you can *never* do what you did last night and expect that the situation will turn out the same."

"It took every scripture I know, every prayer that I've ever prayed, and every prayer prayed on my behalf—for me to leave you last night. You have no idea . . . " Chase smiled. "And if there is any doubt in your mind, I can clear it up by telling you that I am *extremely* attracted to you—in every aspect. I think you are drop-dead gorgeous. Intelligent. Caring. A strong woman of God. It took every ounce of my integrity to walk out of your house. My walk with God and your circumstances dictate that we can't be en-tangled in any way. All I can offer you right now is friendship—a very platonic one." He was serious.

Debra's smile faded. It was a blow to the ego. He didn't want to deal with her. She had too much baggage. "I understand, Chase." Her voice was weakened.

"I hope you know where I'm coming from, Debra. My rela-tionship with God is of the utmost importance. My thoughts alone had me in deep trouble. My policy has always been to *never* get involved with a married woman. It doesn't matter that you're go-ing through a divorce. The bond is there. The papers are still there. You still belong to your husband. I mean, you and me just going out together would look inappropriate. I know the world has its own way. I try my best to follow the way of the Lord. More sleep at night. Less worry."

"I hear you. Listen, I've got some things to do. I'll talk to you some other time, okay?"

He knew she was hurt. He hoped that this didn't permanently damage his chances of being with her in the future, if the opportunity arose. "See you around."

*   *   *

Chase sat on the bench near the basketball court, inside of the private health club he and Corey preferred. Corey had just whipped him again in another game of one on one.

"Don't tell me you're a sore loser, Chase?" Corey teased. "Chase! Where ya head at, man?" Corey said, swatting Chase with a towel.

Chase jumped. "What?"

"What in the world are you thinking about? You are on cloud nine. Did I beat you that badly? I'll give you a re-match right now."

Chase smiled. "No, man. I got stuff on my mind."

"What's up?"

Chase didn't feel like hearing a lecture. "Nothing. It's cool. I just have to work some things out in my mind."

"You tight-lipped with your brother?"

"No—I just know what you're going to say already, and I don't want to hear it," Chase chuckled.

Corey had a good idea of what was bothering Chase, but decided against an overbearing approach. "Look, you know we're brothers—nothing is off limits—and I promise to talk to you as your *brother*—not your assistant pastor. So please, tell me what has got you zoned out."

"Last night—with Debra."

Corey let out a breath, looking suspiciously at Chase, but he was determined to keep his promise. In the calmest voice he could muster he said, "Tell me what happened."

"The Metropolitan Culinary Arts Association held the annual High School Cook-Off Competition, and I attended because Noni, the student I'm mentoring, was a finalist—she won by the way. Debra had already asked me to stop by after the event, and given the circumstances, I didn't think it was that bad of an idea. I mean, I thought about the fact that it might not be wise with the way I feel about her but—"

Corey cut him off mid-sentence. "Man, you're worse than a suspense novel. Get to the point," Corey said playfully.

"We started talking and Debra started to cry—blaming herself for everything, just kind of feeling like a failure. So I just tried to comfort her—I hugged her."

"Uh-huh," Corey said with increased suspicion. "Then what happened?"

"Debra sort-of came on to me—the way she was touching me."

"Uh-huh. Then what?"

"I mean . . . she kissed me, and uh . . . I was struggling in my mind because I wanted her—very badly—really bad."

"Uh-huh. Then what?" Corey said eagerly.

"Well, it was like that cartoon where the little angel is on one shoulder talking to you, and the little devil is on the other."

"Which one did you listen to, Chase?" Corey eyed him directly to make sure he'd give up a confession.

"I left."

Corey smiled, unbelieving. "You kiddin' me?"

"No—I left—for real. Do you have *any* faith in your best friend?"

Corey burst into laughter. "Of course, man. It's just that I know how things happen. I'm saved—not sinless. But let me get this straight, Debra touched you and kissed you and you didn't do *anything?*"

"Correct. I did nothing except leave, but it took all the strength I had in me and a double dose from God. Debra's lips were like fire on my mouth. I was in another world when she kissed me. My heart was beating so fast and loud, I thought I was about to have a heart-attack! I don't think I've ever wanted to be with a woman that badly. I knew if I did anything—touched her—kissed her—anything—it would have been over!"

Corey stood up. "I'm proud of you, Chase. That means you're really growing in the Spirit, but didn't I—*swat!*" The gym towel Corey was holding smacked against Chase's skin. " . . . tell you—*swat!*—to stay—*swat!*—away—*swat!*—from that—*swat!*—fine woman?!" Corey said, emulating a parent issuing an old fashioned whipping as he hit Chase with the gym towel.

Chase laughed aloud. "Man, get away from me!" he yelled blocking Corey's hits with his forearm.

"You're blessed that the Lord helped your fool behind out of that one," Corey said seriously.

"I know."

"And I hope I don't have to tell you again, if you just have to see Debra, you need to do it in public places *only.*"

"I know."

"Now, come on Hot Lips, let's go get some grub!"

"Corey, I'm in love, man."

Corey shook his head. "Aw, Hot Lips . . . you better pray!"

31
All Fall Down

Debra returned from her spur-of-the-moment, five-night Cancun trip, feeling refreshed. She'd felt like a heel initially because spring break had passed two weeks prior and she had taken plenty of days off before then. Usually, she took vacations during the scheduled school breaks. She had to admit getting away had been worth it. Debra could sleep at night again. She'd taken Dr. Buckley up on his offer to see his friend, Dr. Erica Buchanan, for sleeping pills and they worked. Debra felt rested in the mornings and she wasn't cranky from not getting any sleep at night like she had been. Cancun wasn't a bad place to work on getting yourself together either. Debra had taken advantage of the spa services and the food at the Fiesta Americana Grand Coral Beach hotel in Cancun. She'd even gotten a tan and picked up at least six of the ten pounds she'd lost. That was a good thing.

If it weren't for her father, Daniel, she might not have gone.

She mentioned it to him while wrestling with the thought of leaving her babies for a few days. He sweetened the pot when he told Debra if she went, he'd pay for it. That one gesture sold her. Normally, she'd refuse when Daniel offered money. Bryce had always told her that accepting money and gifts from Daniel made him feel like he wasn't doing his job as a husband.

Bryce was gone now, and Debra was working hard to restructure her life emotionally and financially. Going on a two-thousand-dollar trip courtesy of someone else was a deal she couldn't say no to. She thought about that as she pulled out of the airport parking garage and headed home. Night was just starting to seize the sky. Debra had enjoyed her trip immensely. She hadn't thought much about her situation either—that is until now, when heading to her new home reminded her that life was different and would be different from now on. There was no getting around it. This new life seemed so foreign—like it just wasn't supposed to be this way.

Debra turned on the car stereo and pushed the CD button. The sounds of a jazz-flavored gospel tune piped through the speakers, filling the car with praise and worship music. Debra felt guilty. She didn't feel like praising God. Did He deserve it? Yes. Was it due Him? Yes. Her heart just wasn't in it. "Lord God, what is happening to me?" she asked, disappointed and ashamed that she'd let life and Bryce rob her of her praise. Debra just didn't know how to get it back. "Help me Lord. I don't know how to get my life back," she said steering onto the freeway. "The only good things I've got going on in my life are my babies at work. I desire so much more than that. What about my own children? What about everything I've ever asked you for Oh, Lord? Why has my life just fallen apart like this?" Debra didn't hear God's answer to her questions at that moment. That made her cry.

She wondered how God made decisions about who received

the "happily-ever-after" and who didn't. Who woke up in the morning with cancer, and who didn't? Which children got to live in a country with plenty, and which children would starve to death? It was all too much to think about. It hurt, and it was confusing. Everything Debra ever learned about God, reminded her that He was loving, gentle, kind, and just. How did those characteristics apply in every situation? Certainly, a child starving to death couldn't be considered just—not by human standards, anyway. She started to feel as confused as a non-believer. "Lord, I don't understand You at all. I thought I did, but I don't. I don't know why things are the way they are. I can't wait for heaven to get a happy ending. I need something right now—on this side of heaven!" Debra's truthful confession shocked her. She was glad that she said the words aloud. It took the fear away. Didn't God know what she was thinking anyway?

She was half-way home when she noticed her Blackberry on the passenger seat. She'd missed a dozen text messages and calls. She picked it up. Six calls from Noni. Four calls from Maya's dad. Two calls from Chase. She felt a churning in her stomach. Something didn't feel right. She hit the mail icon. EMERGENCY. PLEASE CALL. That was the last text Noni left. What could be happening at eight-thirty on a Sunday night? She instantly forgot about her own problems. Debra's heart thumped. She pulled into a gas station lot and fumbled around in her purse for her Bluetooth earpiece, but couldn't find it. Frustrated, she dialed Noni's number without it.

Noni's voice was weary. "Oh my God, Mrs. Myles . . . we shouldn't have left her . . . "

"Noni, what is wrong?"

"We . . . shouldn't . . . have left her . . . "

Debra couldn't make out anything else Noni was saying because she was crying so profusely. "Noni, left who? What is going—?"

"Hello, Mrs. Myles. This is Elaine Hudson. How are you doing?"

Debra didn't have time for pleasantries right now. She wanted answers. "Hi Ms. Hudson, what's going on?" Debra asked nervously and full of fear.

"It's Maya . . . apparently she had some sort of break-up with her boyfriend. She overdosed on some of her father's sleeping pills."

"What?! Is she okay?"

"She's alive. We're at Beaumont Hospital in Troy. Maya and her dad don't have any other family members here in the city. I believe the doctor's are still working on her."

Before Elaine Hudson had finished her last sentence, Debra was screeching out of the gas station lot headed toward Beaumont. It seemed like the longest drive Debra had ever taken. A thousand and one thoughts raced through her head. She just couldn't fix her mind on any one thing besides guilt. She'd left them. She was the one who shouldn't have left. A stupid vacation in the middle of the semester. She had cancelled Maya's individual session on Wednesday because she left for Cancun Tuesday after work. Maybe she could have prevented this. Debra felt terrible, like she was going to be sick. It was her fault. She had to snap out of the pity party she was having for herself and focus on her babies. She should have been there for Maya. Debra would have known if something was wrong. She could have warned Greg McIntyre to keep an eye on her. What had she done? "Lord, please forgive me. Let Maya be okay . . . please Lord," Debra prayed aloud. It seemed that life just kept getting worse since Bryce left.

All the traffic lights appeared to be one continuum of color.

The reds blended into the greens into the yellows. Debra couldn't hear the blaring horns or shouts of the other drivers she'd offended. She was robotic with only one goal in mind: Get to Beaumont.

Debra burst into the waiting area of the emergency room looking frantic. Instinctively, Noni ran into her arms and bawled on her shoulder. "I can't keep doing this. Why would Maya do this to me?"

Debra said nothing. She held onto Noni and let go of her own tears. When Noni released Debra, Corey hugged her deeply. Todd Bennett was right by Corey's side with his Bible in his hand. Then Greg McIntyre walked over to Debra and hugged her. "Thank you so much, Mrs. Myles. I know you don't get paid to work on the weekends and stuff," he rambled. "I just didn't know who else to call. I know Maya trusts you. She loves you. She said so . . . " Greg McIntyre's eyes were blood-red from crying.

"It's fine, Mr. McIntyre. I'm here. Maya's really special to me."

Greg wiped his tears with the back of his hand, then he cried openly. "I've been working at this . . . raising Maya by myself . . . I just don't know what else she needs. She's a different girl, you know. We've been to counseling—everything. The best schools . . . I don't know what to do. I feel like I've failed . . . and I . . . I just want us to be a normal family."

Debra squeezed Greg's hand. "You've done your best . . . let God finish the job." The words were a revelation to Debra as they rolled off her tongue. They resonated in her spirit. She'd done her best also. It was time for her to allow God to complete the work. Debra spotted Chase and Mona entering the room from the opposite door. Noni had called him. Being a good mentor he had come right away. He and Mona were toting hot chocolates and coffee for everyone. Jason, Todd, Corey, Elaine, and Noni swarmed around

Mona and took the cups from her, welcoming the liquid treasure. It was something else to focus on other than the reason they were all here. Chase walked over and handed Greg a strong cup of black coffee as he had requested.

"Thanks, man. I really I appreciate you," Greg said. It was his second time meeting Chase and there was something about him that was genuine. They'd been introduced just a few weeks prior at the annual high school cook-off. Usually a very private person, Greg didn't normally take to a stranger the way he was taking to Chase. It was odd, but for some reason, he wasn't threatened by Chase knowing his personal business. He could see that both Chase and Mona were good people. He missed that in his life. Despite the church he had been attending in order to make some connections with others in the city, he still lacked true intimacy with friends. He had moved around so much in life trying to get ahead, he had never settled long enough to build enduring relationships.

"No problem. If you need anything else, just let me know," Chase said before turning his attention to Debra. "How are you?"

"I'm doing," Debra nodded letting her tears flow.

Chase spoke quietly into Debra's ear. "It's not your fault."

Debra smoothed her hands over her hair that was tucked neatly into a ponytail. "Well, why do I feel like this?"

"Because you're human."

"Is that the reason? I don't know what I am anymore. The inside of me is raw, Chase. I feel like I'm just a person existing without a soul."

It hurt Chase to hear Debra speak those words. He wanted to wrap himself around her and fill her with a love so powerful, it would only be second to Christ's. "God knows and cares," he said. He was careful this time not to say too much or to offer any advice. He didn't want to minimize what Debra was feeling at the moment. He had no idea what she was actually going through right now. He could only imagine that it wasn't a good place to be. He could see the pain in her eyes that stemmed from something deeper than Maya's situation. It was a culmination of hurt.

Greg had eased back over to them. "Mrs. Myles, I think you should take a look at this," he said unfolding a piece of pink stationery with roses bordering the top and bottom of the page. "Maya had left this on her door." He walked away as quietly as he had walked over. He needed to sit and think about something else until the doctor returned.

Debra opened it slowly and read the words. She trembled as she held the delicate paper in her hands.

Dear Dad,

I'm sorry that this is our fate. I know you love me and that you try really hard to be the best Dad you can. You've been a good father to me. As a matter of fact, you're a pretty good mom, too (LOL). We've traveled together, and lived in some neat places—especially Michigan. This was a good choice. I've finally found some real true friends in Noni and Corey. I love them. They love me for me and they are like the sisters I've never had. And Mrs. Myles is the bomb! I've learned so much about myself from her. I'm sorry for whatever pain my decision will cause you and them. Please don't blame yourself, Dad. It's me. I'm tired of the pain of this world. It hurts too much. I've figured out that I'm just not strong as other people I know. I can't take pain. I just want to have some peace in my life, Dad, and I don't think I can have peace on this side.

You were right about Devin. He doesn't care about me, but in my heart, I love him. I thought that I'd finally found a true boyfriend. Well, I was wrong. Mrs. Myles and the girls were right about him. Devin doesn't love me. He told me he just wants to be friends now. That means he wants someone else. And it's too late for friendship because I've already given him all of me. But I wanted to believe in something so much, I couldn't see what you all were saying, Dad. But now, I want you to focus on your own life—meet someone and get married. I know you want to have a girlfriend or a wife one day. You've spent too much time worried about me. And if you ever talk to my mom one day, tell her that I wish I could have gotten to know her. I think we could have at least been friends. I'm not mad at her for leaving. It just hurts sometimes when I think about it. Now I won't hurt anymore. Good Bye. I love you.

                                        Maya

Debra couldn't compose herself any longer. She ran until she could feel the outside air against her skin. She hadn't realized that

Chase was right behind her. She sat on a cement bench near the entrance of the hospital. She rocked back and forth, trying to keep herself calm. A part of her wanted to scream aloud. Burning tears flowed steadily. Chase had scooted next to her, but Debra couldn't feel him anymore. She felt nothing but the heaviness of this world. She understood what Maya must have felt when she penned those words—when she realized that Devin was just another shattered dream—just like her mother. It had to have been an overwhelming hurt that caused her to want to escape this world—to take her own life.

Debra had always thought of people who committed suicide as selfish individuals who didn't consider the pain that taking their lives would cause the people who loved them. She would ask herself questions like: *Why would someone inflict pain on the people who loved them? Couldn't they just stop to think about someone other than themselves?* Right now, at this crossroad in her own life, she felt Maya's pain—the pain of failure.

Debra knew what it felt like to want something so badly and then watch it crumble right before your eyes. She understood the pain of rejection, and how damaging it was to one's spirit. She sat for the longest time crying before Chase covered her hand with his and squeezed it. He brought it to his lips and planted a kiss on it. Then he put his arm around her shoulder and squeezed her with the love of Christ. Debra laid her head on Chase's shoulder until the crushing of her heart relented. Then she gathered herself and returned to the waiting room to join the others. She'd been so upset earlier, she hadn't noticed Savannah sitting in a chair in the far corner of the room watching her portable pink DVD player. She looked adorable with little pink headphones covering her ears. Mona was nearby tapping away on her laptop. Greg had fallen asleep. Noni and Corey were both sleeping as well, resting on their respective "boos." Jason and Todd nodded. Debra smiled. Elaine walked up and hugged her. "You are a wonderful person with a beautiful spirit, Mrs. Myles. The Lord is going to reward you for your dedication to these kids."

"Thank you. It's just so hard for kids these days. People don't understand what they go through."

"Well, that's why God has blessed them with you."

"Amen," Chase said.

32

Dynamite

Debra sat in Dr. Buckley's office removed from his conversation. His lips were moving, but she couldn't hear
a thing he was saying. She didn't want to hear. She
thought of a million other things she could be doing at the moment. What was the point? Obviously she was stuck with the life
God had given her. Now what?

Dr. Buckley was more intrigued than agitated by Debra's disposition. "Debra do you have plans or something? Or is therapy
boring you?"

"Actually, Dr. Buckley, to be honest, I don't want to be here."

"I see. I appreciate your honesty."

Debra said nothing. She shot him a quick glare before divert-
ing her eyes away again. What was there to talk about today? Did
he understand that she'd failed at the very thing she'd taken pride
in—being a good therapist for her babies? Surely he wasn't so

dense that he couldn't figure that out. Now Maya was tucked securely in an inpatient psychiatric hospital for youth, serving out her thirty-day sentence.

Both Debra and Greg agreed that was the best decision for Maya. It still bothered Debra that she hadn't seen it coming. No extreme depression. No change in attitude—nothing to make her think that Maya would do such a thing. Maya had made such strides in treatment. It was almost inconceivable that she would do something like this, judging from the way things had been going. Debra questioned Noni and Corey extensively and they both agreed that Maya had been her normal self up until the night she'd told them that she'd broken up with Devin. They had planned to go on a triple date to a movie that Sunday evening with their boyfriends.

Maya had told them she just wasn't in the mood after her argument with Devin. She didn't even elaborate on the break-up. She had been no more upset or less upset than anyone who'd just had an argument with their boyfriend. They'd offered to stay with her, but Maya had assured them that she just needed some alone time—a couple of hours. She said she had a headache and was going to get some rest. She asked them to come by after the movie and they'd go out for ice cream together, just the three of them and she'd tell them everything.

When they returned, there was an ambulance outside of the McIntyre home. Greg had returned home early because he'd forgotten something. If it hadn't been for that, Maya would probably be dead. The thought made Debra shudder. She still couldn't figure it out. She had had extensive suicide prevention training. She was a certified suicide prevention counselor. She ran all of this through her mind while Dr. Buckley said whatever it was he was saying.

"You know what your problem is, Debra?" Dr. Buckley said. "You have a God complex."

An aggressive fire shot through Debra. "What are you talking about!"

Dr. Buckley didn't back down. "I bet you've been punishing yourself all week. Moping. Feeling like you failed at your marriage, failed at keeping your student from attempting suicide, failed at saving the world. But you know something? You're not God. You call yourself a Christian, yet you don't even recognize God as the Supreme Ruler that He is. Somehow in your twisted little mind, you've convinced yourself that it's your job to keep things running smoothly—that you and you only make the world go round. Well you know what? That is the biggest untruth I have ever heard. Get over yourself, Debra."

Debra jumped out of her seat. "Are you crazy! What don't you understand about what I've told you? I could have done more for her, if I had stayed!"

"How do you know that, Debra? Huh? You're a certified suicide prevention counselor. Didn't you learn in training that some folks don't fit the vignettes or the case studies . . . they don't exhibit the same clear symptoms that we can identify as being suicidal? Surely you remember that from your training."

"Why am I here?!" Debra shouted. She snatched her purse and coat from the chair and headed for the door. Dr. Buckley's cold response made Debra want to turn around and choke him to death. "Does running away put you in control, Debra?" He had grown tired of her self-condemning, self-berating statements. Tired of her feeling sorry for herself. God had so much more to offer her. Every assignment and exercise they'd done was to help her understand more fully that God saw her as precious and important, and worthy to be loved by Him because of her relationship with Christ.

Over the last few months, Dr. Buckley had watched Debra's confidence and energy level of vacillate. One week she was concentrating on "living," the next she was so depressed it was like a black cloud followed her into his office and dimmed the light as soon as she walked in. If only Debra's emotions were consistent. High highs led to low lows. If she came in excited one week, he could just about predict that the next week she'd be in a spiritual valley. It was almost like watching a bipolar person, although he hadn't considered that as a diagnosis for her. The mood changes—the depression was a result of her "perfect" syndrome. She'd failed at being "perfect."

Debra turned around slowly with fire in her eyes that was succumbing to tears. "What do you want me to do, Dr. Buckley, pretend that my life is all good when it isn't?"

"All things work together for good to those that love God, to those who are the called according to His purpose," he quoted from Romans 8:28. He handed Debra a Bible off his desk as a peace offering. She reached out for it reluctantly. "Read it. Tell me what you think that really means, Debra."

She took the Bible from his hands and plopped back down in her chair. "It means that everything will work to my benefit in the end because I belong to God."

"Absolutely," Dr. Buckley nodded. "So let's get unstuck Debra. Let's focus on pushing through your depression. I'm sorry that I can't tell you when things are going to get better for you. I just know that they will. You've got to use your faith on this leg of the journey, plain and simple."

Debra cried. "Can't you see that my faith is all busted up?" Her eyes were tired and empty.

"That may be, but busted up faith is better than none. God can work with busted up faith. You be honest and tell Him that it's busted up. Tell Him you need Him to increase it."

"I'm tired . . . " The words dragged out slowly.

Dr. Buckley's response was more sensitive. His voice was quiet and calm. "I know you're tired Debra, but you can't give up. That's what your student did. Don't you see that? She gave up. You can't give up, Debra—no matter what. Everything you're going through now represents a brick wall trying to block your path as you journey on your way to be like Christ. God has given you the power to bust through walls—through setbacks, and unexpected events in life that bring you pain. What you've got inside—that Holy Ghost power—is like dynamite. You've got to use your dynamite right now. You've got to pray and praise your way through this thing, Debra. I promise you'll smile again."

Silent tears flowed. Debra read the scripture aloud and swallowed the lump in her throat. She turned the pages of the Bible and read Isaiah 54:17. *"No weapon formed against you shall prosper . . ."*

"That's it. Read it!" Dr. Buckley said excitedly.

"Yet in all these things we are more than conquerors through Him who loved us," Debra quoted from Romans 8:37.

"That's right, go to 2 Corinthians 12:9"

Debra turned slowly and read aloud again.

Dr. Buckley joined in with her. *"My grace is sufficient for you, for My strength is made perfect in weakness.* Okay, so let's say we concentrate on God's promises instead of Debra's failures, huh? I want you to really meditate on those scriptures you just read, Debra. Only the Holy Spirit can remind you of God's promises. God *will* keep His word—you just trust and pray. That's your only assignment for this week. Can you handle that?"

"Yes . . . " Debra said weakly.

"Remember, you've got to use your dynamite, Debra."

"Okay," Debra said. At least she would give it a try.

33

What Love Feels Like

Debra eased her car into her parents' driveway. She didn't have the garage door opener Daniel had given her, so she parked at the curb and walked up to the front door. The traditional white colonial was regal with glossy black shutters. The bright red door had always been a welcome symbol until tonight. She could hear Daniel and Sheila's inimical discussion from the porch. She felt like she was in the Twilight Zone. Growing up, she'd never once heard her parents have a full blown *shouting* match like they were having now. She wondered what in the world they were arguing about. She knew how Sheila could get under Daniel's skin at times with her snide comments and nonchalant attitude, but she'd never heard them shouting like this. Sometimes Debra wondered what her father saw in her mother. They were total opposites. Then again, how could anyone be on the same page as her mother? Sheila was a different type of person.

Debra's relationship with her had always been strained. Sheila could be so critical and uncaring—mean. It was hard for Debra to imagine a man being intimate with her mother. Debra opened the door and called out. "Hello . . . " Her voice was drowned out by Sheila's screaming.

"I am so sick and tired of trying to prove myself to you, Daniel Prince!"

"I'm not asking you to prove *anything* to me Sheila! All I *have* asked you to do is be a good wife, but even that's too hard for you!" Daniel shouted back.

"Here we go again. That was thirty-something years ago. You need to let that go. I'm sick of hearing about it and I don't want to talk about it anymore!"

"I wasn't talking about *that*, but since you brought it up, it's easy for you to let it go. You weren't the one being cheated on—you were too busy living out some fantasy with somebody else!"

"Okay, Daniel! "I cheated on you! I had an affair! I slept with another man! Are you happy now!" Sheila screamed at the top of her lungs.

Daniel's response was tame. "At least that was honest," he said sullenly before walking out of the kitchen to the garage. He slammed the door ceremoniously on his exit.

Debra was shocked by what her mother had admitted. *That* couldn't have happened. She walked slowly into the kitchen. Sheila stood over the sink crying hard. Debra had never seen her mother cry—never seen her broken. For the first time in her life, despite what she'd just heard, she felt sorry for her mother.

Debra reached out and touched Sheila's shoulder gently. "Mama . . . "

Startled, Sheila jumped, quickly covering her beating heart with her hand. She let out a breath of relief when she realized it was Debra. "How long have you been here? Did you hear us?" Sheila asked, embarrassed.

Debra nodded in the affirmative.

"So I guess you hate me more, huh?"

"No," Debra said quietly. The situation with Maya had caused her to realize just how short life could be. How a person could be here one minute, and in the twinkling of an eye, be gone the next. She no longer wanted to be trapped in the feelings she felt or didn't feel for her mother.

"Sit," Sheila said motioning Debra to the bar stools.

Debra took a seat and took her jacket off. She hung it on the back of the chair.

"I'm not some monster, Debra."

"I never said you were, Mama."

"I am not perfect—I'm a woman. That's all. I have never tried to be anything other than what I am. I've never tried to live in a world that wasn't true. I love your father with everything in me. Somewhere inside that crazy heart of his, he knows that. But when a man closes his heart to you, there is no getting back in. I've learned that over the years. I once had a space in his heart, and now I don't. So there, that's the truth. I don't know why he has stayed this long. I can't wrap my mind around it."

Debra thought of Bryce and how she'd once had a space in his heart, but now it was filled with another woman. "Daddy loves you," she said. It was spoken as a comparison to her own situation. Sheila picked up on the juxtaposition.

"Not like he once did—not tonight."

"Love hurts sometimes," Debra said.

"Yes it does."

"At least he's here—he's been here, no matter what happened in the past."

Sheila took the opportunity to say the words she'd wanted to say for months, but never felt the time was right. "Bryce isn't what you need. He's weak, Debra. It seems like he has everything under control, but he doesn't. He's so confused, he isn't even aware of it. I bet right now he doesn't know if he is coming or going."

"I understand him wanting another woman—loving another woman, but not the coldness."

"Coldness is the only way to justify what he's doing. He has to make himself be angry—be cold, in order to do what he's doing. He knows you've done nothing to deserve it."

"I didn't think my life was going to be this way. I had no idea it would turn out like this."

Sheila snapped back. "You sound as if it's over because Bryce isn't in your life anymore."

Debra wondered how long it would take for her mother's cynicism to creep out. "It just feels that way sometimes, Mama."

Sheila chose her words carefully. "*Feels* that way, but it's not true. You're only thirty-five years old Debra—you've got so much ahead of you. This will be like a drop in the bucket twenty years from now. You probably will have re-married, had children—be on your way to having grandchildren—this won't matter."

The mention of children saddened Debra. She wasn't getting any younger. She knew that a first pregnancy after thirty-five was considered high-risk, despite modern technology. When would she have the heart to get to know, let alone *love* another man? "I've just about given up on having children, Mama."

"Are you kidding me? You want to rob Daniel Prince of being Super Granddaddy?" Sheila said gesturing with muscled arms and tight fists like a superhero. "Don't tell him that."

Debra smiled deep, imagining her father being the Superhero grandfather she knew he would be. "That would be a sight to see."

"Honey, if Daniel Prince has to find you a husband himself, you are going to have him some grandbabies one day. That's all that man talks about now."

Debra looked surprised. Daniel hadn't mentioned anything to her about grandkids. "What?"

"Yes. He probably hasn't said anything to you because of everything that has been going on, but he definitely wants to be a granddaddy. So don't you give up on your life before it gets started."

"Why were you and Daddy fighting?" Debra asked, changing the subject.

"Who knows," Sheila said exasperated. "It always starts over something simple, you know. Then it turns ugly—like it did tonight, and your father walks out of here and stays gone for hours at a time. I'm inclined to think he has another woman somewhere."

"Mama, that's not true and you know it," Debra said defending her father.

"I said that's what I *think* sometimes, Debra. You don't have to protect your father from me."

It took all of Debra's might not to say what was on her mind. *Somebody has to.* "I'm just saying that Daddy isn't that kind of man—he tries to live by the Word of God, Mama."

Sheila got up and poured herself a glass of wine. She stared out the kitchen window with her back to Debra. She sipped from her glass slowly. "That he does . . . " she said in a low tone.

Debra asked the question she wanted to ask her mother for years, but never had the courage to. She had asked her father a thousand times, but he always laughed it off without a response. "Why are you so mean to him?" her words hung suspended in the air for minutes before Sheila acknowledged them. She stood in the same spot looking out of the window, sipping her glass of wine as if life were okay. Finally she turned to Debra.

"People love the way they know how, Debra Ann Prince," Sheila said with evil eyes penetrating Debra so hard, she felt like her mother was casting some sort of spell on her.

"Love isn't mean, Mama. It's nurturing and tender . . . and kind."

"And just who do you know that loves that way, Debra? You? Daniel?"

"*Good love* is gentle and uplifting."

"How do *you* know that?"

Debra's anger rose. She felt like Sheila was taking shots at her because of her failed marriage to Bryce. Frustrated she said, "Because it's evident in God's Word."

"Well, apparently love is more than all that mushy stuff you just mentioned, otherwise people wouldn't get divorces, now would they?"

Debra stood. "Forget it," she said retrieving her keys from her purse. "I'm not about to go there with you tonight, Mama. I've had a very long day."

"Stop running, Miss Goody Two-Shoes! Sit down." Sheila and Debra entangled each other in a staring match. "Sit down, please. Tonight you and I are going to talk *woman to woman,* since you think you've got me figured out so well."

Debra let go of her irritation with a cool sigh and reclaimed her seat reluctantly. Sheila poured another glass of wine and handed it to Debra. She sat across from Debra with eyes that were brimming with tears.

Debra took a sip and tried to relax. "Mama, we don't have to do this . . . it doesn't matter. It's between you and Daddy anyway."

"Debra, would you just *listen*? You are so much like your father sometimes. Sheila poured herself another glass of wine. Gently she made circular motions with her wine glass causing the liquid to swish. She seemed hypnotized by it. "I was raised by my mother's sister, Tabitha, mainly because my mother, Dorothy, didn't want me. They called my mother a sportin' woman—a woman a man kept because she looked good. Back then her light skin and long wavy hair made her desirable to white men and black men. My mother had been so used when she got pregnant with me, that it was more important to keep the men and the money that she had grown accustomed to.

"So my aunt Tabitha took me in. Tabitha and my mother had the same mother, but different fathers. My mother's father was a white man and Tabitha's father was a black man—a very dark man. Tabitha looked like her father, she was beautiful. Her dark skin was beautiful, but she must have hated herself. She resented the way I looked—my light skin. There was a part of her that loved me because I was her blood—her niece, but another part of her resented me. She called me ugly names and made me feel so unwanted and unloved. She was cold, Debra, just plain mean. I began to hate myself and the way I looked. I didn't grow up with the love and attention your father and I tried to give you.

"Anyway, I was eighteen years old when I met a young man and fell in love. He worked for a construction company—had the most gifted hands I'd ever seen. He could build the most beautiful things. He was the most loving person I had ever known. He didn't have much at the time, but he wanted to marry me. I was so broken and naive that I allowed Tabitha to convince me that I would be throwing my life away by marrying him. I ruined that relationship.

"I met your father shortly afterward. He was a kind man. He had been in the military and had just gotten a good job at the auto plant. He didn't know the Lord then, but he was good to me. We ended up pregnant with you, so we got married. I didn't believe that I deserved to be loved. I thought I was going to wake up one day and it would all disappear," Sheila said with tears streaming.

"So I did a stupid thing one Christmas, something I have regretted for over thirty years. I had an affair. Daniel took me back because we had you and we wanted you to have the life neither of us had growing up. Daniel grew up without his father and he didn't want our family to be broken. So I stayed and loved your father the best I knew how. In these thirty–five years, I have never loved anyone as much as I have grown to love Daniel Prince—and that is love, Debra."

Debra swallowed, wiping her own tears. She got up and hugged her mother. The two of them cried together. For the first time in her life—right, wrong, or indifferent, Debra understood her mother. She knew who her mother was. Their tears broke down the barriers that had prevented them from fully loving one another over the years. Sheila pulled apart gently, cupping Debra's smooth face in her hands. "Live your life, baby. Let go of Bryce and live your life to the fullest. Love will find you again. I promise." Debra nodded and the two embraced again.

34
Second Chances

Maya was discharged from Honeywood psychiatric hospital for youth on a Sunday. Greg had insisted that the staff not allow Maya any visitors for the 30 days she was in treatment. He wanted her to focus solely on being healthy. He did however, allow notes from the girls and he delivered them to Maya himself. Maya had but one request today. She wanted to see the girls, but she wasn't quite ready to be out in public, so Greg arranged for Noni and Corey to have dinner with him and Maya. He'd even invited Debra to stop by. She promised she would after church.

Greg had cooked dinner—pot roast and cornbread. That was Maya's favorite. Noni brought a few of her mini sweet potato pies. She knew how much Maya loved them. Both she and Corey had written poems for Maya. They planned to read them to her. Noni and Corey had made Maya a scrapbook devoted to their happy times and beautiful blossoming friendship. It was filled with photographs of the girls' various adventures together, with comedic anecdotes and poems Noni and Corey had written.

Maya burst into tears as she turned the pages. "You guys, this is the most special present I've ever received. I don't deserve this. . . " Maya cried pushing herself back against the sofa.

"Yes you do, girl. We love you," Noni said. She and Corey wrapped their arms around Maya giving her a group hug.

The three of them cried on one another. Greg piqued out at them from the kitchen. He tried to control himself, but he wept silently overwhelmed by the girls' emotion.

"Don't you ever try to leave us again. We love you, and we need you. I was so mad at you—you know you can always talk to us. We're your *sisters*," Noni said lifting Maya's chin with her hand.

"That's right, there's nothing we can't get through together, Maya. We are the real Three Musketeers! Don't you ever forget that."

"I won't. I was so selfish," Maya cried. "I'm so sorry to have hurt you—especially you Noni, I know you just lost your parents—I was just hurting so much that day. I wasn't thinking . . . please forgive me."

"Shhh . . . It's over. You made it. We're right here." The three of them hugged and cried until Greg thought he was going to faint from being so emotional himself. Each of them had puffy, swollen red eyes and a mangled lion's mane from squeezing so closely together, smashing their hair into one gigantic bush. They looked a pitiful, happy sight.

"Okay . . . " Noni said pulling back gently. "I promised God when we got together again, I would pray a special prayer of deliverance and thanks. I prayed that God would bring you through,

Maya, and He did. Now let's thank Him for His faithfulness." The three of them put their foreheads together and Noni led them in prayer. "Dear Father, You are our rock and our salvation. There is none like You. You are our healer and protector, Dear Lord. We thank You for our sister Maya, whose life You spared and to whom You gave another chance so that Your name could be glorified. We thank You for Your saving grace and new mercies. We thank You for Mr. McIntyre letting us be sisters again. Now Lord, watch over us. Protect us and keep us near the cross, until death do us part. Amen."

Their Amens were said seriously and in unison. They squeezed each other tightly and cried some more. "Wait a second," Corey said after they had cried on each other for another couple of minutes. "I think Noni just married us—didn't you say till death do us part?" Corey laughed.

"Yes, I did and both y'all fools said Amen!" Noni laughed.

"Unh-uh. Y'all cute and all, but y'all ain't that cute—not to be married to anyways," Maya laughed.

Noni grabbed both of them by their necks and put them in headlocks. "Wanna bet?"

"No, we give . . . " Maya and Corey said in unison.

The doorbell rang and Greg was grateful. He could no longer take the sight of those three little women with their mascara streaking down their faces and their swollen eyes that looked like a triple case of severe hay fever—not to mention that untamed ball of hair they now shared. Too much crying. He had to sniff it in. He smiled as he swung the door open, but just cracking his jaw slightly was giving him a headache now that the girls had overwhelmed him.

"Hi Mr. McIntyre, how's everything? Have the girls made it here yet?"

"Have they? They have been in there crying and laughing and crying for the last hour. They've got my head hurting!"

Debra smiled. "Yeah . . . that sounds like them."

"They love each other, you know. If I didn't know, I do now. They're like real sisters."

"Yes, they have a very strong bond. It's good. I think it's going to follow them through life."

"I certainly hope so. I just don't know how I'm going to deal with *three* girls from now on," Greg chuckled.

"You better think of something quick Mr. McIntyre 'cause we're here to stay," Noni said as the three of them walked up behind Greg to see who had just entered the house.

"Mrs. Myles!" Maya screeched running into Debra's arms. Noni and Corey gathered around and they all started their hug-crying ritual again. Greg snuck away.

"Hey sweetie, how are you doing today?" Debra said hugging Maya.

"Great. Just great."

"That's good, because y'all look a hot raggedy mess!" Debra laughed. Just then Greg had returned and snapped a picture of the three—soon to be four raccoon women.

"Daddy!" Maya chased her Dad through the house.

"I'm going to put this on Facebook if you don't stop chasing me!" Greg said, running into his office and shutting the door.

Maya stood in front of her father's closed office door. "Daddy you can't stay in there all night. We've got company."

"I can stay in here long enough to load this on Facebook. Back away from the door."

The girls laughed hysterically. "You know you better get away from that door, girl. I can't afford to have my reputation tarnished by that picture your dad just took," Corey said.

"Alright, Daddy. You win . . . but just remember there is such a thing called pay back. Now let's eat! I'm starvin'!"

The girls raced to the kitchen, fixed their plates and sat at the dining room table like a family. Greg and Debra joined them. Noni and Corey brought Maya up to date on all the happenings at school. Greg had heard enough high school gossip to last a life time, but his spirits had been genuinely lifted by the girls' presence and seeing his daughter so happy. He was grateful to Debra for going the extra mile.

"Oh, by the way, Chef Chase said to tell you hello, Mrs. Myles," Noni said with a straight face.

Debra smiled on the inside because she knew Noni was trying to get a rise out of her. She kept a poker-face. "Well, tell him I said hello as well," Debra said casually.

"Sure will."

Debra could just choke the little woman.

Corey burst into laughter, which caused Noni and Maya to laugh too. Debra rolled her eyes.

"Did I miss something?" Greg asked puzzled, scanning the Three Musketeers' faces for answers.

"Noni has this theory that Chef Chase is sweet on Mrs. Myles . . . and we think it's so funny," Maya explained.

"If I were you Miss Noni, I wouldn't spread rumors about people," Debra chided playfully.

"I didn't say a word," Noni defended.

"Your theories are just that, Miss Noni."

"Well, if it is true, I couldn't blame Chase. Mrs. Myles is a beautiful and caring woman," Greg said.

"Oooh . . . beautiful and caring!" Noni mocked.

"Daddy, there is a beautiful and caring woman out there for you too," Maya said.

"I know. I met her already."

"Daddy, you met somebody?"

"Yes, as a matter of fact I did."

"When was this?"

"About a couple of months ago on a job site. She's a construction engineer. Her name is Valerie. You'll be meeting her soon."

"Well, go Daddy! Why haven't you said anything about a girlfriend?"

"Well, I wanted to wait until I knew it was steady."

"When did it become *steady*?"

"Last weekend."

"So, Daddy, how did it all go down? Did you say, 'I like you, let's go *steady*?'"

"I hope not," Noni laughed. "That is weak!"

"I mean . . . " Corey piggybacked.

"Please . . . I'm *Greg McIntyre*," Greg teased. "I said, 'Valerie, you're a very beautiful woman, mentally and physically. You have been a total blessing to my life these past couple of months and I'd like to have the opportunity to bless you in a committed relationship that I hope will lead to marriage.'"

"Alright! Mr. Mac got game!!" Noni shouted. The three of them clapped like fools.

"Hoot. Hoot. Hoot!!!" Noni and Corey shouted, pumping their fists in the air as if they were at a sports event.

"Well, Daddy it's about time!" Maya got up and kissed her father on the forehead. He stood and hugged her in a tender embrace. He loved to see her skin glow that way—to see her smiling. She looked just like her mother. Greg McIntyre squeezed his daughter and prayed on the inside that God would keep their small, but love-filled family together.

They settled enough to have dessert, courtesy of Noni. They

were all sitting at the table with their stomachs full. Debra thought hers would burst open if she swallowed another bite to eat. She felt like unbuttoning her pants. For that, she'd have to wait until she got into the car. "Well, it has been a beautiful evening, Mr. McIntyre. Thank you for inviting me. I have to get home before you guys have to roll me out of here."

"Thank you for coming. Let me get your coat." As Greg stood, Maya burst into tears.

He hurried over to where she sat. "Maya what's wrong? What's the matter?"

"Oh my God, Oh my God . . . " she repeated. Everyone stood, perplexed by her sudden outburst.

"Maya, talk to me!" Greg pleaded.

"He saved me . . . He saved me . . . He let me live. He gave me a second chance," Maya said tearfully remembering Noni's prayer.

"Yes, He did, and I am so happy that He did, baby. You're the most important thing in my life Maya—you're all I have. I need you to be around to take care of me."

"I need to give my life to Him. I want Jesus," Maya said tearfully.

Before another word could be spoken, Noni walked over to Maya and took her hands. "It's just like we talked about before, Maya. All you have to do is admit that you have sinned against Him, confess with your mouth the Lord Jesus and believe that God raised him from the dead, and you'll be saved. Pray it out Maya."

Maya inhaled slowly and sniffed in deeply. She'd just realized the gravity of what she'd done—trying to kill herself. She fully understood the grace God had shown her by allowing her to survive and not die in her sin. That broke her emotionally, right down to the bare soul that seeks the Father. "Lord, I confess that I have sinned against you . . . please forgive me. I confess that You are Jesus Christ—the One True God, crucified for my sins, and risen from the dead. I believe it in my heart Lord. I need you in my life to be my Lord . . . I can't do this on my own . . . help me, Jesus."

"Amen," Noni said gently in Maya's ear as she embraced her.

35
Glue

Greg had allowed Maya to take another week off before returning to school. He'd made arrangements with Maya's teachers through Debra to get all her homework assignments. Most of the teachers allowed Maya to turn in assignments online. Greg had taken a week off work to devote to getting Maya adjusted and just spending quality time with her. They continued the family counseling that was set up through the psychiatric hospital and Maya was scheduled to continue seeing Debra while at school. She saw her for individual and group sessions. Today would be their first group session since Maya's suicide attempt.

Debra felt inspired by the prospect of having them all together again. She praised the Lord in her heart for all three of her little butterflies. She knew that He had sent them to comfort *her* at this time in her life. Debra had never felt better about life. For years, she'd wrapped her whole life around Bryce. But lately, God had shown her in so many ways that her life had to be devoted to serving Him first. She was glad she was able to do that by working with her students. She absolutely loved them.

As usual, Debra heard them coming before she actually saw their faces. She wondered how they could do those high pitched screeches at seven-thirty in the morning, when most of the time she still had a frog in her throat. The amount of energy they had this early in the morning was unbelievable. Today she surprised them with breakfast—chicken and waffles. She'd deep fried the wing-dings at home an hour earlier and made the waffles in her office with the waffle-maker she'd brought from home so that they'd be piping hot when the girls arrived. She had spread a beautiful butterfly table cloth over the table and found some fancy pink plastic ware from the Dollar Tree. It looked like a set-up at a nice restaurant.

"Ooh, it smells good up in here!" Debra heard Noni say.

"For real. I am super hungry!"

Debra stepped into the hallway. "You're supposed to eat at home, Miss Maya."

"I had a piece of toast—you said eat *something*."

"Yes, I did," Debra conceded. "What were you hungry little monsters going to do if I hadn't brought breakfast?"

"We were going to sneak out and go to the IHOP down the street. Mrs. Sanchez and Mr. Forbes are absent today."

"How do you know that? School hasn't even started yet."

"Mrs. Sanchez is at some bilingual teachers' conference or something, and I heard Mr. Forbes tell Ms. Jones he wasn't going to be here today—taking a mental health day."

"You sure do hear a lot, Miss Noni."

"Hey, it's not my fault if teachers talk too much in front of students."

Debra laughed on the inside. She and her colleagues had discussed it before. They had to be extremely careful talking around students. Even when it seemed like the kids weren't listening they always were. The four of them ate and then Debra got down to the business of therapy. She knew she'd missed these group sessions as much as the girls. They brought purpose to her life at a time when she needed something else to focus on besides herself.

"Ms. Myles, I just want to say that this is the first time in my life that I have truly appreciated therapy, it has really helped me a lot. I have a lot to live for! I really like being with you and the girls, and I look forward to coming, especially since you surprise us with breakfast sometimes."

"I'm glad to have been part of your growth process Maya. I hope that therapy has been beneficial to all of you."

"You know, Mrs. Myles, we've been thinking, and we came up with a great idea about something that this school *doesn't* have, Noni said."

"What's that?"

"Well you know how Millicent and Scotlyn are a part of that little sorority T.B.O.—which I recently found out stands for *The Beautiful Ones*—"

"Give me a break!" Corey interjected.

"I'm dead serious," Noni said rolling her eyes. " . . . Well, we came up with something that would benefit girls like us—you know young women who are a long way from 'perfection' but who love God—a Christian club for young women."

"It's called G.L.U.E. Girls" Corey said.

Debra looked puzzled. "*Glue?*"

"Yep. It stands for God Loves Us Eternally," Noni explained. "Actually Maya came up with the name."

Debra smiled. "I think that's great!"

"Well, you know we have to meet after school because it's a religious organization and stuff, and uh . . . we also need a faculty sponsor. We were wondering if you would be our sponsor."

Debra raised her brows. Why did everything with these three turn out to be an adventure? Now what was she getting herself into? They looked anxiously at her awaiting an answer. "Well, what days were you planning to meet?"

Maya spoke up. "We figured Tuesdays would be a good day—if that works with your schedule."

"Well, I guess it wouldn't be a problem—just give me a little write up about what your club will be doing . . . purpose and all that."

"Thanks, Mrs. Myles. This will be great! We can have Bible study and everything once we get going. There's a minister at my church that said he would be interested in teaching Bible study at the school in the evenings. I think this will really help people at the school—those that are saved and those that want to know more about God," Maya said.

"*Glue,*" Debra said to herself as the girls started a side conversation about getting the word out about their club and inviting members to join. She realized that these three little women had been part of the glue God had used to hold her together the last few months, enabling her to keep going when she felt paralyzed by all that had happened in her life. What a blessing they were.

36
Planting Flowers

Debra pulled up to her parents' home and smiled. Daniel was working diligently on his knees planting impatiens in the front yard inside his raised flower bed that was bordered by a red stone retaining wall. Debra was amazed at the great shape her father was in. She watched him choose his flowers carefully, digging perfect six-inch residences for each of them. It was a ritualistic enjoyment for him. He had a neurotic practice of getting them all planted by Mother's Day, which was the coming Sunday.

Sheila stood over him with a glass of homemade lemonade, directing him as to which colors would look good in what spots. A sparse row of white impatiens was reinforced by a row of pink. Daniel had bunches of flower trays lined up to choose from. The delicate flowers curved around the inside perimeter of the flower bed sprinkling color on Daniel's mature hostas and other greenery.

Sheila never put her hands in the dirt. The thought of it caused her to shiver—especially when she thought about *worms*. Debra watched as her mother gingerly handed the glass of lemonade to her father, and then lovingly blotted his brow. With his knee-pads dug firmly in the wet soil, barely reaching Sheila's waist, he looked like a miniature man. He gulped the sweet drink and nodded in approval of its taste. Sheila bent down and kissed him and he anchored one leg up as if he were proposing to her and pulled her down onto his leg. Sheila squealed before Daniel kissed her passionately, all while keeping his balance.

Debra got out of the car and mumbled to herself. "Now that's a first." She grabbed her pink gardening kit out of the trunk and walked up to them unnoticed until she said, "I thought military guys weren't supposed to engage in public displays of affection."

Daniel and Sheila took their time pulling their lips away from one another. "We have to make exceptions when it comes to women as beautiful as your mother," Daniel said finally when Sheila let *him* up for air.

Debra stood over them chuckling. "Uh-huh. Well the neighbors might be video-taping this little scene here for future extortion,"

Daniel released Sheila and she stood, giving Debra a sly wink. She took the glass from Daniel.

"You want more?" Sheila asked

"Tonight," Daniel said, grinning mischievously.

"Y-u-c-k!" Debra teased covering her ears.

"Girl, please," Sheila said to Debra. "Stay out of *grown* folks' business young lady—didn't your mother teach you that?"

Debra smiled. "Nope."

"Now you know you just broke a commandment, little girl," Sheila said.

The three of them laughed. The interrupting ring of the telephone sent Sheila racing into the house. "That's probably Beverly calling me back. She said she had something *very* important to tell me."

Daniel twisted his lips. "You know good and well all Beverly does is gos—"

Sheila hushed Daniel with a finger over her lips. "Be nice," she said before dashing into the house.

"Looks like you two have done a 360," Debra said to Daniel when Sheila was out of earshot.

"You could say that. A lot has changed in the last few weeks around here." His face was serious.

"Must have been a visit from alien body snatchers. I can't remember the last time I've seen you two acting like that. What brought that about?"

"Well for starters, your mother and I decided to take a marriage challenge class at church, which has proven to be one of the best decisions we've ever made."

Debra fastened on her knee pads and climbed into the flower bed. She bent down on her knees across from her father and began handing him impatiens from the nursery crate, while Daniel continued to dig.

"Oh yeah? Whose idea was that?"

Daniel smiled. "Actually, it was your mother's."

Debra's eyes bucked wide. "Wow. That's *national news.*"

Daniel chuckled. "Well, your mother said she had a long talk with you one evening, and while she was talking, she felt as if God were revealing her "true-self." She decided she didn't like what she saw and wanted to make some changes. So I guess I can say that I owe much of your mother's 'new attitude' to you, Princess."

Debra thought to herself wondering how much of their conversation her mother had shared with her father.

It was as if Daniel read his daughter's mind. "She didn't go into details about what you two talked about. She just said that you had a pretty good heart-to-heart conversation about life in general. Whatever it was, it made her reflect on our marriage— which turned out to be a good thing. It's like they say, God works in mysterious ways, Princess."

Debra nodded in astonishment. "That He does."

"You know, your mother and I have had our challenges over the years. There were some things she did that caused rifts and some things I did to keep the rifts going. I had never thought about how deeply *not* forgiving someone could hurt a relationship—it sure took a toll on ours."

Debra held a pensive gaze. She could only think about how mean her mother had been to her father over the years. She hesitated before saying, " . . . um . . . Daddy . . . all I ever saw was her being mean to you and I never understood why." After having that heart to heart with Sheila, Debra understood that Sheila had never really learned to love the way most people think of love, but she wanted to finally hear what her father had to say about it after all these years.

"I'm sure it seemed that way, Princess, but I hurt your mother, too—with the things I did and said—not forgiving her for her mistakes. I'm just as guilty as she is for that. I didn't understand that when your mother and I married, she still had baggage from her childhood—poor self-esteem, not knowing how to really love anyone. And she had unresolved issues from a past relationship. It makes for a bad mix when you consider marrying. She was a young girl—feeling her way through just like I was."

Debra nodded remembering her conversation with her mother. "Well, I'm happy that *you* seem so happy, Daddy. That's really important to me."

"Thank you, Princess. I know it is. Marriage is one of those things that have to be worked on and tended to—just like what I'm doing out here with these flowers. Once I plant them, I can't just leave them here to fend on their own. They have to be nurtured and cared for. Your mother and I made some mistakes, but we're not going to live in the past anymore. We have learned in our class to live and love in the moment—to nurture our relationship—and it feels really good."

Debra reflected on her own life. For the past couple of weeks she'd been trying to do just that—live and love in the moment. She'd been loving God and serving Him through the teens he had blessed her with. She felt like she had enough energy to move forward, despite her impending divorce. She wasn't boxed in by guilt or failure anymore. She looked at her father and said simply, "I love you, Daddy."

"I love you too, Princess."

It wasn't long before Debra had eased into the house under the guise of needing to use the bathroom. She had to talk to her mother. The whole interaction between Sheila and Daniel was unbelievable. She had to hear Sheila's side of the story. It was incredulous the way the two of them seemed to be clicking. It was *strange* to see them this loving toward one another. They showed affection on occasion, but it was rare, and this was certainly different.

"Mama . . . " Debra started.

Sheila was pouring warm liquid Jell-O into molds for Daniel. She looked up at Debra. "What is it, sweetie?"

"I just wanted to say that I'm glad that you and Daddy seem so happy with each other. It's good to see you like this."

"Why thank you, Debra Ann. God has really made a difference in me—in my marriage. I'm thankful to have been blessed with a man like your father. I am learning how to be the kind of wife God wants me to be, and it's benefitting both of us."

Debra was proud of her mother, glad to see that it was never too late to grow. Sheila had never been too interested in God or church. This was a great start for her. Debra put her arms around Sheila and hugged her. "I love you, Mama."

"I know . . . and I love you more. Life is just getting started. Remember that."

"Thank you."

37
The End?

D ebra dressed in slow motion. She purchased a new white suit for this fine June day. She wore a peach colored cotton shirt underneath the short sleeved jacket. Her skirt ended just above the knee. She oiled her legs and put on her peach tie-up wedges. Her toes were cute. She looked down at them and smiled. She'd gotten a pedicure the day before, just for this occasion. Her make-up was flawless. She'd practiced with the make-up artist at the day spa until she could mimic some of the tricks herself.

It was going to be a gorgeous day. The forecast was eighty degrees and sunny. Perfect. Debra stared at herself in the mirror. She wasn't the same broken spirit she'd been a few months ago. She smiled again. God had pulled her through. She didn't feel like a failure. She didn't bear the burden of her failed marriage alone— it was Bryce's fault too. She'd tried. She didn't feel doomed, like life was over—or that she could never marry again. The Word of God from 1 Corinthians 7:15 resonated in her heart. *But if the unbeliever departs, let him depart; a brother or a sister is not under bondage in such cases. But God has called us to peace.*

She had struggled with divorce and pained over what it meant for months before Dr. Buckley had gone over that scripture with her. She felt released by it. She'd been incorrectly told by so many people that as long as Bryce was alive, she could never marry again or she would be guilty of committing adultery. This scripture had helped to allay her fears about that. It was Bryce who had departed. It was Bryce who was struggling with God's Word— who didn't know what he believed. Debra picked up her brown leather briefcase and walked to the door. She stood for a while with her hand on the door knob feeling a sudden rush of terror.

She felt as if she was going into battle, instead of saying goodbye to her life as Mrs. Bryce Myles. She began to pray. "Oh, Lord God, Your Word says that Your strength is made perfect in weakness. I'm weak right now, Lord. Help me, Jesus." Debra fought back tears. This wasn't the time to come un-glued. God's Word came back to her clearly. *Do not be afraid. Stand still, and see the salvation of the Lord, which He will accomplish for you today. For the Egyptians whom you see today, you shall see again no more forever. The Lord will fight for you, and you shall hold your peace.* "Thank You, Jesus," Debra said with strength enough to twist the knob. She walked directly to the trash can in front of the house and tossed in the destroyer. It was the small unopened packet that had turned her world upside down. She didn't know why she had held onto it this long. She thought it ironic that it was advertised as *protection*. The only protection one needed was God's. It was over now. The last evidence of residue from her life with Bryce was in the trash can. She could hear the garbage truck around the corner.

She smiled. The sun splashed across her face, warming her on the outside and inside. It was as if the Lord was smiling on her. Every doubt gave way to peace. A peace that was sound and complete.

* * *

Nervously, Debra walked through the metal detectors at the City County building. The sheriff handed back her purse once she proceeded through. Debra picked up her leather briefcase from the table and slung it over her shoulders. She walked to the elevator and pushed the up button. She looked up in the air, checking to see if God was still with her. She smiled. When she got off on the 19th floor, the first person she saw was Helena. She rushed over to Debra and explained once again what the protocol would be in the court room, what the judge would say, and what she should say in return. Debra nodded, but most of what Helena said didn't register. It floated somewhere above Debra's head on clouds.

She was focused on Bryce talking with Bailey a few feet away. Suzette stood right next to him with her fingers threaded through his. Her stomach protruded under the red and white flowered baby doll top. She was wearing white capri pants with red ballerina flats. She still had on her sunglasses. Bryce looked up and made eye contact with Debra briefly. It was as if he could feel her penetrating stare. His face looked ashamed. Suzette looked in Debra's direction and whispered something to Bryce. He nodded in the affirmative.

Debra returned her attention to Helena who sensed her ambivalence—the sadness one must feel when a part of their life vanishes, never to return, like a death. Helena rubbed Debra's shoulders. "You'll be fine. You've been through the hardest part already." Helena couldn't be more right. The hardest part had been coming to the realization that Bryce wasn't the man that Debra thought he was. That he didn't love her or want her like she loved and wanted him. Bryce was convinced that Suzette was his soul mate and there was nothing Debra could have done to make him stay in their marriage. It was over between them, and God had made it okay. She could breathe again.

Helena excused herself and talked with Bailey in private. Debra turned when she heard Helena's soft snicker. Helena and Bailey talked for a few minutes before Helena returned to Debra's side.

"What was that all about?" Debra asked.

"Bailey has short patience for girlfriends who show up at court with men who are divorcing their wives. She thinks it's tacky."

"It is what it is," Debra said.

"Are you okay?"

"I'm fine."

They entered the court, and less than an hour later, Debra was standing before the judge. She thought it strange that it took months to plan a wedding ceremony, but the legally binding contract of marriage itself could be dissolved in less than fifteen minutes. Debra was like a robot. Helena had nudged her when it was time for her to answer the judge's inquiries. Debra had floated off somewhere. "Excuse me your honor, I was on an island someplace in the Caribbean," Debra admitted. Chuckles emerged from the small court room. The judge chuckled as well. Before Debra knew it, it was over. She had her name back, and her life back. She exited the courtroom with Helena. Bailey, Bryce, and Suzette followed.

Debra felt like a gigantic ball and chain had been loosed from her neck. She hugged Helena. "Thank you so much."

"You're welcome, honey. Life is going to take you higher

from here on out. You'll see."

"I believe that," Debra said. When Suzette and Bryce passed her, Debra spoke her heart. "I hope one day you both find out what it feels like."

"Whatever," Suzette snapped, pulling Bryce toward the elevator. But there was something telling in Bryce's eyes, a sorrow and unsettledness.

"You are one incredible sister," Bailey said to Debra. She shook her hand.

"Thank you."

"Debra, I'll let you know as soon as the judge has signed the decree," Helena said.

"Okay, see you later, Helena," Debra said. She heard Bailey and Helena discussing where they were going to eat lunch. The three of them ended up on the elevator together. A sheriff stepped onto the elevator. Bailey eyed him deliciously. The three of them laughed. Bailey made all kinds of googley eyes at the tall handsome man behind his back. Helena's olive skin had turned beet red, trying to stifle her laugh. Debra didn't know Bailey was this much fun. She could see why Chase had been attracted to her. Bailey flirted with the gentleman before stepping off the elevator. The three women pushed through the revolving door outside to the nice weather. A voice stopped them.

"Ms. Prince . . . "

A smiled beamed across Debra's face. "Hello, Chase," Debra said surprised. Mona stood at his side.

"Where are you parked?"

"Around the corner in the cheap lot."

"Why don't you give Mona your car keys, and she'll take your car to the restaurant. I was thinking that this is a beautiful day for some ice cream. It's nice enough to walk to Greek Town. What do you say?"

She handed Mona her keys and briefcase. "I'd love to."

"Good," he said taking her hand in his. The two of them strode down the sidewalk hand and hand weaving in and out of the downtown crowd. Chase swung their arms like a little kid and Debra laughed hysterically at his silliness. It was a beautiful day for ice cream.

38
Happily-Ever-After
(Eighteen Months Later)

Debra lay across Chase's lap watching television in his high-rise riverfront condo. He stroked her hair lightly, trailing his fingers over her face and neck. Debra looked up at him and smiled. Chase cleared his throat and spoke, "Debra Ann . . . I need to talk to you about something."

Debra sat up. "What's the matter?"

"Nothing really. It's just that . . . spending time with you has really blessed me. And I think Savannah has fallen in love with you, too. I was worried about her getting too close to you initially. I didn't want her to be disappointed if our friendship didn't work out the way I planned." He had a tendency to drone on.

"Chase, spit it out."

"Well, Debra, it's like this . . . when I approached you about dating after your divorce, you asked me for at least six months to be alone and collect yourself, and I agreed. I gave you your six months. To be honest, it was really hard to back off, because I had been backing off ever since I met you. So now, here we are one year after that. Our friendship is beautiful—being with you has been good for me—it's been good for Savannah. Wait a minute . . . " he said getting up.

He went into his bedroom and came out moments later. He stood in front of her just looking at her, taking her in. She was everything he wanted. There was no doubt in his mind. He brought his hand from behind his back and dropped to one knee. In his hand was an engagement ring nestled in a black velvet box. It held a princess cut diamond mounted atop a platinum band with single diamonds on each side of the center stone, which appeared to be paying tribute to the royally elevated gem. It was an exquisite setting with a baguette band. Debra looked at the beautiful ring and back at Chase. Her eyes watered, but she didn't speak. She didn't know what to say. There were too many thoughts swirling around in her head.

"I'm asking you to marry me, Debra Ann," Chase clarified.

"Chase . . . I love you with all my heart . . . I do."

Chase became worried. He prayed that this moment wouldn't go down in history as one of his most embarrassing ones. He began to perspire. "Then say *yes*."

"It just seems so soon, I don't know what people would think if I—"

"Debra, listen to me. Tomorrow isn't promised to anyone. Who knows how long either of us has left on this side of heaven? What is there to wait for? I don't want to waste a moment of my life worrying about what someone else thinks. Do you love me?"

"Yes."

"Are you in love with me?"

"Yes."

Chase sighed from relief. "Do you believe that I would be a good husband to you—that I would *honor* you as my wife?"

"Yes. I have no doubts about that, Chase."

"Okay . . . let me try this again. Debra Ann Prince, will you marry me?"

"Yes, I will . . . " Debra cried, throwing her arms around his neck. Then Chased kissed her until he was lost in her. He pulled back slowly.

"Allow me to place this ring on your finger." Chase removed it from the box.

"It's so beautiful," Debra said.

Chase slid the sparkling stone on Debra's ring finger. She held her hand out and watched it glisten. "I bought it after we had our first *official* date, Debra. There has never been any doubt in my mind that you are the one for me. I'm sure of it."

"I love you, Chase Martin."

"And I love you . . . and I don't want to wait anymore. How soon can we make this official?"

"Well, its July so maybe during winter break?"

"No. That's too long, Debra."

"Okay, when would you like to do it?"

"If it were up to me, I'd drag you off to some chapel right now," he chuckled. "But I was thinking maybe we could do a wed-dingmoon—I've checked out some places online in Jamaica that are awesome. How do you feel about that?"

"I'd like that. I just want something intimate and meaning-ful—I need to talk to my parents and see what their schedule is like. They travel a lot."

"I've already talked to Daniel. He said their calendar is clear for the rest of the month. You're off work. Is two weeks enough time to find a dress?"

She didn't utter one rebuttal. "Yes," she said. She'd make it work.

"Well then, let's do it this month. We can honeymoon for a week and come back and take Vannah to Disney for a few days."

"Okay," Debra said before kissing Chase with the intention of making him feel everything she felt on the inside.

"You better be good, Debra Ann, I've been a good boy longer than you know. I'm busting at the seams," he laughed.

"Sorry," she said with an insincere smile.

"You are not the least bit sorry."

"You're right," she said before spellbinding him with another kiss.

* * *

Debra's toes sank in the sand. Wisps of her hair blew slightly with the breeze coming off the ocean. The remainder of her tresses were pulled elegantly on top of her head in a loose pile of curls that was pinned delicately with small hair pins decorated with pearls. Her white satin mermaid dress fit her body superbly. The red-orange sun eased down in the backdrop and the ocean show-cased its reflection as a fire globe in the middle of gently moving blue glass. It was a scene that was fit for the vows that would take place this Friday evening in July. Chase stood confidently dressed in a white tuxedo with his best man, Corey Perry by his side. He eyed Debra both lovingly and passionately sending a nervous quiver up her spine. He'd been abnormally flirtatious since their engagement just two weeks ago. Debra could call it frisky even. It was a whole other side of him that she hadn't seen before. The transformation tickled her. Corey's father and mother were nearby admiring the young couple. Mona stood as their maid of honor.

Daniel and Sheila watched the ceremony with joy in their hearts, while Virginia Carlton and her husband admired how beautiful everything was.

Chase had written his own vows.

"I, Chase Arman Martin, promise to be the man God created me to be, rightfully assuming my position as God's priest in our home, seeking His knowledge and wisdom above everything else to guide our family in the direction that He would have us to go.

I promise to love you as Christ loves the church, sacrificing for you to the point of giving up my own life.

I promise to be a strong enough tower for you to lean on, but gentle enough for you to find comfort in my arms.

I promise to honor and uplift you with the words of my mouth, never allowing anger to cause me to take for granted the gift that God has given me in you, knowing that the wrath of man does not produce the righteousness of God.

I promise to be faithful to you in heart, mind, emotion and flesh, fixing my heart on the love we share in our holy union, allowing nothing and no one to destroy our holy covenant.

I promise to love you through all manner of sickness, shortcomings, or any other earthly devastation, until the Lord shall call one or both of us home.

I take you Debra Ann Prince to be my lawfully wedded wife."

Debra's eyes were so teary that she couldn't see the beautiful man that stood before her professing the deepest of love. She blotted her eyes with the handkerchief Mona had given her and read her vows, while Chase held her hand in his. She felt his strength and power. She felt God's Holy Spirit in him. She couldn't hear herself speaking when she said her vows. Ever so often, she looked up from the index card she held and drowned in Chase's eyes, taken to a place where they shared each other fully.

"I take you Chase Arman Martin to be my lawfully wedded husband," she said. She heard the minister pronounce them man and wife. She heard him tell Chase that he could kiss his bride. She heard the clapping and cheering, but all she could feel was Chase's caress. His deep, soft, urgent kiss. And God's unfailing love for her.

"I take it, it's going to be a short reception," Corey teased, poking fun at the way Chase kept drowning Debra in kisses that were reserved for privacy.

Chase came up for air "Believe that. Real short reception. As a matter of fact, we can cut that cake tomorrow morning." The guests laughed. Chase scooped Debra off her feet and twirled her, and Debra squealed joyously.

Reading Group Guide

 SHERRHONDA DENICE

1. Debra's discovery of the "destroyer" in Bryce's suitcase was the catalyst that eventually led to the upheaval of their marriage. Do you think their situation would have been different if she hadn't found it?

2. GLUE touched on self-esteem issues. Debra wondered if Suzette was more attractive to Bryce than she was because of physical differences. Sheila had issues related to skin color. Maya had self-esteem issues related to acceptance. Do you think self-esteem severely impacts our relationships with others or God? If so, how?

3. Debra initially felt like she had done all the "right" things in her attempt to live for Christ and yet she still suffered tragedy. What does this tell us about the human condition and about God?

4. It was clear in the novel that love and commitment are choices, evidenced by the decision Bryce made in relationship to his marriage, and also the decision Daniel made in relationship to his marriage with Sheila. Do you think each of these characters' decisions is representative of issues dealt with in today's marriages? Explain.

5. GLUE dealt honestly with teen love and teen relationships. What are your attitudes or feelings about this particular topic? Were you comfortable or uncomfortable with the way teen relationships were portrayed in the novel? Explain your position.

6. Chase and Debra's friendship could have been misconstrued as inappropriate by some. What are your feelings about their relationship? Can you share any scriptures that support your feelings?

7. The Christians portrayed in the novel all had flaws. Were their flaws realistic? Could you relate to one character in particular?

8. What was your favorite scene in the novel? Why?

9. Who is your favorite character? Why?

10. Statistics show that Christians divorce at the same rate as non-Christians. Why do you think this is true? What are your feelings about divorce in comparison to what the Bible says about divorce?

Take Five with the Author

*What made you decide to write **GLUE** and how personal was it for you?*

The idea of **GLUE** actually came to me a couple of years after I went through a very emotionally devastating divorce. In talking with other women who shared their horror stories and lessons with me, I sort of pulled those thoughts together. **GLUE** is very similar to my life in that, like Debra, as a therapist, I know what it feels like to be responsible for someone else's emotional well-being when you are trying to keep it together yourself. But there is nothing in the novel that happened to me or anyone that shared with me, exactly the way it appears in the novel. I have a lot of respect for my privacy and the privacy of others. I tried to concentrate on conveying the emotional pain one experiences in a situation like Debra's.

The teenagers in the story have some very adult-like problems—complicated issues. How realistic do you think the teen characters' reliance on God was in comparison to teens today?

Well, as a youth ministry leader and worker, I have had the opportunity to mentor and meet some very dynamic teens—ones who have been really sold out for Christ. So I see the teens in the novel as very realistic. And then, I have met and mentored some teens who have made some horrible mistakes—like the rest of us—and have experienced how God is still able to pull them through. I feel that following God's Word is "do-able." I don't at all feel like it's unrealistic for a teenager to remain a virgin/celibate or do any other thing the Bible commands. It is an act of will. When you depend on God and continually go to God for help, you can be successful regardless of your age, or mistakes.

You dealt with adultery through characters other than Debra. Why did you choose to do that?

Well, speaking of complicated issues . . . in my own family, adultery has caused some very complicated issues that have affected more than one generation. Actually, I'm planning to write a book about some of those things. I think it's a problem that needs to be addressed. In speaking with others, some have had similar experiences, so I feel it's worth putting on the table for discussion and hopefully some resolution. God gives us guidelines for a reason. The messes we have made in some families, simply because we haven't listened to God, are unbelievable.

Who is your favorite character in the novel?

I would have to say Debra—then Chase. I think Debra represents a lot of women who get blindsided by that "happily-ever-after" myth. You don't know what life is going to bring you. You just have to keep your hand in God's hand and move forward. You can't get stuck in despair. I think Debra was eventually able to do that and to see that even though you are going through something, you can't stop serving others—no way! And Chase, I love him because he exemplified the ultimate self-control and strength of character as a Christian man. There are some men who are serious about their walk with Christ. He held firm to what he believed in, and got the ultimate prize in the end!

So what's next for you?

My next project is **A Man's Heart**. It's a story about a minister who essentially finds himself torn between his love for Christ and his love for the woman in his life. It explores how faith in Christ can sometimes either intersect or collide with our earthly relationships and desires, and the struggle one experiences when that happens. It raises the question: *How much are you really willing to give up for the love of Christ?*

I'm also working on the first installment of the **G.L.U.E. (God Loves Us Eternally) GIRLS** young adult series entitled **Worthy**. It's a story about a young lady named Jaye, who finds herself involved in a relationship with a young man that is plagued with secrets that are detrimental to her emotional and physical well-being, as well as her relationship with Christ. Jaye has to make the right choice before it's too late . . .

CPSIA information can be obtained at www.ICGtesting.com
Printed in the USA
LVOW041153281012

304752LV00005B/20/P